Deceiving the Duke

Scandals and Spies, Book 2

Leighann Dobbs
Harmony Williams

This is a work of fiction.

None of it is real. All names, places, and events are products of the author's imagination. Any resemblance to real names, places, or events are purely coincidental, and should not be construed as being real.

Chapter One

Morgan Graylocke, the tenth Duke of Tenwick, concealed his irritation as he leaned back in the red velvet-upholstered chairs of his private box. The opera, *Il matrimonio segreto*, drew near to the close of the second act, with nary a sign of the man he had arranged to meet. Morgan's life was composed of enough secrets for him to voluntarily watch an opera about a secret marriage. His mother and sister would rejoice if he one day returned home with a wife. They'd made it their mission this Season to see him married and on his way to producing an heir, now that he'd reached the age of thirty.

Morgan didn't have the time to find a wife, certainly not after his brother and fellow Crown spy, Tristan, had taken an untimely vacation in order to honeymoon with his new wife. Usually stuck behind a desk cooling his heels as he waited to compile reports and ciphers, he was finally given a chance to do the dangerous fieldwork his younger brother usually took upon himself. And,

the very night his stint in the field was due to begin, Morgan found himself...bored to tears.

He adjusted the cravat around his throat and
straightened the cuffs of his eveningwear jacket—
black, so as to fade into the shadows when he left.

A portly, balding man dropped into the chair
to his left. Morgan glanced over his shoulder. The
scarlet curtain that separated his box from the
gold damask-carpeted corridor twitched as it settled into place once more. They were alone.

"It's about bloody time you got here."

Morgan faced forward at the grumbled re-
mark. He clenched his fists, clad in thin gloves. *I'd
like to say the same to you.* Clement Strickland,
the Lord Commander of the spy network in
Britain and beyond, didn't refer to Morgan's
opera outing this evening. Over the past two
weeks, Morgan had been held up at his ancestral
estate as he prepared to return to London.

When something went wrong, it seemed like
everything else did, too. The fallen domino leading to all the others had been the attendance—and
death—at the annual Graylocke house party of
Lord Elias Harker, a member of the peerage and a
French spy. Ever since he'd darkened Morgan's
doorway, his carefully cultivated plans had turned
awry. Some, like Tristan's marriage, were cause
for celebration. Others caused Morgan more
headaches than triumphs.

He sighed. "I had some business to tie up. If I'm to go into the field, I need to ensure that Keeling, my assistant, is well-equipped to handle the influx of work."

"You trained him, did you not?"

"I did." Keeling, and half of Britain. Morgan worked as Strickland's unofficial second-in-command. He read all the reports from agents afield, he decoded the correspondence intercepted from the enemy, and he trained every man and woman destined to enter into the business. What he hadn't heretofore been permitted to do, since he was the Duke of Tenwick and without an heir, was to enter the field himself.

One more reason to thank Tristan for getting him into this mess and then leaving on a tour of the Lake District. If Tristan had been available, he would have been the man Strickland assigned to ferreting out Harker's replacement in the *ton*. Morgan would be reassigned to his eternal slew of paperwork. At least this way, he was finally *doing* something.

Even if, never having done this before, he didn't quite know where to start.

"Your assistant will do fine in your absence. Your assistance in this matter is paramount." Strickland drummed his stubby fingers on the arm of the chair, a sure sign of anxiety. Drops of sweat beaded his wide forehead and darkened the

6

brown hair ringing his pate. His jaw was stiff and clenched.

On the stage below the private box, a woman raised her voice in a penetrating aria. The sound rang through the theater, smothering all hope of conversation. The stone pillars between the scarlet-decked private boxes, stacked row by row on either side of the stage and extending over the public seating toward the door, only seemed to amplify the sound, drawing it out longer. The air vibrated with the collective intake of breath of the crowd. After the actress held the note for an impossibly long time and drew it to a close, the other sounds in the room boomed in contrast to the ringing silence. The rustle of clothing as the patrons shifted, Strickland's even breathing to his left, even the thump of Morgan's own heart.

"What do we know?" His whisper emerged like thunder.

"Next to nothing." Strickland's voice was curt, almost cutting. He ran his hand over his clean-shaven chin. "None of Harker's known associates have yielded any clues as to who has inherited Bonaparte's London-based operations. They must have someone new in the *ton*."

"What if the new ringleader isn't in the *ton?* If I were to install someone, I would place them in a servant position, less visible."

"Also with less access," Strickland pointed out. He half turned, pointing his finger at Morgan for emphasis. His dark eyes glittered with determination. "A peer could get into parties and meetings where even a servant or slave might be remarked upon."

Morgan pressed his lips together at the mention of slavery. His family had been among the first to lobby for abolition of the slave trade. With luck, the Foreign Slave Trade Abolition Bill would pass through Parliament next week, and Morgan would be there to further the cause with his vote.

In the meantime, the import and export of slaves, a vile occupation in itself, provided ideal circumstances for French spies to be ferried in and out of the country. The sooner it was stopped, the better.

Oblivious to Morgan's disgust, Strickland added, "Rest assured, I have others searching in the lower classes, agents with more freedom of movement than you would have in those spheres. Even if the new French ringleader is not among the *ton*, they will certainly need an agent among the peerage with access to different information and more funds at hand. Someone in London is bored and wicked enough to take up the French's offer."

Morgan didn't want to believe that a British peer could be so easily swayed. Unfortunately, that had already been proven, with Harker and with multiple agents before him.

"Do you have any inkling of where I should start my search?"

Morgan read most of the reports sent to Strickland—in fact, he compiled the information into more easily readable documents for the Lord Commander. However, Morgan handled the information sent from abroad, not from London. Strickland might know something he didn't.

A suspicion was confirmed when Strickland whispered, "The Society for the Advancement of Science. They meet monthly on St. James's Street. I've heard rumors that the French may be ferrying messages through the inventions of the Society members."

"I'll look into it." Morgan stood, unwilling to sit through another minute of the opera.

As Morgan rounded the chair, Strickland, still seated, added, "The next meeting is Saturday at seven of the evening."

Morgan nodded. Strickland leaned back in the plush chair, taking in the opera as he hooked one ankle over the other. The stance was a clear dismissal. Fingering the white streak in his black hair, situated at his right temple, Morgan slipped past the heavy drape and into the corridor.

Two days was not a lot of time to prepare to infiltrate an exclusive club.

Two days later

Morgan turned his collar up to shield the nape of his neck against the cold spring drizzle. It wrapped around him like a fog, muffling his booted footsteps on the cobblestones and soaking through his greatcoat and eveningwear, into his very bones. He tucked his chin into the collar as he pulled his topper lower over his forehead.

The twilight gloom blanketed the night, premature for this time of day due to the thick clouds overhead. Anyone with any sense drove in a closed carriage or remained indoors. Not wanting to draw attention to himself with the ducal seal on his coach door, Morgan had instructed his driver to wait near Piccadilly. The clatter of carriage wheels trundled past Morgan, splattering murky water from a puddle onto Morgan's Hessian boots. He clutched his greatcoat closer to his person. He breathed shallowly through his mouth. The humidity of the night increased the stench of the street.

At last, he found the door to the club. It was a five-story townhouse, squashed wall-to-wall with its neighbors, the third in a row of six. The brick façade was identical to the others in the line, worn from years and weather into a long, benevolent visage. Light spilled from the glass windows in its cheeks, lighting Morgan's path up the beaten stone steps to the red-painted door. He grasped the brass knocker and rapped sharply.

An eternity seemed to pass before the door yawned open, revealing a butler in somber black livery. Brass buttons gleamed from his coat. He, like the townhouse, sported a long, narrow face weathered from the passing years.

"May I help you?" He dragged out the words as he swept his gaze over Morgan.

Annoyed, Morgan bit the inside of his cheek. He swept the topper off his head despite having yet to enter the club. Satisfaction swept through him, chasing away the chill brought on by the drizzle, as the butler's eyes widened. The wrinkled man's jowls quivered as his gaze fixed to the white streak in Morgan's hair. The telltale marker that the oldest Graylocke brother graced the house, not one of the younger three.

Bending at the waist, the butler stepped to the side, holding the door open for Morgan to enter. "Forgive me, Your Grace. May I take your coat?"

Morgan relinquished his coat, topper, and leather gloves. The snowy-haired butler tucked them away in a nearby closet. Once he finished, he gestured for Morgan to follow him down the hall. "This way, Your Grace."

A green runner patterned with fronds ran the length of the squat corridor. At the back, a wooden staircase disappeared into the shadowed depths above stairs. Indecipherable chatter from deeper in the house spilled down, interrupted by the creak of the staircase as they passed to the higher levels. As they neared the third floor, other sounds intruded, including something that sounded like eerie thumping. Reflexively, Morgan grasped for a pistol he'd left in his greatcoat pocket.

The third floor overflowed with light. The flames cast a reflected, amplified light in mirrored contraptions mounted in sconces on the walls. The flames burned bright, but gave off surprisingly little heat given the amount of light. In fact, when Morgan squinted and leaned closer, he saw that the flame itself was barely larger than his thumbnail. It gave off as much light as one the size of his hand.

Standing a few feet down the hall, the butler coughed into his fist. Morgan straightened, following as the man led him to an open door at the end of the corridor. When the butler looked as though he intended to announce his presence, Morgan brushed his fingers over the man's shoulder, a hand lower than his own. He slipped the man a shilling. "I'd prefer to watch unimpeded."

"Of course, Your Grace." The butler bowed and took himself off.

Morgan straightened the cuffs of his jacket, dove gray tonight. He checked his pocket watch. Five minutes to seven o'clock, though from the cacophony seeping from within the room, it sounded as though the meeting was already well under way. He thrust his shoulders back and stepped into the room.

Like the corridor, the room was brightly illuminated with the strange mirrored lights. They chased the shadows into the very corners of the large, rectangular chamber that must have stretched from the front of the townhouse to its rear. The far wall of the room was lined with shelves stuffed with books, the spines a jumbled, disorganized array of colors and sizes. A damask patterned rug running the length of the room was faded along the edges from many booted feet. In the center of the room, an oblong table ringed with chairs was packed with men, shoulder to shoulder, in varying displays of wealth. Some wore pristine jackets and elaborate cravats—others battled with unkempt hair and rumpled, ink-stained clothes. Morgan was surprised at the variety of quality of their clothes. The Society for the Advancement of Science required a yearly membership fee which he doubted some of those gathered could afford.

The men around the table clutched inventions of all sizes, from the fist-sized nugget one man absently rolled from hand to hand, to a contraption so large that it obscured the man seated behind it. On either end of the room, overstuffed furniture in dark colors sat beneath the windows overlooking the street. Morgan slipped into the room, unnoticed but for a few furtive glances by those engaged in heated conversation, replete with hand gestures and sarcastic expressions. Not wanting to attract attention, he chose a leather armchair in the corner and sat to take in the proceedings.

The meeting didn't proceed for some time. Members continued to pour in, some lugging inventions to be set up on the table, others empty-handed who, like Morgan, took chairs along the perimeter. A few of the lesser-dressed gentlemen were accompanied by peers, clearly their patrons in the proceedings. Morgan memorized each face, running over what he knew about the various peers. The Billingsley heir, a young fop with a tendency to get half-sprung and race horses down Rotten Row, more interested in impressing women of ill repute than in attending to his studies or the family estate. Baron Abinger, a hefty middle-aged man with a reputation for investing on the ground floor of profitable ventures in steam and other technology. Lord Coleville, a thin, sour-faced old man who didn't often enter into Society. Viscount Folkestone and his friend Baron Marchwood, always trying to out-do one another through their various bets.

Morgan counted at least five other peers of note among the men gathered. One, the Earl of Wycombe's second son, earned himself a position at the table, seated in front of a contraption covered in a white linen sheet. He spoke to no one, eyeing those who ventured near with a wary glare, as if they meant to peek at whatever secret he concealed beneath the cloth.

Any one of these men might have changed their allegiances and decided to ferry information to the French through the sale of their inventions. Morgan paid close attention to the conversations—those who stood in pairs debating, those who demonstrated their device to whoever cared to watch, those who whispered to one another along the perimeter. He watched for the exchange of money or messages. Those who aroused his suspicion, he placed on a mental list of people to investigate.

Two men strode through the door, the shorter with a parcel tucked under his arm. Despite the difference in their heights—nearly a foot between the shorter and the taller—they were obviously related. Both sported auburn hair; the taller man, who looked as young as his companion, neither appearing old enough to sport facial hair, wore his in a fashionably short style with a longer forelock that dripped onto his pale forehead. The shorter man, narrower in the shoulder but thicker in the waist and rump, wore his hair in a long queue. Both had relinquished their hats, but sported hat-head, wisps of hair escaping in disarray. Without preamble, the shorter man claimed the last seat at the table, leaving his grumbling compatriot to find a spot along the perimeter to lounge. The fellow looked bored. He idly contributed to conversation with the man standing beside him, a pudgy blond youth whose whiskers were so pale as to be invisible.

Meanwhile, the shorter man grinned as he fielded questions from the men seated alongside and across from him. He tucked the parcel into his side, refusing to reveal its contents as he shook his head with a smile. His sharp chin was softened by the fluffy white cravat tied around his neck. The curve of his eyebrows looked a bit too precise—a dandy, to be sure—and they betrayed his excitement when he spoke, raising and scrunching in turn. Something about him set Morgan's senses to tingling, but Morgan couldn't put his finger on what. Perhaps the mischievous way his lips curved, as if he knew a salacious secret.

Trusting his instincts, Morgan paid particular attention to this young man as he interacted with other inventors and shook hands with the peers.

At half past seven, according to Morgan's pocket watch, the doddery old man at the head of the table raised his hand. The room fell silent in turns as the occupants noticed him. He coughed into his fist, jiggling his jowls and the unfashionable powdered wig he wore.

Once underway, the meeting flew by. With difficulty, Morgan wrested his attention from the wonders the inventors displayed. Wycombe's son revealed the prototype for a two-wheeled contraption he called a running curricle. Another man unrolled a design for a man-sized flying machine that somewhat resembled a kite. He paid particular attention to the wealthier patrons of the group, citing costs and the time it would take to build and test a prototype. At one point, his eye turned to Morgan, trying to get his attention. With a small shake of the head, Morgan leaned back. As tempting as it would be, he didn't have the time to invest to become the benefactor of an inventor. Judging by the gleam in Folkestone and Marchwood's eyes, the man would have lavish offers heaped upon him by the end of the meeting.

Throughout the meeting, Morgan's eyes continually returned to that short, peculiar man as he tried to name what about him irked Morgan to such an extent. More wonders were revealed, though not the parcel the young man had tucked under his arm. At long last, the meeting disbanded. Out the window, the twilight had deepened into full, inky night.

As Morgan predicted, Marchwood and Folkestone immediately swooped on the man designing the flying machine. Various others jockeyed around the inventors. The noise in the room swelled to a roar as everyone tried to speak at once. In the chaos, Morgan was hard-put to keep his eyes on the groups, searching for anything that exchanged hands.

As he stood, stretching his legs, he found himself near the short young man with the queue and the impish smile, along with that man's lanky relative. The shorter man all but jogged through the room to reach the door.

"Phil—" The taller man brushed a lock of hair out of his eyes, looking harried.

"I'll meet you down by the carriage in twenty minutes. I need to take care of something first."

As the shorter man slipped through the door, his companion clenched his fist at his side. He lingered in the room, staring at the open door with hostility. Something was about to happen, and the lanky young man, about eighteen or twenty at most, would miss it at this rate.

Morgan made no such mistake. Squaring his shoulders, he slipped through the door. His instincts had been clamoring all night, and they were about to be confirmed.

This had to be the spy meeting he'd been waiting for.

Chapter Two

Miss Philomena St. Gobain lengthened her stride as she slipped into the corridor. The herd of inventors would be on her heels in minutes. If she wanted to escape the deluge without being delayed, she had to complete this meeting quickly. She'd slipped an invitation to her "cousin's" upcoming soiree in two days into the hands of every peer crowded around the table. To the men of the Society for the Advancement of Science, she was Phil, the bright cousin of a brilliant but eccentric heiress. Men were fickle. She was certain more than half of her patrons suspected that Phil and Miss St. Gobain were one and the same, but so long as she didn't flaunt her gender during the meetings, they were content not to say a word against her. A word in the wrong ear could bring censure down upon her and lose business.

The money was the bottom line. As a woman, she only served as her brother's regent—the inheritance was his, not hers. Without her clientele among the peerage, she would have nothing. Not that Jared would turn her out, but he might at some point marry and encourage her to do the same. Tie herself to a man who would curtail her freedom and her creativity? That, she would never do.

Her only recourse was to squirrel away money against that eventuality. For that, she plied the interest and curiosity of rich peers with an interest in science. When they turned up at her townhouse on Monday evening, she would use the cover of the ball to arrange for a private tour of her invention room and, with luck, earn herself a few more commissions. Perhaps not Folkestone and Marchwood, who seemed enamored with the thought of racing to their deaths in midair, but several others had probed her for information as to what her "cousin" was currently working on.

The goggles dug through her jacket, waistcoat, and shirt and into her side. With just one small adjustment, she should be able to make them work. She'd painstakingly replicated every single component of the original light-enhancement goggles, or LEGs as she liked to call them. Left to her by her father, their creator, upon his death, they were one of the many mysteries she had sought in the past four and a half years to recreate. Now, she was so close to success she could taste it.

Crossing the fern-patterned runner to the staircase, she descended one floor to a dimly lit hallway. Her eyes adjusted slowly to the faint light as she followed the T corridor by rote, pausing near the junction as she spotted a man's silhouette. He was stocky in the shoulders and chest, only a hand taller than her with a plump face that seemed to dwarf his nose.

Squaring her shoulders, she infused her stance with confidence. She didn't much like dealing with him, but since the pieces she needed to complete her invention had been created in France, she had no choice. Without that particular cut and material of prism, her LEGs wouldn't amplify the ambient light properly—which made them no better than a bizarre fashion choice.

As she stepped abreast of his form, tightening her hold on the package beneath her arm, the stocky man blurted, "Do you have the money?" There was a slight twist to his words, the hint of a French accent.

For a moment, it conjured the image of her father, explaining how one of his fantastical devices would one day change the world—and her life.

She shut her eyes, banishing the image. When she opened them again, she squinted to see her contact, Mr. Lefevre. The light drifting from the rest of the manor was dim. "I do. One moment."

Taking a step back, she reached up to the light in the sconce on the wall. It had been devised by the Society's chairman. A thin cylinder on the side served as a switch. When she rolled it between her fingers as quick as a snap, the inner workings struck the flint and steel together and ignited the small flame. The lamp's angled mirrors did the rest of the work by amplifying the light, much like her LEGs—albeit the LEGs turned the light in toward the eye, whereas the lamp turned it outward and took up a much larger space to do it. The mirrors stretched almost a foot long in places, scalloped like a seashell.

As the light bloomed, Lefevre scowled. His mop of blond hair fell onto his wide forehead. He didn't bother brushing it away.

Phil juggled the parcel under her arm, pulling on the twine that held it closed. The brown paper crinkled as she peeled it away from its contents—not only the goggles, but also a fat purse. It clinked as she handed it to Lefevre. At his insistence, she had brought coins, not a banknote. As she rewrapped the paper around the goggles to keep them from accidentally slipping to the ground, the Frenchman pulled the drawstring on the purse to peek inside.

Phil scowled. "It's all there, like you asked. I trust you have the product?"

With a sneer twisting his plump cheeks, Lefevre thrust his hand into his pocket. He emerged with two identical, intricately-cut transparent rings of glass. His disdainful expression falling from his face, he thrust them into her hand and strode toward the window at the end of the hall.

Her mouth dropped open as she juggled the thick jewels, trying not to drop them. Her parcel slipped from beneath her arm instead. She dove to catch it, fumbling and thrusting her hands beneath just in time to cushion the impact. She winced.

Please don't break. She ran her hands over the parcel, but it felt intact. Quickly, she stuffed the prisms into her pocket. She turned her attention to the window in time to see Lefevre slip onto the sill and grasp the rickety trellis.

What the devil had gotten into him?

The vibration along the floor hailing the approach of footsteps gave her the answer. She tilted her face up to spot who had intruded upon the transaction. Her breath fled as the light illuminated a face she hadn't thought ever to see this close.

The Duke of Tenwick. She'd interacted with his youngest brother, Lord Gideon Graylocke, enough times to recognize the family resemblance. When had he arrived—why? He'd never attended any other meeting. Ordinarily, she might try to interest him in her inventions, but the forbidding set of his sensual mouth warned her that he wasn't in an investing mood. His gray eyes pierced the air like silver bullets.

If his mouth wasn't set in a scowl, he would have been handsome. Devastatingly handsome, in fact. Ebony locks of hair swept over his forehead, punctuated by a vivid white streak at his right temple. His chiseled jaw held the barest kiss of stubble, a shadow framing his mouth and chin. Phil curled her fist, fighting the urge to touch him and feel the rasp beneath her palm. His wide shoulders filled out his dove-gray jacket to distraction. The color seemed to make his eyes gleam —or maybe that was a trick of the light.

Her heart galloped as he neared. Hastily, she sprang to her feet, hoping to meet him on equal footing. It was in vain. He loomed over her, towering even taller than her brother. Her nose scarcely reached his chest. Even if he believed her a man, it was clear from his imperious expression that they were far from equal.

She clutched her parcel to her chest. A glance behind her showed the window ajar, a breeze of cool night air gusting through. Climbing down the trellis was starting to look very appealing.

He's only a man. Titles meant little to her. Her family might not have one anymore, but thanks to her inventions and ingenuity, she was richer than most peers.

Still, as he raked that shiver-inducing gray gaze over her, she couldn't decide if she wanted to flee or press closer.

"Is there a second meeting down this hall that I am unaware of?"

Phil shifted in place. The duke's deep voice was as sinfully sexy as he was. It swept through her like a warm gulp of brandy.

Did he notice her reaction to him? If he did, he would surely guess at her gender. She bit the inside of her cheek as she schooled her expression to a blank mask.

Deepening her voice, she answered, "No, your grace. I was just saying goodbye to a friend." A friend who slipped out the window. "If you'll excuse me..."

She almost curtseyed before she caught herself. How bacon-brained was she? She used the bend in her knees to slip around his form. She arrowed for the staircase at the end of the hall. The bright light cast a long shadow ahead of her, like a pointing finger aiming away from danger.

The duke caught her by the arm before she took more than two steps. His large hand easily wrapped around her bicep. His grip was inescapable, but not punishing. It burned through her clothing, seeming to brand the shape of him into her flesh. Her breath caught. A strange ache blossomed in her gut.

"What do you have there?" His voice was pitched low, intimate. It was the kind of voice that convinced women to strip themselves bare.

Pretend you aren't a woman. Usually, she had no difficulty keeping up the pretense. Society meetings were a time to discuss science, when it was her mind that mattered, not her body.

Her heart stuttered as his gaze dipped from her eyes to her bosom. Did it show? She glanced down, but the paper-wrapped parcel covered her. On a normal night, she might eagerly show it to him, but tonight she clutched it closer. It wasn't complete.

"I'm not at liberty to show it to you. Perhaps at next month's meeting."

His eyebrows swooped down over his eyes like birds of prey, hailing the same predatory mood. "I insist, Mr...?"

Her heart jumped into her throat. She couldn't give him her name!

The stampede of boots on the stairs interrupted the tense moment. The duke retracted his hand immediately, fisting it at his side. Glimpses of the other members came into view.

Phil darted into their midst. She elbowed the lead man aside as she slid into position in front of him. As she escaped down the staircase, the rest of the grumbling line shielding her from her pursuer, she glanced up toward the second floor. His piercing eyes snapping with irritation, the Duke of Tenwick stared after her, mute and motionless. Unable to help herself, she waggled her fingers at him in a little wave a moment before she stepped out of sight.

She didn't know why the duke had singled her out, nor why he was so avid to peek into her parcel, but at the very least, he could pursue her no more. Her life would return to normal, and she would never have to see him again.

Chapter Three

Phil's heart hammered so fiercely, it was a wonder it didn't carve its way out of her chest. Frantically, she turned the pockets of her men's jacket inside out. Her waistcoat earned the same treatment. A single prism bit into her bare palm; she couldn't find the mate.

Canting her head, she hollered, "Meg!"

Where was her maid? Maybe Phil was searching the wrong jacket. If Meg had washed it in the two days since the Society meeting, she might have put the other prism somewhere else. After calling her maid's name again, Phil searched the drawers of her vanity, thinking that it might have been misplaced in there.

"Phil?"

The call was thin and weak; Phil barely heard it.

"I'm in the bedchamber," she yelled back. "Come here a moment!"

The noise that followed sounded uncannily closer to bird wings than it did to the slap of slippers on the wood floor. The sound ceased as abruptly as it began. Phil turned toward the open doorway, but no one appeared. She exhaled sharply with irritation. "Me—"

She scarcely began her maid's name before a sing-song voice pierced the air. It did not at all resemble that of her maid.

"You're...in...a...*pickle!*" The words dragged through the air, stretched to their limit until, at the last, the parrot thrust his head through the top frame of the door, where he must have perched on the other side. The bird's beak was parted in his version of a grin.

Phil shook her head, unable to keep from smiling. "Indeed I am, Pickle. Which is why I called for Meg and not you. You're no help at all in a crisis."

Taking no offense, the bird spread his scarlet wings and soared into the room. For a moment, as he crossed the velvet drapes shielding the bed, he camouflaged so well that the indigo and emerald feathers in his wingtips and tail seemed to move independently. Stirring the air with his vigorous wingbeats, he settled onto the broad perch next to the vanity, installed for his use. Phil had others like it in every room in the manor. The window, facing west, poured in a vibrant orange light that made Pickle look as though he was aflame.

"Have you seen Meg?" Phil lifted her forest green, silk skirt above her ankles as she slipped her feet into the thickly-embroidered slippers

31

resting on the Oriental rug. She crossed to the doorway, her heels clicking as she passed on to the wood floor. A few servants passed through the halls, the footman in the olive-and-white St. Gobain livery, but none resembled her mousy young maid. Phil called her name again, to no avail.

When she turned, she found Pickle examining the prism she had set on the vanity for a moment. He grasped it in his beak, running his tongue across it.

"No, Pickle, drop that at once! It wouldn't make a very good meal." She dashed across the length of the lavish room, startling her pet into flight. He flew over her head and dove out of her bedchamber and into the corridor.

Hiking her skirt to her knees, Phil raced after him. "Pickle, give that back. I need it for a very important project."

One of the most important projects that she'd ever worked on. Upon her father's death, she'd discovered that all the designs for his inventions had been contained in his mind. He hadn't entrusted anything to paper. All she had left of the mind she'd adored so much were the remnants of his past inventions—at least, the ones he hadn't taken with him that fateful day he'd gone to demonstrate his talent. The handful that remained proved an enigma to her as she puzzled out their construction. With the LEGs, she was on the cusp of success.

If she could find the second prism, and *if* Pickle didn't accidentally break the one he carried.

Flapping his wings, spanning over three feet from tip to tip, Pickle soared down the hall and smoothly turned through another open door. Phil skidded in after him a second later.

He'd taken refuge in her secret invention room. The door—an archway with a section of the wall that flipped open upon the press of a hidden switch—had been left open when she'd rushed to retrieve the prisms. Devoid of windows, the secret room was lit entirely by small, glass-paned lanterns to prevent their falling and wreaking havoc on the inventions. Even so, they were placed at intervals well out of reach of the rolled parchments she kept on one side of her work table along the wall. Instead, she placed them on the rare empty shelf in the jumble of machinery, glass, metal, wood, and other materials. Most of the materials were being used for one device or another. The inventions, in various stages of completion, some her own design and some an attempt to replicate one of her father's, were strewn across the room in a jumble of organized chaos, one that Meg often chided was decipherable only to Phil. In the center of the room, a wide perch with a basin beneath—Meg's attempt to confine Pickle's droppings—served as the parrot's throne.

However, instead of sitting his rump on that, he flew to the wide work table. Dropping beside the brown paper-wrapped parcel she'd set there, he abandoned the prism in favor of chewing on the twine. She snatched up the prism, turning it over in her hand to verify that it hadn't chipped. Either Pickle had been unusually delicate in his handling, or the glass was much less fragile than Phil feared.

With her free hand, she shooed the bird away from the parcel. "Stop that, you. That's delicate."

Cocking his head in indignation, the bird spread his wings and glided to the stand in the middle of the room. As he got there, he told her, "Your feet smell like...*pickles*."

"I certainly hope not."

Cackling, the parrot bobbed his head in circles, repeating the word *pickles* all the while.

She stuck her tongue out at him. "It's a lucky thing I'm wearing shoes and no one can smell my feet, you big turkey."

"You're a turkey."

She cocked an eyebrow. "That's not very original now, is it?"

"You're original."

"Why, thank you. I do try." Pursing her lips, she turned to the parcel. "You did have a good idea, for once. Maybe I stuffed one of the prisms in with the LEGs."

"You're a leg."

With a wry look at the bird, who was now grooming his wing, she informed him, "No, my dear. I *have* legs."

He twisted his head to study her with one golden eye. "I have legs." As if to demonstrate, he lifted one of them and curled his claws into his belly.

"Indeed, you do."

When she unwrapped the parcel, he set down both his legs and spread his wings. She whisked the twine into the embroidered reticule hanging from her wrist, out of sight.

"Oh, no. You stay over there."

He froze with his wings half-spread and strained his neck, as if to see where she'd put the string. "What's over there?"

"You are," she told him with a smirk.

The witticism was lost on him.

The paper crinkled as she opened it, speaking to her pet at the same time. "You can't have the twine, my dear. You might swallow it and choke. Even if you don't, it will feel exceedingly odd coming out your other end."

Pickle squawked, indignant. "How do you know?"

"I'm extrapolating, based on the assumption that you won't be able to digest it properly." She shook her head. Sometimes, he sounded as intelligent as a human.

"Meg ate the cackling cheat!"

Other times, he said things like that. Though Phil would be interested to know which of Meg's brothers had taught Pickle *that* particular phrase.

A huff sounded at the doorway. When Phil turned her head, her hands still on the parcel, she found Meg glaring at the parrot. Meagan O'Neill, one of the many O'Neills employed by the St. Gobain family, had been with the family ever since they had arrived in London. Granted, then she had been far too young to work and had been Jared's playmate instead, as they were closer in age. The moment she'd grown old enough to do steady work, she'd latched onto Phil. When Phil had made her bows as a marriageable young woman, she had begged Meg to take up the position of her lady's maid despite the fact that she was four years older than Meg. She'd never regretted the decision. Whether she needed a hairdresser or a confidante, Meg was always close at hand.

After brushing her pale brown hair away from her heavily-freckled cheek, Meg jabbed her finger at the bird. The other hand scrunched around a pair of silk, white gloves. "If I cared to eat you, I'd take you down to mam first and have her roast you. Then you wouldn't be singing no song, I'd say."

Pickle whistled, innocent-looking. When he unfolded his wings, looking like he might take flight, Meg flinched and shuffled from the doorway into the corner, beside the work table. Pickle cackled.

"You did no one any favors when you brought that blighted bird home with you." Meg's voice was weak, her freckles stark against her milk-pale skin.

Phil shrugged. Meg constantly lobbied for her to get rid of the parrot, but Pickle amused her. And despite his occasional threats, he never bit or landed on Meg. Though the latter might be due to the fact that whenever he took to the air, Meg hid beneath the nearest table. She was only brave from across the room.

As Phil lifted the goggles from the paper, she didn't find a prism beneath. She set the one in her hand down on the rough wooden work table. "Have you seen another bit of glass like this? I'm sure I put it in my jacket when I left the Society meeting the other night."

Sidling closer, Meg didn't take her eyes off the parrot. Even her irises were pale, to match the rest of her. A light, icy blue, much darker than Phil's storm-cloud-blue eyes. Meg licked her lips before she answered the inquiry.

"You only had the one in there. I set it on your writing desk when I cleaned the tailcoat."

Phil sighed. "That's where I found this one. Maybe I took it out and put it on the work table for some reason?"

Muttering under her breath, she systematically searched the table from end to end. Meg ventured out of the corner, hovering at Phil's elbow as she alternately tried to convince Phil to give up the venture and argued with the parrot. Phil tuned the pair of them out. When she reached the end of the table only to come up empty handed, she started along the shelves.

Beside her, Meg wrung the gloves in her hands. "I do not smell like pickles, you overgrown canary!"

Phil fought the urge to grin. She pressed her lips together until she had herself under control. Pickle loosed a rude whistle.

"You know pickle is his favorite word."

Meg made a face. It scrunched her freckles together until they looked twice as big. "Then maybe you shouldn't have named him that."

Absently, Phil answered, "It's a bit too late to undo it, now."

She cut a beeline across the room, heading for another shelving unit. Meg skirted the edge, giving the perch and parrot a wide berth.

As her friend rejoined her, Phil added, "Besides, he was in a pickle when I met him, thanks to that horrid old hag. The word seemed to amuse him."

"It still does," Meg grumbled.

No prisms caught Phil's eye. She sighed. Where had she put it? She had one, so the other had to be around here somewhere.

Meg caught her arm as she turned away. "Maybe now isn't the best time to search. In fact, you should put on some gloves, I think." She held up the pair in her hand. "And I'll fix your hair."

"My hair is fine."

Meg raised her pale eyebrows. "It's falling free of your pins again."

"So? Let it fall. In fact, let's take it out."

The young woman rolled her eyes. "I doubt your guests would appreciate your unkempt appearance."

Phil frowned. "What guests?"

"You forgot that it's Monday, didn't you?"

Phil pressed her lips together.

Meg sighed. "The ball?"

"Hell and damnation!" Phil snatched the gloves from her hand and tugged them on.

Pickle reacted to her vehemence, flapping his wings with a vigorous *thwap-thwap-thwap* as he clutched his perch and repeated the expletive.

Phil prayed for patience. "You shouldn't say that, my dear. It's rude."

"Hell and damnation!"

Wonderful. Now he would be repeating it all the night through and her guests would think her savage.

With a sigh, she turned her back to Meg, who was an inch or two taller than her. With a brisk, businesslike touch, Meg coiled the tendrils of Phil's auburn hair escaping the coif and pinned them in place. The moment she finished, Phil turned toward the door.

"Have the guests started to arrive?"

"About half an hour ago." Meg gave Phil a pointed look. "I've been searching for you ever since. I should have known to look in the invention room."

Phil patted her shoulder, the signal for Pickle to fly over. The moment he launched from his perch, Meg squeaked and ducked into the corridor.

"Don't let him—"

Pickle's wing buffeted Phil's coif as he landed on her left shoulder. His claws dug into the thin silk and her flesh beneath. Stifling a wince, she tapped his foot to tell him to ease up. As he settled his wings into a half-folded position for balance, he loosened his clutch on her.

Meg sighed. "That dress cost a fortune. If he soils it..."

Phil shut the door to the invention room. Pickle ran his beak lightly over the shell of her ear, tasting the curve with his tongue. When he reached where the top fused with her skull, he relinquished the exploration and butted her cheek with his beak instead.

"Kiss, kiss."

As requested, she gave him a peck on the beak.

Meg scowled. "You two deserve each other."

Phil tickled the parrot's chest as she grinned. "I certainly think so."

The maid rolled her eyes. "If you need my help after he ruins your hair or your dress, I'll be in the kitchen playing loo."

Phil shrugged with the shoulder not currently weighed down by her pet. "You know I don't much care about my appearance."

"You might decide otherwise after you meet the guests. You have a duke in attendance tonight."

Phil's stomach lurched. She stopped walking as her knees turned weak. Surely Meg didn't mean...

No. The Duke of Tenwick had never attended one of her balls before. He couldn't have connected her to the man he'd met at the club, either. She hadn't given him her name. No, it had to be someone else.

"Are you all right?"

Phil didn't like the worried look on Meg's face. She could be worse than a mother bear, given the smallest semblance of cause. Phil feigned a smile.

"I'm fine. Have fun playing loo. Don't let your brothers cheat you out of your wages this time. If you do, I might as well start paying them instead of you."

Shaking her head, Meg turned on her heel and strode in the opposite direction. She muttered something under her breath that sounded uncomfortably close to, "Why couldn't I have chosen a normal mistress who cared more for ribbons and embroidery than beastly birds and machines?"

I inherited you. So there.

The spiteful words didn't come close to the truth. The O'Neill family was as loyal to Phil as she was to them. She would never turn them out. In fact, she loved them as though they were her own family, even though it wasn't quite true.

The only family she had was Jared.

Pickle squawked in her ear as he dove to nibble on her earring.

And Pickle, too, of course.

She batted him away with her fingers. "Don't chew on that. I have to look presentable tonight, and I won't if you pop the gem out of the setting."

The parrot stopped his chewing. Leaning very close to her ear, he bumped her with his beak and whispered, "*Pickle.*"

Chuckling, Phil strolled down the corridor. The scattered candelabra lit this portion of the townhouse, which was destined to remain unoccupied for the duration of the evening. Save, of course, for those she accompanied up to her invention room. As she passed by the window, she saw that the sun had disappeared beneath the horizon. The sky was a grayish purple, deepening to inky black overhead as the stars began to wink into being.

As she reached the bannister on the staircase, the babble from below rose upward with a swell and burst like the bubbles in a champagne glass. She descended into the corridor. Although the scattered guests moved to and from the sitting room, where card tables had been set up, the bulk of them were contained behind the open double doors leading to the ballroom. Unlike many in London, Phil's townhouse was nearly as big as some ancestral mansions. Four years past when the house had fallen to her as Jared's regent, she had expanded from the original structure, sacrificing the garden out back in order to make room for the ballroom.

The ballroom was a vast rectangular room with wide, costly windows and a vaulting ceiling.

Several chandeliers twinkled from the heights, ringing a larger one in the center. The floor was a marble mosaic, bewitching to the eye. Porcelain pots from China decorated the area between neo-classical pillars on the far end of the room. On one side was a line of chairs, for wallflowers, chaperones, and the infirm; on the other, the orchestra sat on a raised dais as they prepared to play.

This early in the evening, the dance floor was vacant, the dozen or two guests who had arrived early chattering around the edges of the floor in little knots. As Phil paused in the doorway, her appearance caused a stir. Two women in their sixties, one tall and thin with a chemisette filling in her neckline to the chin and the other short and plump with a daring cut to her dress and narrowed eyes, twittered to one another. The first, who Phil recognized as Mrs. Biddleford, a notorious gabble-grinder, had to bend nearly double to press her head near her companion, Miss Maize. They squawked nearly as adamantly as Pickle, who reared his head to transfix them with a pugnacious look in his eye.

"Pudding house."

This, to him, was a grievous insult.

Raising her chin, Phil ignored the busybodies. Let them say what they would. She had only invited them because of Mrs. Biddleford's connection to the esteemed Lord Strickland, the son of Biddleford's older sister.

Several others on the guest list tonight had been invited simply because not to do so would be a grievous insult. Phil didn't care to embroil herself in *ton* politics; she only cared for the revenue opened by the deep pockets of her patrons. Although she craned her neck, she didn't spot anyone she had invited with an aim of showing one of her inventions. In fact, this early she didn't spot any of the richer peers. Those who typically showed up at this early hour were those with the most to gain from rubbing shoulders with the titled peers, along with desperate matchmaking mamas. In fact, Jared was ensconced right now with a woman in a golden dress, and he didn't look happy about it. The back of her brunette head was to Phil.

Pickle whistled provocatively, gaining the attention of several nearby guests. Phil smiled at them, offering a word of greeting to counteract Pickle's name-calling as she strolled around the perimeter of the ballroom. Where was this duke Meg had announced? Phil made it a point to familiarize herself with the physical appearance of all the highest peers in the country, especially the ones called eccentrics. As she toured the room, her rapid pulse slowed. He wasn't here—not the

Duke of Tenwick or any other duke. Meg must have been mistaken.

"What a charming bird."

Phil turned with a smile at the young woman's voice. She was about seventeen, taller than Phil and not as round in the hip and breast. Her inky black hair was coiled atop her head and threaded with pearls that looked real to Phil's inexpert gaze. A double string of pearls lined the young woman's throat, following the lace-edged bodice of an embroidered muslin dress over a creamy underdress—an appropriately pale color for a debutante. Phil, who had no designs on marrying, didn't give a fig's end whether or not she conformed to the fashion standards of the *ton*. Let the gabble-grinders call her long in the tooth if they wanted.

Without a care for her pristine, white silk gloves, the young woman lifted her hand to stroke Pickle's feathers. She giggled when he gently took her index finger between his beak and ran his tongue along the length.

"It tickles." Her cheeks turned rosy. Her deep brown eyes twinkled.

Phil couldn't help but smile. Anyone charmed by her bird was a good person, in her books. "He's very gentle, though he likes to pretend to be a bully sometimes."

46

As if to prove her point, Pickle released the young woman's hand and said, "Meg ate the pickle!"

The girl laughed, clapping her hand over her mouth. "Who's Meg?"

"My maid. She's a bit afraid of him."

"Who could be?" The young woman stroked Pickle's chest. "Does he help you with your inventions?" Several expressions crossed her face, shock and chagrin among them, before she gushed, "Forgive me, that was terribly forward of me. It's just that I've heard you are an inventor. I find it fascinating. I'm Lucy, by the way."

"It's nice to meet you, Lucy. Call me Phil." Normally, Phil wouldn't be so intimate with a woman she'd just met, but it would feel odd being called 'Miss St. Gobain' by a woman whose surname she didn't know.

Despite Lucy's obvious innocence, a flush of caution swept through Phil. How had Lucy known she was an inventor? Phil liked to keep knowledge of her hobby restricted to certain clientele that could afford to purchase what she created, but the excited gleam in Lucy's eye made it difficult not to feel at ease around her. Not to mention that if the pearls she was practically enshrouded in were, indeed, real, then the girl had money. Maybe she would be interested in purchasing something.

Beaming, Lucy asked, "Do you find it difficult, being a woman inventor?"

"It can be challenging at times. Men like to think they are the masters at everything, including the ability to generate ideas."

Lucy rolled her eyes. "I have four older brothers. I know exactly what you mean. I'm a writer and they don't understand my desire to research."

Phil smiled. "Yes. Well. I'm sure they mean well." Not that she knew any such thing, but it seemed like the proper thing to say.

Lucy shrugged. "Yes, I suppose they do. Actually, it's wonderful that we've met." Lucy reached out, almost as if she meant to take Phil's arm, but Pickle's presence on Phil's shoulder barred her from doing so. After a moment's hesitation, she let her hand fall and leaned closer instead. "I have so many questions I'd like to ask you. Would you mind if I called on you some time?"

"Not at all." In that, at least, Phil could be genuine. "If you come sometime in the morning or afternoon, I'll show you a few of my inventions."

"Smashing!" Lucy's wide smile dazzled. "The heroine of my latest book *was* going to be a swashbuckling princess, but now I'm thinking it might be best for her to do some inventing. Perhaps she creates her own guns."

Phil blinked twice before she found the words to answer. "She sounds like...a very capable woman." An eccentric woman, to be sure. Being an eccentric herself, Phil could appreciate that.

Smugly, Lucy answered, "All the best women are."

I agree. Phil pressed her lips together, though a smile teased at the corners of her mouth.

With unbridled enthusiasm, Lucy asked, "Have you ever created a gun, Phil?"

"I have not."

"A pity. Perhaps you ought to try."

If you have the money to invest, I'd be willing to design anything you like. Phil didn't dare venture the phrase aloud, not with an acquaintance she'd met five minutes ago. Although her penchant for inventing was well known, the fact that she sold her creations was a well-kept secret. If widely known, she—and her brother's social statuses would be reduced, much the way the rich men of industry were treated. The indolent *ton* preferred to embrace those who appeared, on the surface at least, to be every bit as unambitious.

"Have you met my brothers?"

Phil's head spun at the abrupt change in topic. "No, I have not. I hope you don't mean to ask me to shoot one of them."

Lucy laughed, a loud, unrestrained sound. "No, of course not." She half-turned away. "Come with me, and I'll introduce you. I left them with Mother."

The young woman left Phil with no choice as she turned her back and sashayed across the room. Phil quickened her step to follow. They approached a group in the corner, consisting of a woman near the age of fifty with chestnut hair threaded through with gray, wearing a ravishing violet dress, and two impossibly tall, broad-shouldered men with black hair who had their backs turned. Lifting her skirt above her ankles with one hand and waving her other through the air, Lucy called, "Giddy!"

Pickle took up the cry, repeating the word over and over again.

The taller man, slightly lankier than his companion, turned. His hair swept over his forehead, his sideburns lining the hinges of his chiseled jaw. The rest of his chin was dark with the shadow of stubble, a beard battling to come to fruition despite his attempt at shaving. His cravat was askew, likely having been tugged on a half-dozen times until it hung off-center. Phil recognized that long nose, slightly turned up at the tip, and the shrewd green eyes that seemed brighter in contrast to his black evening jacket.

Lord Gideon Graylocke.

Phil faltered. Unfortunately, she was too close to the group. Lucy snatched her hand and dragged her across the last pace until she stood between the two men. Lord Gideon, on her right, inclined his head.

"Miss St. Gobain. It's always a pleasure to see you."

Shakily, Phil returned the greeting. She kept her face turned away from the man on her left, even though his gaze felt like fire licking at her profile.

Lucy looked disappointed. "So you have met them."

Phil forced a smile. "Only Lord Gideon, I'm afraid. We've attended several lectures and meetings together." In fact, she had at one point tried to interest him in commissioning a better irrigation system for his plants. He had insisted that he preferred to water them himself, and have that personal touch.

At Phil's words, Lucy Graylocke brightened. "Then may I introduce you to my oldest brother, the Duke of Tenwick? Morgan, this is—"

"Miss St. Gobain." Phil blurted her name as she turned, not wanting Lucy to use the same nickname she used at the Society for the Advancement of Science meetings. The smile she tried to fix to her mouth immediately fell away.

It was definitely him. The man who had cornered her at the meeting, who had nearly uncovered her identity. His Brutus haircut was perfectly styled, the kiss of stubble lined his jaw as he inclined his head to her. His gray eyes pierced her, as if rooting through her soul to uncover any other secrets she kept from him.

Her breath caught. Did he recognize her? Would he expose her, have her barred from future meetings? He was a duke; he had the power to do anything he liked.

Something caught the light as he fiddled with something near the pocket of his royal blue jacket. He turned it and for a moment, her heart stopped beating. It was her prism, the piece she needed to complete her LEGs. She must have dropped it at the club. Did he know?

Paralyzed, she raised her gaze to his.

Pickle squawked in her ear. "You're in a *pickle.*"

Indeed, she was. And she didn't know how she would get out of it.

Chapter Four

"Kiss, kiss."

Miss St. Gobain looked as panicked at the parrot's words as Morgan was. The color drained from her cheeks. Her thick eyelashes fluttered wildly in front of her stormy blue-gray eyes. Her lips half-pursed, sending an inconvenient tingle through his chest and lower. Surely the bird didn't mean for him to kiss her!

She bussed the parrot's beak instead. An odd sweep of mingled relief and disappointment washed through him. With her heart-shaped face, secretive curve of her lips, and curvaceous figure, kissing her would be far from a trial.

He didn't have the time to succumb to her temptations or that of any other woman. He had a spy to find. Every minute he spent at this ball and others like it was a minute wasted.

Unfortunately, his mother had insisted on his attendance, and he didn't deny his mother anything.

As if his thoughts of her drew her attention, she laid her hand on his sleeve, every bit as tenaciously as the bird perched on Miss St. Gobain's shoulder. "What a delightful animal," Mother exclaimed. "Don't you think, Morgan, dear?"

Morgan exchanged a glance with his brother, on Miss St. Gobain's other side. Gideon, a foot-and-a-half taller than the hostess, shrugged as if to say, *Well, don't you?*

Morgan put on his most charming ducal smile, the one he kept reserved for soirees like this one, when he was expected to be a duke first, a man second, and pretend he had no connection to Britain's spying efforts at all. It chafed.

"He is a charming parrot, Miss St. Gobain." There. That should absolve him of all obligations to lavish attention on the bird. Although the parrot was charming in his own way, Morgan itched to circulate. Someone in the *ton* had changed their allegiance to side with the French. He didn't have time to stand here talking about parrots. He had to find that person.

The parrot sidled closer, twisting his head at an odd angle to survey Morgan with an astute golden eye. His claws dimpled the fine silk of her emerald gown, an unfashionably dark color for an unmarried woman. Could she be engaged? An uncomfortable feeling pinched Morgan's stomach.

Her marital status is none of your concern. Even so, he couldn't tear his gaze away from the sweep of her décolletage. The line of lace flirted with the ample swell of her bosom, and the rich color of the dress gave her skin an even creamier cast. A lock of auburn hair had escaped from her coiffure to caress the curve of her neck. He found himself enthralled by the sight.

The parrot squawked, as if he noticed Morgan's straying gaze. Gathering himself, Morgan chanced a glance at his family to see if they'd noticed his momentary preoccupation. Apparently, mere heartbeats had passed. It felt like an eternity.

All the more reason to make his excuses and circulate. He balled his fist at his side to keep from adjusting his cravat.

"Your nose looks funny."

Morgan frowned at the parrot. "I beg your pardon?"

The words scarcely left his lips before the bird drew himself up. "Like a *pickle*."

Lucy sniggered, elbowing Gideon in the side. From the way Mother pressed her fan to her mouth, she attempted to hold back a laugh, too. None of them were any help.

Cocking an eyebrow, Morgan tried to replicate his brother, Tristan's, usual joking air. "I do believe I've been insulted."

Apparently, he failed. The pert bow of Miss St. Gobain's pink lips parted. She raised her hands, which only jostled the bird, who squawked in indignation.

"I'm terribly sorry. Your nose does not at all resemble a pickle."

Lucy and Gideon lost the battle to contain themselves and burst into raucous laughter that had them both clutching their sides as they doubled over.

Miss St. Gobain raised her voice above their interruption as she reached out, laying her hand on his sleeve. "Your nose is attractively shaped, I assure you." She snatched her hand back, leaving his arm tingling in its absence as she wrung her hands in front of her waist. "I mean, um, Pickle... He didn't mean anything by it, of course. Pickle, apologize at once."

Thrashing Miss St. Gobain in the back of the head with his wing, the bird erupted in a ringing cry of, "Funny pickle! Funny pickle!"

Color stained her cheeks. If anything, it added to her allure. "No, Pickle, you are *not* funny. You are rude. Your Grace, please forgive his precociousness."

Morgan smiled tightly. Her distress leeched the amusement from the moment. "He's only a bird, Miss St. Gobain. I doubt he understands what he's saying."

Relief crossed her face. She stopped wringing her hands in front of her. When she opened her mouth, her bird screeched instead.

"Kiss, kiss!"

With an exasperated look, Miss. St. Gobain puckered her lips and leaned forward.

The ornery bird turned his head. "Not you."

Was he staring at Morgan? Good God, surely the bird couldn't be asking for a kiss from him. That would make all the scandal rags, if the Duke of Tenwick was seen kissing a bird.

Puffing out his chest, the parrot flapped his wings, buffeting both his mistress and Morgan. Pickle had a surprising wing span. And strength— the blow stung for a second.

"Kiss, kiss," he demanded.

"He must be agitated from meeting all these new people. I should stow him away someplace quiet. Your Grace, Lord Gideon, Lady Graylocke, Lady Lucy." Miss St. Gobain spewed her words in a high, hasty voice as she dipped her knees in a shallow curtsey.

Morgan, who had already bent forward, resigned to his fate, wasn't prepared for her to flee. His nose brushed the top of her tower of curls and he inhaled a whiff of her perfume. Beneath the ladylike floral scent was something sharper. Was that mineral oil?

Without looking at him, she turned on her heel and marched into the growing crowd. Morgan straightened, dumbfounded. What had just happened? And why hadn't she looked him in the eye the entire time?

Wiping her eyes but still chuckling, Lucy straightened. "I like her."

"Of course you do," Morgan muttered under his breath. Knowing his sister, he would have a devil of a time convincing her not to adopt a bird after a spectacle like that.

Confirming his suspicions, Lucy added, "We should get a parrot."

"No, we should not."

Her mouth dropped open at his abrupt tone. He never spoke sharply to her.

Mother smacked him in the arm with her fan. "Morgan! Don't speak to your sister that way."

He took a deep breath, and added in a more calm tone, "Forgive me. I didn't mean to raise my voice. But, Lucy, you don't have time to devote to a pet. You have research for your novel, remember?"

Heaven help him when he was using that unfortunate habit of hers to get his way. She would never let him live it down.

She pouted. "I suppose you're right... I am terribly busy. But maybe Giddy could—"

Gideon shook his head, his mouth flattening into a stubborn line. "Not on your life."

Lucy's face fell.

Mother laid her hand on Lucy's sleeve. "I could look after the bird while you're busy, my dear."

"Mother." Morgan groaned.

She met him stare for stare, raising her eyebrow. "Morgan."

With his index and middle finger, he rubbed circles over his right temple, where his pulse throbbed violently. "Very well, I wish you well with your bird."

Lucy squealed in delight. Although the soiree hadn't yet gone into full swing, the noise drew the attention of several nearby gentlemen and ladies. Once they noticed the woman making the sound, the men's looks grew appreciative. Morgan glared at them. His gaze, he'd been told, pierced like steel. Their grins slipped as they averted their gazes.

Mother laid a hand on his arm, drawing his attention. "Thank you," she murmured, her voice soft.

Gideon was looking remarkably harried as Lucy latched onto his arm and regaled him with all the fun they would have together with their new pet. In fact, he looked a tad nauseated.

Mother added, "It will be nice to have a pet in the house, to add to the cheer, especially if we can find a bird that speaks as charmingly as the one Miss St. Gobain has."

"Charming?" He almost choked on the word. "The bird accused me of having a pickle-shaped nose!"

Mother shrugged. "If you do, you get it from your father."

Morgan didn't know if he meant to cough or laugh. The strangled noise that issued from his throat was something in between.

Mother tugged him toward the chairs at one end of the ballroom. "Come now, dear. Have you met Miss Mandeville? She trims a darling bonnet."

As if he cared about a woman's ability to add ribbon to a bonnet. Unfortunately, now that he was in his mother's grasp, she refused to let him go. He had no choice but to meet the unsuspecting debutante.

Then, perhaps, he would be able to sneak away and survey the guests for possible traitors.

***

Morgan did not get away. His mother dragged him from one debutante to the next, throwing him into the arms of several in an effort to convince him to dance. The one woman whose dancing skills he wondered about remained resolutely on the edges of the ballroom—when she was in attendance at all. That loud, insulting parrot on her shoulder made her presence abundantly known.

Despite her claims, she hadn't stowed him away in another room for the duration of the ball.

Perhaps it was for the best that she always seemed to be flitting to the next guest, a step ahead of him. There was something about her that made his skin tingle with awareness, his spy senses on high alert. Did he know her from somewhere? If so, he would certainly have remembered her. She wasn't like any other woman in his acquaintance.

Most, if not all, unmarried women of his acquaintance threw themselves at the Duke of Tenwick. Some of the married ones, too. Miss St. Gobain, on the other hand, made a point never to meet his gaze, let alone cross paths with him. Was she playing a game?

Perhaps it was better if he never found out. It would be blasted difficult to dance with a woman while a parrot perched on her shoulder.

Even so, the moment he and his family stepped foot in the Tenwick townhouse, he resolved never to repeat tonight. As his mother and sister disappeared upstairs to the bedchambers on the third floor to get undressed, he latched onto Gideon's arm.

"You have to help me with Mother."

Giddy shook his head, pulling free. "Oh, no. If she doesn't have you to pair off, she'll undoubtedly turn to me. This business with Tristan marrying has only encouraged her."

Morgan swallowed. *I'm only thirty. I'm not ready to marry.* Was he? Marriage was a perfunctory arrangement meant to bring the estate an heir. He knew how to perform in the marriage bed, even if, with this business of the war and the responsibility of maintaining the dukedom's reputation, he'd abstained for far too long.

You don't have what Tristan and Freddie have. Maybe not, but did he need it? Tristan was head over heels in love. It was nauseating to watch. He barely recognized his brother in the devoted, attentive husband he'd become. Before Tristan had met his wife, Morgan hadn't realized that his brother hadn't truly been happy.

Am I happy?

It didn't matter.

"Please," he begged his brother. "I don't have time to hunt for a wife right now."

"You could let Mother make the choice for you. I'm sure everything would be settled inside a week."

For the first time in his life, Morgan understood how those wilting, delicate debutantes felt when they swooned. "Zeus, anything but that."

Giddy laughed. "I was only teasing."

Morgan shook his head. The light of the single candelabra in the foyer blurred. It reflected off the lines of gilt on the large vase next to the door. The white marble floor shimmered in the light. The polished oak bannister gleamed as it rose toward the second story of the house. Shadows swathed the doorways leading away from the foyer.

Gideon gripped Morgan's shoulder, squeezing. "Are you all right? You look pale."

"I'm in the pink of health."

"Is this about Mother's matchmaking? If you feel so strongly about it, tell her—"

Morgan shrugged off his brother's hand. "I said I'm fine. But I have important business and Mother and Lucy's machinations are curtailing my movements. I need your help."

Giddy narrowed his eyes. A lock of his dark hair fell into his eyes. He didn't appear to notice. He lowered his voice to a hush. "Is this the kind of business you and Tristan normally have?"

Morgan opened his mouth to answer, but he couldn't find the right words. How did Gideon learn of his and Tristan's extracurricular activities? The two brothers had done their damnedest to keep their family away from their business as spies. Lucy was the hardest to keep in the dark, since her curiosity often led her to places she shouldn't be at inopportune times. But Giddy... He spent the majority of his time in the orangery, away from everyone, including Morgan.

At Morgan's speechlessness, Giddy drew himself up until he loomed over Morgan, though he wasn't quite as intimidating with his cheeks still a bit soft with youth, his hair in disarray, and his lankier build. Morgan noticed a glint of Tristan's rebelliousness in their youngest brother's eye.

"You aren't as inconspicuous as you'd like to think you are. If this is family business, I'd like to know about it. I'm almost twenty-four. I'm not a child."

Morgan released a breath. He raised his hand to fiddle with the lock of white hair at his temple. "It isn't family business."

Giddy raised an eyebrow, his mouth set in a stubborn line.

After glancing around to ensure that no servants eavesdropped on the conversation, Morgan reluctantly admitted, "Tristan and I serve the Crown."

Giddy's shrewd green eyes gained a calculating look. Morgan could almost see the cogs spinning in his head as he sifted through the information. His lips barely moving, Gideon murmured, "As spies?"

Morgan neither confirmed nor denied this. He didn't want to bring his family into the danger. Tristan had narrowly missed enough scrapes for Morgan to know exactly how dangerous field work was.

With a gleam in his eye, Giddy stepped closer, blocking Morgan's path toward the stairs. When the botanist crossed his arms, Morgan was surprised to notice solid muscle shaping the fabric of his tailcoat. At six and a half feet tall, he would likely have frightened any man other than Morgan. Morgan was suddenly struck with the reality that his brother *wasn't* a boy any more. He was a man.

"I want to take over Tristan's position. Let me help."

At twenty-four, Morgan had already been Duke for four years. Granted, he had been young to inherit the position and the responsibility had matured him. But he'd never been able to grasp things as quickly as Gideon, nor had he been as studious. Giddy was likely better able to take care of himself than Morgan had been at his age.

Morgan dropped his hand from his temple. "Tristan is in Tristan's position. He hasn't retired."

"No, but he's not in London, is he? He's on his honeymoon, and you need someone to watch your back."

Tristan was usually the man in the field, with Morgan providing additional support as needed. However, Morgan decided to keep that fact to himself. Even if he was willing to sit idly behind a desk—which he was not—his brother wasn't properly trained. The training of spies fell under Morgan's jurisdiction, but with a pivotal mission on the field and Strickland breathing down his neck to finish the job, he didn't have the time.

Gideon added, "If you won't accept my help, I'll tell Lucy about this endeavor." His voice was light, as if he didn't care one way or another. He shrugged one shoulder.

He was a terrible liar. He wouldn't put their sister in danger any more than Morgan would. Even if neither of them were children any longer, Lucy was a thousand times more reckless than Gideon. At least Morgan could count on Giddy to think his actions through before he made them.

With a sigh, Morgan shook his head in disapproval. "Blackmail, Gideon?"

His brother hiked up his chin. Throughout the evening, he'd gathered the deepening shadow of stubble along his jaw. All the Graylocke brothers were thus afflicted; Morgan had to shave twice a day if he hoped to keep his appearance presentable. Some days, he prayed for beards to come back into fashion, just to save him the trouble.

Giddy said, "You need my help. You said so yourself. That's the price for putting myself in Mother's matchmaking sights."

"And Lucy. Don't forget about her."

The younger man made a face. "The day she tries to convince me to marry is the day I resume leaving frogs in her bed."

"She'd probably adopt one as a pet."

The glimmer of a smile crossed Giddy's face. He didn't argue.

Morgan jabbed a finger at his brother. "You will stay out of the field."

He nodded, more of his hair falling into his eyes. "Done."

"And do what I say."

"How is that different from any other day?"

Morgan clenched his jaw. "*Gideon.*"

"Fine, yes."

The weight started to lift from Morgan's shoulders as he warmed to the idea. He had been nervous about entering the field without Tristan. He could do it, of that he had no doubt, but the idea of doing it alone left a sour taste in his mouth. However, if Tristan had been in London, he would have taken over the investigation and left Morgan on the sidelines.

Morgan was always left behind. He couldn't go off to war because he was the duke and needed to beget an heir. His position in the spy network, that of a secondary spymaster to Strickland, had been crafted for that very reason, as well. He was too important, to the family and to England. In reality, it was Morgan's position as Duke that was important, not him. He compiled reports. He trained spies.

This mission was his chance to prove that he could do more.

Morgan caught and held his brother's gaze. "If you want to help, you cannot under any circumstances tell Mother or Lucy." A shudder crawled down Morgan's spine as he thought of their reactions. Mother would likely worry herself into an early grave. Lucy would march up to Strickland's house and demand to be included, even though she was the most conspicuous person Morgan knew.

Given the look on Giddy's face, the same horrifying thoughts crossed his mind. "Agreed."

"Then let's continue this conversation in the study."

Morgan's study in the Tenwick townhouse was located on the second floor nestled between a sitting room overlooking the street and the formal library. As he and his brother mounted the stairs, their footsteps echoing in the eerily silent house. Most, if not everyone, had gone to sleep.

The second floor was dark, without a single candle to light their path, but Morgan knew the way by rote. He found the right door and let himself in, cocking an ear for anything or anyone out of place. Silence. As he crossed to the mantle, he used a tinderbox to light a pair of candles. Once they cast a rosy glow around the room, he snuffed the tinder and returned the box to its place on the mantle.

Giddy claimed one of the leather chairs in front of Morgan's desk. Papers stacked neatly, in pile after pile, on the surface. Since his return to London three days ago, the spy reports had been directed to the townhouse instead of the ancestral estate. He tried to skim as many as he could before forwarding them to his assistant, recuperating from a gunshot wound in the country.

As he stretched out his legs in front of him, Gideon laced his fingers behind his head. "So, why are you in London?"

Morgan poured them both a snifter of brandy before he dropped into the chair next to his brother, rather than his usual position behind the desk. He didn't want this to feel like a formal instruction. They clinked glasses and he took a sip, relishing the warm burn, before he answered.

"It begins with Harker."

"Elias Harker? The one who died at Tenwick Abbey earlier this month?"

Morgan nodded. He took another sip before he confessed, "Harker was a French spy."

Gideon's mouth dropped open. "That weasel? Who would want him?"

"The French, apparently."

Shaking his head, Giddy shrugged, incredulous. "So you killed him?"

Morgan didn't flinch. He had killed a man before, in the line of duty. If at all possible, he didn't want to repeat it, no matter their allegiance. "I didn't, personally. I tried to arrest him, but he refused to be taken alive."

Giddy clawed off his cravat, letting it hang loose. His throat worked as he took a sip. After he finished processing the information, he ventured, "Sounds like he was on his way to the hangman's noose, anyway. What does he have to do with your sudden urge to return to London?"

"Harker's allegiances were well known, for years. We had someone in place, monitoring him and reporting on his movements."

His new sister-in-law's mother, in fact. She and her other daughter, Charlotte, had returned to Harker's estate to gather what belongings they could before the Crown seized the house. He had extended them his hospitality, given that they had nowhere else to go.

Morgan rubbed the streak in his hair. "We weren't supposed to interfere with Harker."

"Ah."

His brother, usually much more verbose, said nothing more.

Morgan added, "As punishment, I have to uncover his replacement in the *ton*. Strickland—our spymaster—is convinced France will push to have someone fill Harker's shoes."

Gideon raised an eyebrow. "You aren't convinced?"

"I think a spy in the servant class would have more freedom of movement and won't draw as many rapt gazes, eager to dig up a scandal. But I've only been doing this for half a decade. What do I know?" With those bitter words, he gulped another mouthful of brandy. Only a finger remained in the glass. He swirled it, letting it breathe.

"I probably don't have enough information about France's tactics to give my opinion," Giddy said slowly, "but I'm inclined to agree with you. You, of all people, know how nosy the *ton* can be."

Morgan grinned. "I knew you were my favorite brother for a reason."

Although he tried to hide the reaction behind a sip of brandy, Morgan noticed his brother's cheeks turn pink.

"So, where do we start looking?"

Morgan's chest clenched. *Not 'we.' Me.* For all that Giddy was quick of mind, he didn't have the experience Morgan had, nor the training. He couldn't condone sending his baby brother out into the field.

Choosing his words carefully, he said, "I'm following a lead from Strickland at the moment that started with the Society for the Advancement of Science. He handles the reports from London, not me, so I'm working on secondhand knowledge."

Gideon frowned. He rubbed at the stubble on his chin. "That sounds inefficient. Maybe we ought to talk to this Strickland, and have the reports sent here instead."

Morgan shrugged. "I don't have the time to attend to the reports I usually do—Keeling is handling those at the moment."

"Your valet who was shot?"

He raised his eyebrows. "My assistant. Surely you didn't think Tristan and I were the only spies on the Tenwick estate."

"But you left him at Tenwick Abbey."

Morgan shrugged. "I'm borrowing Tristan's assistant for now."

"His valet." Giddy's voice was flat. After a moment to think about it, he shook his head ruefully. "And here I thought Tristan wanted a private holiday with his new wife, without servants to interrupt."

A grin pulled at Morgan's lips. "I'm sure he wants that. He's quite smitten, you know."

"I know." Giddy put his tumbler down on a corner of the desk. He drummed his fingers on the wood. "I could handle the reports, you know. Look for connections. I'm good at that sort of thing. Not as good as you, but a decent second."

Morgan was flattered that his genius younger brother thought he could do something better. "I'll send a note to Strickland."

After draining the contents of his glass, he stood and rounded his desk, fishing out a sheet of foolscap. As he jotted down the request, he added, "I doubt he'll relinquish the originals, but perhaps he can send us the compiled reports from those in the *ton* or those watching high society."

Leaning across the desk, Giddy's eyes gleamed. "What language are you writing in?"

Morgan spared a glance at the words he'd written without thinking. "English. But it's in code, in case the message is intercepted." He sprinkled sand onto the page to dry the ink. "Are you tired? I'll teach you."

Gideon sat straighter. "I'm wide awake."

"Good." Morgan smiled. It was destined to be a long night, but he couldn't regret it. Sharing this part of spy work with his brother, who seemed as enthusiastic about it as Morgan was, felt good. He didn't feel quite so much like a useless ornament tonight.

Chapter Five

Phil rapped on the dark mahogany door hard enough to sting her knuckles. The smooth wood, carved with an intricate scroll pattern in the corners, was nestled between the dusky gray stone walls of a six-story townhouse with a slate roof. The Tenwick townhouse perched on the edge of a square of other lofty homes, separated by a shared mews and dirt alleys leading to spacious gardens behind. In the center of the square was a fenced park of graveled walkways twining between the trees. The square screamed of money and influence. Phil wasn't surprised at all to discover this was the townhouse of a Duke.

A tall, prim-looking older man opened the door from within, sixty if he was a day. Snowy white hair pulled back in a queue—a wig or his hair?—complemented the silver trim on his azure livery. He raised bushy eyebrows that resembled small snowbanks perched over his clear, blue eyes. His long face ended in a thin-lipped mouth pulled into a neutral line.

"May I help you?"

"That depends if you intend to let me in." Phil fished a calling card from the reticule hanging off her left wrist. The corner of the card was crinkled, but she hoped it wasn't too noticeable. She thrust it into his hand. "I'm here to see Lady Lucy Gray-locke."

Liar. Phil bit the inside of her cheek. She matched the butler's stare.

Hell's bells, given his impeccable composure, his pedigree was probably more pristine than hers was! No doubt his family had served the Gray-lockes since the dawn of time, when the now-lofty ducal house had lived in a cave with their pet dinosaurs. Phil, whose family had literally been turned out of their estate at gunpoint, felt like slime for venturing to the Tenwick townhouse under false pretenses.

Unfortunately, it couldn't be helped. The Duke of Tenwick had something that she wanted—no, *needed*. Desperately.

In a voice that chilled, the butler informed her, "It's ten of the morning."

"Does Lady Lucy like to lay abed?" Phil had been counting on just such a thing. "Perhaps, if you'll let me wait in the sitting room, you can ask and see if she'll see me."

The grizzled man stared at her for what felt like an eternity. Then, with an almost impercepti-ble sigh, he stepped to the right. "Very well, miss."

Phil almost dropped to the ground and kissed the chiseled stone stairs. She didn't know what she would have done if he'd denied her entry. Climbed the wall and snuck in like a cat burglar? That sounded like it would require more finesse than even her inventions could give her.

"This way."

She followed the butler the few feet to the front parlor. To the left, polished wooden stairs climbed to the upper levels of the townhouse. Although she suspected that the women of the house were still abed, the men likely at White's or some other male abode, the house bustled with activity. Maids ducked in and out of rooms, their dresses mismatched but for the azure apron. Footmen in full livery stopped to flirt with them at doorways, a pause in completing their own tasks. The servants seemed at ease here, evidence that the duke wasn't a cruel master.

Lucky for her, because if he discovered what she was about to do, he would not be happy with her.

With a smile, she sailed into the parlor. This one, likely reserved for guests, was a masterpiece in opulence and an odd juxtaposition of masculine and feminine. Sturdy, wing-backed chairs in brown leather were nestled between dark wood tables matching the mantle. The tables held delicate lace doily napkins, a match for the spindly-legged white settee and chairs. The wallpaper was a neutral beige color, which might have been drab if not for the flourish of red roses above the dark-paneled dado. The air smelled sweet with spring flowers stemming from a glazed vase on the largest tables. The vase overflowed with vibrant blooms. Phil expected no different, considering a botanist lived on the premises.

When she snuck a glance over her shoulder, she found the doorway vacant. The butler must have already gone upstairs to wake Lucy. That meant that Phil didn't have much time. If Lucy was as enthusiastic to question her today as she had been at the ball yesterday, Phil didn't have much time to do what she'd come to do.

Somewhere in this house, the Duke of Tenwick had the prism she needed to complete her LEGs. And she was going to steal it back.

As she darted back into the hall, a squeal split the air—and it did not come from above stairs. Fully dressed in a sea-green walking dress, Lucy erupted from a room down the hall. "Phil, how lovely to see you!"

The poor, haggard butler followed in her wake. "Forgive me, miss. You should have mentioned you were a particular friend of Lady Lucy's."

Speechless, Phil stared at the butler while Lucy squeezed the daylights out of her with a fierce hug. "I didn't know I was. We only met yesterday."

Lucy, seeming not to mind the half-hearted conversation going on behind her back, released Phil and stepped back. Phil gulped for air, only to have it flee her lungs in a rush when Lucy latched onto her hand and yanked her into the drawing room. She stumbled, but managed to keep her feet.

"I'm so happy you decided to call. I have so many questions to ask you." With brisk little pushes, Lucy herded Phil onto the settee. "Stay right there. I jotted my questions down in my notebook, which is in my reticule in my room. I'll ring for tea. Stay there."

Phil's ears rang with the velocity and pitch of her words. Before now, she wouldn't have thought Lucy's behavior last night to be restrained. It was charming, if overwhelming. Before she knew it, she found herself alone in a parlor blanketed in blissful silence.

A serene gait broke the silence with a steady *click, click, click.* As Phil raised her gaze, still lost for words, the dowager duchess appeared in the doorway. In the daylight streaming in from the broad window looking out onto the street, the resemblance between her and Lucy was plain. Both had dark hair—Lucy's a touch darker—and a similarly shaped face. The dowager even resembled her sons, in the shape of her eyes and the proud way she held herself. Her eyes narrowed as she swept her gaze over Phil's attire.

Phil hadn't dressed with a mind toward impressing one of the oldest and most powerful families in Britain. She wore an amber riding dress decorated with the barest hint of lace across the dip of the neckline, covered by her modest beige spencer. She wore no jewels and her hair was simply dressed, braided and then pinned to the back of her head. Unruly strands already fought their way free. She hadn't worn a bonnet, and her gloves were kid leather, made for riding, which she'd done rather than drive. A single horse caused less comment than a carriage.

In short, she didn't compare to the splendor of a duchess. Although Lucy's mother wore a simple, dove-gray frock, she had a poise and presence that Phil couldn't hope to match. Most days, she didn't even aspire to. She liked who she was, and didn't care a whit for the fashion standards of the *ton*.

Today, however, a small part of her whispered that with a fraction of the dowager's grace, Phil could draw any man's eye. *And whose eye do you hope to draw?* She refused to think of the man currently in possession of her prism.

The woman smiled, and it occurred to Phil that she didn't even look that old. In her early fifties, at best.

"I hope you won't take Lucy's lack of manners to heart. She is unusually rambunctious this morning."

For some reason, Phil felt disappointed at that statement. Too many of the *ton* spent their lives restraining their true personality and zest for life. The fact that Lucy did not, despite being raised as the sole daughter of one of the most powerful British families, gave Phil a sense of satisfaction. *We don't all have to be that way.*

"Would you care for some tea?"

Faced with an odd urge to defend Lucy, Phil answered, "Thank you, but Lucy has already offered."

One corner of the dowager's mouth lifted in a wry smile. "I should hope so. What she neglected to do was order the tea before she stampeded up the stairs." With the raise of her hand, the woman summoned a young maid, no more than sixteen years old.

The girl curtsied. "Right away, ma'am. Shall I bring a few slices of seed cake as well?"

"Please do." Without a farewell glance, the dowager glided into the room and claimed a chair across from Phil.

Neat trick. Phil bit the inside of her mouth to keep from spewing the words aloud. If she raised her hand in her own house, would her servants read her mind? More likely Pickle would land on her arm and insult her.

The patter of footsteps hailed Lucy's return. She burst into the sitting room with a wide grin on her face. Despite the exertion adding color to her cheeks, not a strand of her hair was out of place. Locks of Phil's hair tickled her neck. She gritted her teeth, resolutely ignoring the irritation. Some women had all the luck.

As she dropped into one of the masculine armchairs, a leather-bound pocketbook and a graphite pencil in hand, Lucy beamed. "Has Mother told you the good news?"

Wary, Phil glanced toward the dowager, who pressed her lips together in restrained mirth, but didn't comment. "I'm afraid not. What news?"

"We're getting a parrot!"

"That's...wonderful news?"

Leaning forward, Lucy gripped Phil's forearm hard, unable to contain her glee. "Isn't it just? I've been up all night trying to settle on the right name. How did you choose yours?"

Phil smiled, recalling that chaotic moment. Pearls flying across the tea shop, an old woman screaming profanity, and Pickle flapping out of the reach of the beastly woman's cane. Phil's heart had been in her mouth. She'd had a bruise for two weeks on her forearm where she'd taken the blow from that cane in his place.

Gently, Phil pried the young woman's death grip off her arm. "I rescued him from certain death after his owner got irritated that he broke her necklace. When I told him he was in a pickle, he made that cooing bird giggle that parrots make. He didn't stop repeating the word for days."

Lucy canted her head to the side, staring into the air as she tapped her lower lip with her pinky. "Maybe I should see what the bird wants to be named. I had hoped that you would be able to help me find a reputable place to buy a bird, though..."

"I'm afraid I found Pickle by luck alone. I will keep my ear to the ground in case I hear of anything."

"Thank you. I don't suppose you'd be willing to help train our parrot when we get one?"

Phil was saved from having to answer as the young maid returned with a tray full of overturned cups, a tea pot, sugar dish, and milk jug, a scrumptious-looking seed cake, and several plates. As the young woman curtsied, miraculously keeping the tray perfectly level, Phil hopped to her feet.

"Could I beg the use of your retiring room for a moment?"

Lucy shrugged. "Certainly. It's down the hall—"

The dowager leaned forward with a smile. "Why don't you use the one on the third floor, Miss St. Gobain? The one down here is in disrepair and that one is much nicer. All the way down the hall at the back of the house."

Phil's heartbeat quickened. Her mouth dried. Did Lady Graylocke suspect that Phil wasn't here for a social call? She swallowed, trying to call moisture into her mouth, before she replied as evenly as she could manage.

"Thank you, Lady Graylocke, I will."

"Please, call me Evelyn."

Phil's lips parted. It took her a moment to muster words. "Thank you. And you must call me Phil."

The dowager waved one hand idly through the air. "If you get lost, call out. Someone will be by to help you in a trice."

"Thank you. I will."

Somehow, Phil managed to put one foot in front of the other and vacate the room before her heart clawed its way out from between the bars of her ribcage. In the fresh air of the corridor, her churning thoughts settled. The dowager duchess—Evelyn—had given her the perfect excuse to venture above stairs.

She took it, quickly mounting to the second floor. A pair of maids hummed as they bustled out of a room at the end with feather dusters in hand.

With servants nearby, Phil didn't dare linger to discover what rooms lay beyond the doorways peppering the corridor. She mounted the stairs to the third floor. At least she had an excuse to be here.

When she opened the first door on her right to display a feminine bedchamber—likely Lucy's, given the books and papers piled on every flat surface—she realized that she'd been directed to the family's personal quarters. *Excellent.* If she were to find the duke's room, she could shut the door and search to her heart's content. This floor was eerily silent compared to the bustle of the last two, with no servants in sight at all.

In succession, Phil opened the door to reveal: the dowager's chambers, what appeared to be an unused bedchamber given the lack of personal effects, a room in slight disarray with a trunk of feminine clothing in the center, and a dark room that smelled earthy. Phil didn't see much of the last, aside from the fronds of a potted plant nestled next to the door. The moment a snore rent the air, she shut the door with haste. Given the plant, it must be Lord Gideon's room—and he must still be abed. With her heart in her throat, Phil tiptoed away, praying that she hadn't disturbed him. When he didn't yank the door open to glare at her, she let out a sigh of relief.

The next bedchamber down the line must belong to the duke. Squaring her shoulders, Phil ghosted down the hall. She laid her hand on the latch and tentatively opened the door.

No snoring. The rich azure drapes were partially shut, tickled by the breeze drifting through the open window. Daylight trickled in from the gap to dimly light the room. More thick drapes were pulled across the bed, their silver cords hanging loose. No motion betrayed that the room was occupied. Phil slipped into the room, easing the door shut behind her.

Thanks to the breeze through the window, the air didn't smell stale. She crept along the plush Persian carpet, a rich array of blues and greens and purples, as she moved to the window to let in more light. When the gray light sifting through the clouds penetrated the room, she studied the panorama, trying to guess where a duke would hide a prism the size of a shilling. Unfortunately, the possibilities were myriad.

The duke's room was neither messy nor devoid of personality, but a curious mix in between. The four-poster bed, the poles carved with the likenesses of dragons, devoured the majority of the space in the room, relegating the massive wardrobe, a chest topped with various books stacked neatly, a blue stuffed armchair, and twin night tables to the perimeter of the room. A spacious marble fireplace, intricately carved in a neo-classical style, faced the bed. The hearth was now cold, though a few logs had been stacked in the grate. Flanking the fireplace were two doorways, one without a door that presumably led into the dressing room, and a second with the door closed. At a guess, Phil imagined it led into unused, adjoining chambers for the future duchess. Over the mantle of the hearth was a breathtaking painting of Grecian shores. The colors popped in contrast to the white-and-blue damask wallpaper.

Where to begin? Phil stripped off her gloves, tossing them on the armchair as she surveyed the room. The duke didn't keep a writing desk in his bedchamber, though he might have stuffed the prism in one of the drawers of his wardrobe. It was as good a place as any to start.

Despite the cool air, by the time she rummaged through the cravats and gloves in the top drawer, Phil's spencer clung to the back of her neck. She shucked it, tossing it atop the gloves on the chair. She toed off her ankle-high riding boots, for good measure. For some unfathomable reason, she could always find things faster when in her stocking feet.

She pulled out the second drawer and found herself gifted with neat row upon row of folded smallclothes and socks. She felt along the inside of the drawer for a telltale lump. Empty-handed, she shut the drawer with vigor. It met the frame with a small *thump*.

Someone stirred on the bed behind her. Her heart skipped a beat. She whirled, pressing her hand to her chest. A gasp escaped her lips, unbidden.

A second later, the bed curtains rustled as a man shot out of bed. Daylight glinted off the metal barrel of a pistol aimed at Phil's chest. But it wasn't the gun that held her immobile. The Duke of Tenwick was completely, gloriously naked.

And by Jove, it was a pleasing sight. His skin was naturally golden, as if sun-kissed. His broad shoulders tapered down to a washboard-flat abdomen and lean hips. His arms, legs, and chest were dusted with hair to match the dark stubble lining his cheeks. The stubble, coupled with the disarray of his black hair and that distinctive white streak, gave him a wild look. And his manhood... Well, suffice it to say that the gun wasn't the only thing he pointed at her, and his manhood was by far more impressive.

He cleared his throat, drawing her attention back to his snapping gray gaze. Phil's cheeks flamed. She'd forgotten for a moment that she wasn't staring at an art exhibit in a book, but was in fact standing before the unclothed tenth Duke of Tenwick at gunpoint.

She didn't have any excuse for infiltrating his bedchamber and he looked bent on exacting punishment for her transgression.

Chapter Six

If this was a dream, it was the most bizarre dream Morgan had ever had. For one thing, if he didn't have a stitch on, he would have thanked his subconscious to ensure that Miss St. Gobain didn't have anything on, either. She'd already started in that mien, given the spencer and boots in the corner of the room by his armchair. The barest ruffle of lace teased the swell of her breasts, encased in amber-hued muslin. The dress gave her skin a rosy cast—or perhaps that was due to the blush mantling her cheeks and upper chest.

Zeus, she was lovely, her blue-gray eyes sparkling with life. She was also very real. This couldn't possibly be a dream.

His gaze darted to the discarded clothing in the corner. Was she trying to trap him into marriage?

He waited for the wash of horror to envelop him at the notion. Instead, his body reacted with a swift, undeniable burn. If he was going to be forced into the parson's noose, it might as well be for a transgression he'd made. He almost took a step forward before he caught himself, the cold metal of the pistol he'd grabbed from beneath his pillow to ward against the unknown intruder cutting into his palm.

What are you thinking? He wasn't. The ache in his loins nearly overwhelmed all reason. For him to have *that* strenuous a reaction to the thought of bedding the alluring, eccentric Miss St. Gobain—

Yes, yes, yes.

—he must be starved for female companionship. How long had it been since he'd appeased that particular ache? Too long. He rarely took even a temporary mistress, for fear of the repercussions against his family name. In fact, he might not have spent the night with a woman since before he'd joined the war as a British spy.

At the moment, the thought of some nameless, faceless woman didn't draw near the appeal of the woman standing in front of him. Her chest heaved with her breaths. Her tongue darted out, teasing a line across her upper lip. He bit back a groan. *Lawks.* He'd never wanted a woman more. Her hot gaze was locked on his cock as she ran her tongue back and forth, back and forth. He felt the force of her stare almost like a touch. It was not at all the demure, scandalized expression he expected to find on a gently-bred young virgin.

He cleared his throat, unable to take the heat of her gaze for a moment longer without acting on it. The pistol in his hand was the one thing that anchored him to the situation, to the fact that she had infiltrated his house, his bedchamber, and reduced him to this.

As she raised her gaze to his, something akin to trepidation entered her eyes. It reminded him that he stood here with a gentlewoman.

Damn it all, he shouldn't be unclothed in front of her! He flung the pistol on the bed in favor of yanking off the sheet and wrapping it haphazardly around his waist. An emotion resembling disappointment flashed across her face for a second before she smoothed it. It did nothing to ease the fierce throb of his desire. The sheet tented over his erection.

He swallowed hard, counting down his last minutes of freedom. "If you intend to trap me into marriage, you might as well have at it. We're not getting any younger." His voice emerged gravelly and aroused, yet more evidence of her puzzling allure. He'd encountered plenty of beautiful women.

Though none quite like her.

Her lips parted. At that moment, it would have been altogether too easy to cross to her and kiss her senseless.

"I beg your pardon?"

Her voice was a little sharp, considering the situation was of her making. She should have considered that he might sleep in the nude.

He started to cross his arms, only to have to juggle the sheet once more so it didn't drop to the floor. "Go ahead. Scream. The servants will arrive in seconds to discover that you and I are very much alone, and I am unclothed."

She took a step—away from him, not toward him. Bald horror crossed her face, chased by panic. She made a strangled sound and whirled to yank open the drawers to his wardrobe. Several strands of her thick auburn hair escaped her pins to caress her neck or shoulders. With frantic, jerky movements, she grabbed garments from the drawers and flung them blindly behind her.

He caught a pair of knee breeches as they hit him in the chest. His grip slipped and the sheet nearly pooled around his ankles once more.

Miss St. Gobain stared at him with a tempest in her wide eyes. "Dress yourself," she demanded, her voice little more than a hiss.

She hadn't thrown any smallclothes at him. Not to mention, how was he supposed to dress himself without dropping the sheet? He sidled closer to the bed, intending to perch on the edge, when he realized that she wasn't screaming for the servants to pound down his door. In fact, she had snatched her spencer and was now buttoning it to her chin, covering her bare upper chest.

Shame.

"You aren't trying to trap me into marriage?"

Her mouth dropped open. Her hands balled into fists. Given the appalled look on her face, if he'd been standing closer, she might have slapped him. "No!"

He dropped to the edge of the bed and fought to bare his ankles from beneath the folds of the sheet. "But...I'm a duke."

She rolled her eyes. "And an arrogant one, apparently."

I am not. Her words cut him deeper than he let on. Her disgust at the thought of marrying him tempered his arousal, at least. With a surly shrug, he shoved his feet into the breeches. "Aren't all dukes?"

"Quite possibly." Her voice was clipped. She dropped onto the edge of the armchair to fight with the laces on her ankle boots, pulling them farther apart before she squeezed her small foot inside.

He couldn't hold both the sheet and his breeches at once as he pulled them up, so in a swift movement he stood, pulling up the breeches and turning his back to tuck in his softening manhood and carefully button the fall. The cloth was scratchy against his bare rump. He turned, bending to retrieve the shirt that had fluttered to the ground between them.

Her gaze lit on the hollow of his throat and moved down over his bare chest in a slow, agonizing sweep. His cock reacted to her again, a swift ache that turned painful. He shielded his groin with the shirt.

"If you aren't here to trap me into marriage, why were you undressing?"

Her cheeks turned a hot, plum shade as she jumped to her feet. "I was not undressing. And I didn't know you were in the room."

Liar. She avoided his gaze. Instead, her eyes were fixed straight ahead, which, given the difference in their height, wound up somewhere in the middle of his chest, over his pounding heart.

He fought the urge to roll his eyes. When it came to interrogations, he'd been told the piercing, unwavering shade of his gray eyes often yielded the quickest results. He took advantage, staring her down until she hazarded a glance at him again. She averted her gaze just as quickly.

"Do you expect me to believe that you entered my bedchamber intending to take a nap?"

The only reason she could have for entering his bedchamber and starting to remove her clothes would be to trap him into marriage. She must have had second thoughts. Unless...

Could she be the enemy spy?

The thought hit him like a chunk of ice sliding down his back. It doused his arousal just as quickly. She couldn't be working for the French...could she? He didn't know anything about her at all.

He stepped closer, hoping to intimidate her with his size as well as his gaze. "What's your Christian name, Miss St. Gobain?"

She worried her lower lip with her teeth, leaving enticing crescents in the plump flesh. His lips burned in response, aching to kiss her.

No. She is the enemy.

He mustered a smile. Leaning his head closer, he said in a conspiratorial voice, "My Christian name is Morgan, as you must know. Tell me yours. You've seen me naked. I believe that warrants more familiar terms."

Something sparked in her gaze a moment before she turned her face away, an emotion too quick for him to identify. Softly, she murmured, "Philomena."

A lovely name that flowed off the tip of the tongue. Uncommon but beautiful, like she was.

Then she added, "Phil."

He fought not to make a face. The masculine nickname didn't fit someone so obviously female. When she was nearby, his body responded to her in the most primal way a man could a woman.

"Not Mena?" It would fit her better.

She raised her chin. "No. Phil."

"Philly?" Even as he spoke, the word felt wrong.

She scrunched her nose. "I'm not a horse. My name is Phil."

When he pictured someone named Phil, he did *not* picture her. "Doesn't it bother you to answer to a man's name?" Lucy would kill him if he called her Luc.

Her hands fisted again. He took a small step back, fearing that he might get slapped, after all. He held the shirt between them like a shield.

"It isn't a man's name. It's *my* name."

She advanced on him. He retreated from the wild, furious look in her eye.

"Are you trying to say that I'm somehow less worthy of the name than a man?"

"What? No—"

She spoke over top of him, raising her voice as she chased him across the room. "I assure you, I can do anything a man can do."

"I—I don't doubt that you can. I didn't mean to imply—" Blast, but he felt exposed, dressed only in knee breeches without a stitch of clothing otherwise. Quickly, he pulled the shirt over his head, letting the open collar hang loose. When the white linen no longer obscured his gaze, he found the room vacant.

Philomena had walked him right to the door and slipped out. He dashed to the ajar door and stumbled into the hall in time to see her whisk out of sight down the stairs. The cool feeling of the wooden floorboards seeped into his bare feet as he stared after her, rooted in place.

Down the hall, another door opened and Gideon poked his head out. His hair stuck up on end. Stubble outlined his face and drew attention to the dark bags under his eyes. They had both been up until sunrise as Morgan explained the various forms of code currently employed by the British spy network.

"What's going on?" Giddy rubbed at his eyes. "Was that Miss St. Gobain?"

Yes. She's a French spy.

Morgan brought the words to the tip of his tongue as he stared after her, but he couldn't speak them. "I didn't catch a good glimpse of her," he lied, his voice wooden. "It must have been nothing."

Until he knew for sure, he didn't want to confess her treachery to anyone, even the brother he was closest to. He retreated into his bedchamber to prepare for the day. He had some inquiries to make.

Chapter Seven

"Are you hiding from Mother or Lucy?"

Morgan fought a groan at the reminder as his brother dropped into the armchair across from him. Seeking a moment of privacy, Morgan had ensconced himself in the farthest corner of the club. The wood-paneled walls muffled some of the sound pouring from the other patrons, of which there were myriad. At eight of the morning, the club catered to carousers who hadn't yet given up their love affairs with their cups, as well as the early-rising scholars and businessmen who hoped to make their mark on the day. The latter sat quietly alone or in pairs in the leather-upholstered chairs ringing the low mahogany tables, perusing the news rags and their correspondence or talking about markets and investments. The former stumbled around the club from the wooden bar in the center housing the betting book to the uniformed maids disappearing through the various doors into hallways leading away from the common room, slurring their words and stirring up mischief.

Morgan got enough mischief at home. He hadn't seen Philomena since she'd rushed out of his bedchamber two days ago. Gideon was helping to mitigate Mother and Lucy's matchmaking attempts, but it helped not a whit once one of their candidates moved into his house. Miss Charlotte Vale, whose sister was newly married to Morgan's brother, had accepted the Graylockes' hospitality upon the seizure of the late Lord Harker's holdings yesterday. Morgan had tried to establish Miss Vale and her mother in the guest quarters on the fourth floor, but his mother and sister had flat out refused the accommodations. Since the Vales were now family, his female relatives wanted to keep them on the same floor as the family. Mrs. Vale was now ensconced in Anthony's old room, as he wouldn't be using it while he still held his position as Captain in the Royal Navy. Miss Vale had been given the vacant duchess's quarters next to Morgan.

Thank Zeus for locking doors.

With a sigh, Morgan sipped at his coffee. Cold. He rubbed at the white streak in his hair. "Put on a blindfold and point. If she's female, I'm probably avoiding her."

Giddy laughed. He stretched out his legs and accepted a steaming cup of coffee and a news rag from a footman, liveried in black and green to match the maids. Gideon shook out the sheet and skimmed it with his gaze as he answered. "The house is a little full, but I think you're over-reacting. Mrs. Vale hasn't done anything to you at all."

"Mrs. Vale shot Harker and embroiled us in this mess."

The paper slipped from Giddy's fingers as his mouth dropped open. He fiddled with his cravat, already askew. "You're jesting."

"I am not." Morgan sighed. He lowered his voice to the barest whisper. "She's one of us."

"A spy?"

Giddy was the genius of the family for a reason. Morgan nodded.

His brother let out a long breath. He leaned his head back against the chair. The top of the chair rested just above his shoulders. The position must have been deuced uncomfortable. Giddy straightened a moment later.

"Then can we use her to help our hunt?"

Morgan pressed his lips together as he hesitated. "I don't think so. Given what she told me, she was drafted specifically to keep an eye on Harker. Without him, her talents are obsolete."

Giddy narrowed his eyes. "She sounds like a capable woman. I'm sure if she wanted—"

"That's just it. I'm not sure that she wants to be involved in the spy business."

The younger man raised his eyebrows. "Have you asked her directly?"

"No. That's Strickland's place, not mine."

Averting his gaze from the disappointment in his brother's shrewd green eyes, he took a gulp of coffee. Still cold. Making a face, Morgan hailed a footman and turned over the offending cup.

Gideon waited for the man to step out of earshot before he replied, "One more thing for Strickland to do. I'm still waiting on those London reports."

He was more eager for paperwork than any newly-drafted spy Morgan had ever trained. A smile teased at the duke's lips. "With luck, we'll have them today. I'll send a note to him about Mrs. Vale."

"Have the footman wait for a reply this time."

Gideon sipped from his cup, letting out a sigh of delight. Morgan glared at his younger brother. Giddy didn't even care for coffee; he preferred tea. He was teasing Morgan on purpose.

With a grin, the younger man asked, "Grumpy?"

Morgan didn't deign to answer.

"Have trouble sleeping last night?"

"I slept fine." Morgan's voice was surly.

Mostly because it was a lie. He hadn't been able to stop thinking about his encounter with Philomena—or the implications of her presence in his bedroom—since that morning. In his dreams, that altercation went very different.

Shoving his hand into the pocket of his waist-coat, he fiddled with the glass ring he'd confiscated from the spy nearly a week ago. It reminded him of his mission, his priorities.

"You aren't dreaming about the lovely Miss Charlotte, are you?"

Morgan groaned. "Not you, too. I don't care a whit for Miss Charlotte's pretty face. Sticking her in the room next to me won't change that." Thank Zeus Miss Charlotte wasn't like the other *ton* debutantes. She was a fast friend of Lucy's, but didn't seem to aspire to marry anyone, let alone Morgan.

Gideon's smile widened. "Miss St. Gobain, by chance?"

Morgan schooled his expression into a neutral mask. "Who?"

His brother cocked an eyebrow. "You know to whom I'm referring."

"I'm afraid I don't recall much more about her except for her parrot," he lied.

Gideon sniggered. "There's a matchmaking pairing Mother hasn't tried yet. Maybe Lucy will adopt a nice lady parrot for you."

"Are you looking for a new profession? You're a regular court jester."

Giddy grinned. He opened his mouth to retort, but a ruckus at the bar counter, in front of the betting book, cut him short.

"You're daft, man!" A young dandy, his blond hair in disarray as it fell over his forehead and his cheeks ruddy, reflecting his foxed state, clapped a second young man on the back. The friendly contact nearly sent the poor man teetering into the betting book. The two men gathered a crowd of young fops. "His brother is a notorious rake!"

Morgan gritted his teeth, pretending not to notice the way the group glanced in his direction. *Please, let them be gossiping about someone else.*

"If *he* succumbed to the parson's mousetrap, you can bet that the duke will be next."

Bloody hell. They were talking about Morgan. He clenched his fists and shifted in his seat, uncomfortable.

"Two hundred pounds says that he'll be married inside the month."

Was that all that his bachelor state was worth, two hundred pounds? He fought the mad urge to laugh. Any number of debutantes would be throwing money at his feet for the opportunity to marry him.

"Ridiculous." The word slipped out on a growl.

After draining his cup, Giddy set it down on the table beside him with a clink. "What's ridiculous?"

Morgan jerked his chin toward the young, bacon-brained dandies, who were now scribbling down amounts and signatures in the betting book.

"These bets. Don't people have better things to do?"

His younger brother shrugged. His hair flopped down in front of his eyes as he turned over the news rag to read the other side in depth. In an absent voice, he answered, "It distracts them from the war. I have my money on two weeks."

"You're betting against me, too?"

Giddy raised his eyebrows. "Well, I'm certainly not going to bet against Mother or Lucy. I have more sense than that."

Morgan rolled his eyes. "Your confidence in me is astounding."

Grinning, Giddy said, "What are brothers for?"

Thankfully, his teasing was cut short as a footman approached with a scandal rag in hand. He set it next to Morgan with a pointed apology for making him wait. As the man bowed and left, Gideon burst, "Don't tell me you actually read those things?"

"Don't you want to hear what they're saying about our dear brother now?"

Giddy made a face, a rich response, considering that he was laying money on Morgan's downfall.

With a sigh, the duke lowered his voice, "It's a message I've been waiting on." In fact, this information was the only reason he had remained in White's for so long.

He unfolded the scandal rag in his lap to reveal a sheet of paper stuffed into the crease. With the aid of a graphite pencil he kept tucked into his pocket, he swiftly decoded the message.

Gideon leaned closer, trying to read it upside-down. "What does it say?"

Morgan swallowed, reading it twice more to ensure that the translation was correct. His stomach sank further with each sentence. *There it is. The confirmation I needed.*

Unfortunately, now that he had it, he wished it had said something different.

"Morgan?"

He glanced up into his brother's concerned eyes. Reluctantly, he forced himself to say, "Miss St. Gobain was born Miss Plaisance D'Aubigny of France."

Gideon's mouth dropped. "She's French?"

"So it seems."

"Then the spy—"

"It must be her." Lord, how Morgan had prayed otherwise. He still hoped that if only he read the missive again, the information would change. His reaction to her—

It didn't matter. If she was a French spy, she was the enemy, and he would treat her as such.

The silence stretched on between the brothers, broken only by the rowdy gibes as a few of the dandies gave up drinking and left the club to seek their beds.

Finally, Giddy ventured, "What now? Do we turn her in to the Crown?"

Morgan tensed. Every muscle in his body rebelled at the thought. *She's the enemy.*

Slowly, he said, "Strickland will want proof."

Giddy gestured to the missive. "Her heritage isn't proof enough?"

"No. We'll have to catch her in an act of treason."

The younger man raised his eyebrows. "And how do you propose to do that?"

Morgan fingered the last sentence of the coded message. "There is another exchange tomorrow. Strickland has included the time and place in this message. I'll attend and intercept her there."

If she showed up, she was guilty. It was as simple as that.

Gideon suggested, "Lucy seems to be quite fond of her. I'm sure we could convince her and mother to pay a visit to her tomorrow morning. If we join them, we can search the house for coded correspondence, find our proof that way."

Morgan shook his head. He slipped his hand into his pocket, fingering the glass piece he couldn't bring himself to part with. It represented a mystery. Had Philomena's man been at that inventor's meeting in her stead? Did the glass piece mean something to her? When he arrested her, he would find out and put to rest all these questions about her accumulating in his mind.

"Not tomorrow. I have to sit in Parliament tomorrow morning."

As Morgan stood, so did his brother. Giddy caught him by the arm. "Is Parliament really more important than the war?"

Morgan gritted his teeth. He nodded. "Tomorrow is the abolitionist vote. How can I fight the tyranny of another country if I turn a blind eye to the oppression riddling mine?"

Giddy's gaze glinted. Whether or not he agreed with Morgan, at the very least he knew better than to press the subject. The Graylockes hadn't owned slaves for well over a century. Morgan's father had been an abolitionist, as had his father before him. Morgan was proud to carry on that tradition, whatever it took.

Keeping his voice even, he added, "We'll get this spy, Giddy. Don't worry on that account."

Chapter Eight

"You're in a pickle!"

Phil batted the fingers of her free hand at the parrot perched on her shoulders. She scoffed. "I am not. I'm just looking for Jared. Have you seen him?"

"In...a...pickle!"

She sighed. Had she expected another answer?

The flame of the candle she held wavered as she descended the stairs in a rush that had Pickle flapping his wings for balance. The glossy wood bannister reflected the light. Her stocking feet slipped on the steps. She gripped the bannister hard to keep from losing her balance.

Where was Jared? He had been avoiding her all week, ever since the Society for the Advancement of Science meeting that he'd agreed to accompany her to, out of the blue. In fact, he'd been acting more and more distant, closed-lipped and moody, even before that day. He was the only family she had left. She had to fix this rift between them and get her affectionate brother back.

"Jared?"

Distantly, she heard a door slam. Her heart jumped into her throat. Was that the front door?

She dashed into a sitting room overlooking the street. Cupping her eyes to shield the light of the candle, she pressed her face to the glass window. That was definitely a man descending the front steps. Given the lanky build, it had to be Jared. He was leaving without telling her where he intended to go.

Again.

She had to catch up to him.

"Meg!"

Pickle took up the cry, repeating her maid's name at the top of his lungs. Phil raced out the door, nearly colliding with her friend, whose cheeks were pink with exertion.

"What is it?"

Pickle continued to scream Meg's name. She glared at him as she inched away, rounding Phil's other side.

"Hush, you silly bird," Phil commanded.

Pickle made an outraged squawk, ruffled his feathers, and remained silent. That was a neat trick. Phil would have to remember it for a later date.

Pushing the thought aside, she told Meg, "My brother just left the house. I want you to ready the carriage. I'm going after him."

She nodded, her freckled cheeks flushed. When Phil turned toward the staircase leading to the floor above, Meg called after her, "Where are you going?"

"I have to change into men's clothes."

"There's no time—"

I know. But if Phil followed in her skirts, she would certainly be noticed. As a man, she was all but invisible.

She hiked her skirts to her knees and sprinted up the stairs. Disgruntled, Pickle took to the air and soared someplace else in the manor. From the startled shriek a moment later, he'd found Meg.

Phil usually ran interference to ensure that her pet didn't frighten her closest friend, but she had no time to find them and sort it out. Hopefully one of Meg's siblings would come to her rescue. Phil employed them all, and her parents, too.

She shucked her dress the moment she entered her room. She didn't have time to bind her breasts flat, or even to wrestle to untie her stays. Instead, she donned her men's clothes over the feminine undergarments and prayed that the swell of her chest wouldn't be noticeable beneath the loose shirt and jacket. Breeches, boots, shirt, waistcoat, jacket. By the time she was fully dressed, stumbling out of the room, her hair had tumbled from its pins. She gathered it in a queue and tied it off with the first thing that had met her fingers, a frilly white ribbon. With luck, she wouldn't be venturing any place that was brightly lit.

She barreled down the stairs, the soles of her boots giving her more purchase this time on the slick wood. As she reached the front door, Meg waited for her. Her hair was in disarray, but Pickle was nowhere to be found.

"Has he gone?"

Meg nodded. "He just stepped into a hired hack. The hostlers are readying the carriage in the mews."

"Thank you. With luck I can still catch him."

"What do you mean to do—"

Ignoring the protests of her maid, Phil yanked open the door and jumped down to the street. A stitch started in her side as she reached the gaping doors of the mews. The night air wrapped around her, thick with moisture even though the bullish clouds refused to shed their burdens. The stables were nothing more than an indistinct form with a beacon of light spilling from inside.

The hostlers were nearly ready with the carriage as she burst in. The strong musk of horses and hay assaulted her senses.

"Miss St. Gobain!" They stopped to pull on their forelocks.

"Forget that. I have to follow the hack my brother just stepped into. Are we ready?"

"Yes, miss. Let me help you in."

The moment the squat hostler let down the stairs, Phil leaped into the carriage under her own power. In the space of two heartbeats, the driver jumped into place, the other hostlers buckled the last clip, and the horses' hooves clattered as the team of four trotted out of the stables and into the night.

The humidity weighed on Phil. Her hair fought the mooring of the ribbon she'd hastily tied into it. Her heartbeat thundered in time to the horses' hooves. Sweat beaded on her upper lip as she unlatched the coach window to peer out into the night. The cobblestone streets were swathed in shadows, occasionally punctuated by the dim yellow glow of a streetlamp, poised on the junction of two streets.

The carriage slowed as it met with the thick traffic. The fashionable *ton* was leaving for their evening entertainments, both a deterrent and a boon. It slowed down the hack's progress, but also made it more difficult to spot. When Phil peered out of the window, she had to wonder if the driver knew who he pursued at all. Phil certainly couldn't pick out the closed hackney cab from among the other black-topped coaches and the phaetons and carriages open to the balmy night air. Her chest ached as the coach navigated the clogged streets, slowing and speeding up in turns.

She realized that she'd forgotten to breathe. She gulped for air.

After what felt like a hundred thousand beats of her rapidly pumping heart, the driver turned away from the fashionable streets of Mayfair and arrowed toward a less respectable part of town. Phil's stomach clenched. *Jared, what sort of trouble are you involved in?*

Ahead, the black coach they'd been following slowed to a stop. Was it the hack? Had the driver been able to pursue it all this way? Phil rapped on the roof, the signal to stop before the occupant of the carriage spotted them. The moment the wheels stopped turning, Phil slipped out of the carriage.

The hack had stopped on the corner of two streets. The streetlamp cast a wan circle of light onto the occupant as he alighted from the coach and paid the fare. That tall, lean build Phil would recognize anywhere, even with a topper.

Jared.

She swallowed heavily before she found the words to instruct the driver to wait while she followed him on foot. She turned up the collar of her redingote and struck out down the street. Her boots clicked on the worn, uneven cobblestones, half of them broken or crumbled to dust around the edges. The houses in this section of the city leaned together, their faces chipping and their windows shut tight with shutters, as the occupants couldn't afford glass. Gaunt faces pressed against the cracked slats in those windows, young faces with dirty cheeks and sunken eyes. Phil lowered her gaze, her stomach shriveling to the size of a raisin.

She knew there were parts of this city where the less fortunate lived. In fact, she dedicated a portion of her invention earnings to giving the less fortunate a better life. She vehemently opposed slavery and donated to abolitionist causes. Even so, on the rare occasions when she passed through neighborhoods like this one, with too many mouths to feed and somber children staring at her with haunted eyes, the knowledge assailed her that she didn't do enough.

She couldn't do enough. Certainly not now. At the moment, her family came first, and whatever Jared was up to, her gut instinct screamed that it didn't bode well. Keeping her eyes on the figure in front of her as he dodged through alleys strung with clothing lines and past skinny, growling dogs and hostile cats, Phil tried not to notice the steady decrease in the quality of the houses.

When she rounded a corner, she did notice that someone else was tailing Jared, too. Her pulse pounded fast and hard, roaring in her ears as she passed beneath the light of a streetlamp. She ducked her head. As she reached the building on the other side of the street, she risked a glance back.

Her heart did a little, strangled dance in her chest. Like her, the other man wasn't wearing a hat. It left his short-clipped, black hair open to the air—along with the distinctive white streak.

It was Morgan Graylocke, the Duke of Tenwick.

Blast! Why was he pursuing her brother? She turned her face forward, away from the greatcoat-shrouded figure hot on her heels. She had to tell Jared he was being pursued. Unfortunately, when she quickened her step, so did Jared.

As did the duke. Maybe she could lead him away.

Abandoning Jared's path, she darted down the nearest alley and strode at a clipped pace down its length. A thin woman wrapped in a shawl and smoking a cheroot, by the smell, raised her fist and yelled an obscenity. As Phil glanced over her shoulder to gauge whether or not the duke had followed her—he had—she tripped over a mangy cat. It yowled and scampered off into the gloom.

"Sorry, kitten." As she caught her balance, she glanced over her shoulder again. Morgan had already traversed half the alley's length.

Hell and damnation! He would catch her at this rate. She gave up all pretense of belonging and broke into a run.

The duke followed.

She darted through alleys, lunged over a low wagon to the obscenities of its nearby owner, startled a mule into trotting into Morgan's path, and got pelted with rocks from a gaggle of children. Through it all, Morgan followed her, growing ever nearer. Her head spun. A stitch clawed at her side. She was hopelessly lost. She ran through a rowdy tavern room stinking of sour ale and sharp smoke, to the shrieks of the barmaids and the shouts of the patrons. She dodged a punch that landed on her shoulder instead of her eye. The ache chased her through the kitchen and out the back, where spilled water from the pump had made the packed dirt slippery. With her feet determined to slide every which way, she stumbled onto the street and found purchase. A grimy street lamp proved a beacon in the sudden darkness in the wake of the tavern. She lunged toward it.

An arm snaked around her waist, pulling her back against a tall, muscular, male body a moment before he turned her and used that body to pin her against the side of the brick building. The light spilled across his face, emphasizing the length of his lashes and the chiseled cut of his jaw. Phil panted, though she could barely expand her chest far enough with his sternum pressing against her. The brick at her back was rough. It snagged at her hair.

Morgan's eyes grew wide with recognition. "Phil?"

What would he do? Fear quickened her heartbeat, spiraling her senses into high alert.

In a swift movement, Morgan bent and pressed his mouth to hers.

Chapter Nine

Philomena tasted like cloves and cinnamon. Her lips parted beneath his, her body arched into him, and he was lost. She felt even better than he'd dreamed. He cupped her neck as he deepened the kiss. She tasted divine.

She's the enemy.

If she was his enemy, why did she feel so damn good? He was definitely starved for female companionship—specifically, hers. He pressed closer, sliding his hand down the coarse fabric of her jacket and breeches, around to her generous rear. The feel of her curves beneath the fabric drove him wild. His spinning head conflicted with the assault of reason invited by the men's clothes she wore. Most women didn't dress in breeches.

Phil wasn't most women. She was a French spy.

Although he ached to press closer, reason won out and Morgan forced himself to lift his head. If he expected to find her expression that of an experienced woman who had just been kissed senseless, he was destined to be disappointed.

Her expression was one of indignation and outrage. She looked like a spitting cat. He took an instinctive step away from her and her snapping, stormy eyes.

Lud, what had he done?

He raised his hands, as if that would fend off all ten stone of her should she decide to launch herself at him.

"Forgive me." His hoarse voice shattered the illusion of stillness induced by the thick, humid air. Noises penetrated his ringing ears; the clamor of a row in a nearby house, the slow clop of a horse's hooves, the yowl of a dog somewhere in the darkness. Drizzle fell from the sky, raising gooseflesh along the exposed nape of his neck.

She didn't look likely to forgive him.

"The impertinence was uncalled for. I shouldn't have kissed you without asking first."

You shouldn't have kissed her at all! He mentally kicked himself.

Phil narrowed her eyes. Strands of her hair had worked free of her queue to frame her heart-shaped face. She thrust her chin out, mulish.

He took another step back. "I'll marry you, of course."

Wait...*what?!* Had he just proposed marriage to an enemy spy? He was the worst field agent in all of history. His instincts as a gentleman had nothing to do with the battlefield. For all that he was on British soil, this was a battle—a battle of wits between spies.

Phil's mouth fell open. Morgan braced himself to be slapped soundly. Instead, she leaned against the wall, laughing.

"By Jove, did you..." A fresh wave of amusement overwhelmed her. She doubled over, clutching her stomach. The movement pulled her jacket tight against her pronounced womanly figure. Tears glistened at the corners of her eyes, reflecting the lamplight. "Did you just propose marriage? After a kiss?"

He flew his colors like a battle ship. Ducking his head, he rubbed the back of his neck to hide the heat in his cheeks. "It was a knee-jerk reaction. You're a delicate young woman of good standing—"

Phil laughed louder, drowning out his words.

He glared at her. "Forgive me if I've offended you—again—but it was the honorable thing to do."

It was the foolish thing to do.

Phil wiped her eyes as she sidled along the wall, farther away from him. He couldn't blame her. Could he make a bigger idiot of himself?

With a grin, she teased, "I didn't know being kissed in the middle of a deserted alley was the magic formula to prompt a proposal from a duke. I could sell this information, make a fortune."

He gritted his teeth. "I assure you, you are a singular case."

"Am I? Then is it possible you *don't* propose to every woman you kiss in decrepit alleyways?"

He clenched his fists. "I don't go around kissing women in alleyways."

"No?" Her gaze twinkled. "Men?"

"No."

"Pity." She gathered the stray strands of her hair and retied her queue. Was that ribbon edged with lace? How could she hope to pass off as a man?

Then again, given the darkness clinging to every building and street, he hadn't realized he wasn't pursuing a man until he'd caught her and pressed up against her. Only then had he realized that the Phil from the Society for the Advancement of Science meeting and Miss Philomena St. Gobain were the same person—and nestled against him. Her scent still clung to his clothes, stirring his desire.

With a saucy smile that twisted his innards, she added, "No wonder you're out of practice. With the proposal, not with the kiss. That was... pleasant."

Turning her back, she strode away from him, toward the dusty streetlamp. Her heart-shaped rear swung with her decidedly feminine walk. He groaned inwardly.

Wait—he was letting her get away!

"Oh, bugger it," he muttered under his breath. He'd made enough of a fool of himself tonight. Letting the enemy walk away when he'd had her in his clutches was the least of his embarrassments.

He turned on his heel, his mood blackening. How was he going to explain this cock-up to Strickland?

***

Gideon roared with laughter. He doubled over, stumbling into Morgan's side as he struggled to breathe. Morgan shoved him back, into the flower-patterned wallpaper over the wood paneling. Giddy braced his hand on it as he gasped for breath, tears streaming from his eyes.

"It isn't that funny," Morgan grumbled under his breathe.

"You...*proposed!*" He bit off the last word on a strangled laugh.

"Hush!" Morgan pretended not to notice the curious glances of the four women in the room.

Mother, Mrs. Vale, and Lucy were perched on the off-white settee. They sipped from delicate, gold-rimmed white china cups. The cups clinked in the saucers as the two dark-haired women—seated on either side of Mrs. Vale, who shared her daughter's blonde coloring albeit hers had gone to gray—set aside their cups. They exchanged a devious look.

"What was that you said, dear?" Mother asked, her voice light.

Simultaneously, Lucy jumped to her feet and demanded, "What's so funny?"

Mrs. Vale pressed her lips together and held her cup steady on the saucer in front of her. From the glint in her eye, she wanted to learn of the secret, too. In fact, Morgan would do well to watch her. A seasoned spy like Mrs. Vale might have her own methods of uncovering the truth, especially now that she wasn't on an active assignment.

The only person in the room who seemed oblivious to the conversation was Miss Vale. Curled up in an armchair she had dragged to the window much earlier in the day to take advantage of the natural light, Miss Vale bent over her embroidery. Her golden curls fell into her face, an annoyance judging by her expression as she batted them away. She narrowed her eyes as she strained to see by the light of the candle on the windowsill.

Beside Morgan, Giddy straightened. He grinned, "Oh, Mother, nothing you'd be interested in at all."

Mother scoffed. As she refilled her teacup, her sidelong look betrayed her indecision. Judging by her suspicious look, she believed him to be engaged in the worst sort of depravity.

That would almost be preferable. His gloves smelled like Phil, a floral scent mixed with mineral oil. Bizarre at first, but the longer he'd been shut in his carriage without reprieve, the more he'd come to ache for that scent. It conjured the memory of her body pressed against his, of the taste of her lips. Carnal thoughts which shouldn't be repeated and couldn't be quenched. He shifted on his feet and avoided his mother's gaze, uncomfortable.

Unfortunately, Lucy wasn't quelled by the excuse. She stormed forward, her arms akimbo. "Tell me," she demanded, staring at Gideon. "I want to know."

Morgan bit back a groan. *Yes, well, I want to be anywhere else but in this room. We don't always get what we want.*

Giddy held up his hands in surrender. "I can't tell you, or it'll ruin the surprise."

Lucy's dark brown eyes lit up. "Surprise?"

Morgan smiled tightly as his sister glanced between him and his brother. What in blazes was his brother going on about?

Giddy's wicked grin widened. "Oh, yes."

She latched onto his arm. "You must tell or I won't let go."

"Are we children again?" The closest to her age, Lucy had latched onto Gideon during her formative years, when Giddy wasn't tottering after Anthony, three years his senior.

Lucy pouted. "Giddy!"

He laughed, extricating himself with a wink. "Very well. Morgan's found you a parrot."

"He has?"

I have?

"He has," Gideon confirmed. "In fact, he's arranged for the bird to arrive sometime tomorrow."

With a shriek of delight, Lucy launched herself into Morgan's arms. He struggled to breathe as she clutched him tightly. He glared at Gideon over her shoulder. *Why,* he mouthed.

Giddy shrugged, as if to say, *Why not?*

He wasn't the one who had to scour London for the bloody bird overnight. Morgan might feel like a dastard tonight, but he couldn't bring himself to disappoint his sister.

Or his mother, either. She set down her cup and rose from the settee, her arms outstretched to embrace him, too. She beamed.

Lud, he hadn't seen her look that happy since Tristan had announced his engagement. Ever since the death of his father, Mother spent the bulk of her time constantly worrying over her children.

And she didn't even know that two—now three—of them were spies.

Her hug was much gentler than Lucy's. While he was bombarded by questions from his youngest sister—How big was the parrot? Was it male or female? Did it have a name? Could it speak?—Mother engulfed him in a gentle squeeze and stood on tiptoe to kiss his cheek.

"Thank you," she murmured. "It'll be so lovely to have a pet in the house."

Because his townhouse wasn't full enough.

"You're not listening to me," Lucy complained, her voice shrill.

Giddy sniggered. He nudged Morgan. "That's not even the best thing happening tomorrow. Mother, why don't you tell Morgan your news?"

Morgan's stomach dropped. He tried to hide his trepidation behind a smile. It felt wooden.

Mother, on the other hand, beamed. "I received an answer earlier today. Miss St. Gobain and her brother have accepted our invitation to visit Vauxhall Gardens tomorrow evening. Isn't that wonderful?"

Bloody hell. He glared at Gideon. His brother must have known from the second he walked in.

Morgan had made a fool of himself proposing to a woman tonight and he had to face her again tomorrow and pretend as though nothing had happened.

It was going to be a long couple of days.

Chapter Ten

Phil jolted out of a brazen dream during which she clung to Morgan as he kissed her passionately. She bolted upright in the armchair and nearly fell to the floor. What had woken her?

On his perch next to the candle that had nearly guttered out, Pickle ruffled his feathers and launched into a rousing rendition of, "You're in a pickle!" The tune resembled the sea shanty *London Julies*. Where would he have learned *that?*

A man swore. A moment later, a lanky figure crossed the hallway, his hands clapped over his ears. Jared. Phil's heart kicked into a gallop. She'd been waiting for him to return. What time was it? She fumbled for her pocket watch and held it next to the guttering light. It was half three of the morning!

"Jared!" Phil jumped to her feet, fiddling with the wrapper she'd donned over her nightgown.

His footsteps stopped. A mutter was likely another profanity. Pickle cut off his song and ruffled his feathers, muttering sleepily as he tucked his beak beneath one wing. He kept one golden eye fixed on the door.

With slow, plodding steps, Jared reversed to stand in the doorway once more. His cravat poked out of his jacket pocket and his shirt gaped at the throat. The candlelight emphasized the copper strands in his hair, lank against his forehead. In contrast, his skin looked unhealthily pale. A groove furrowed the space between his eyebrows. The fluttering light cast dark shadows around his eyes.

Phil clasped her hands so tightly in front of her that pins and needles pricked her fingertips. "Where have you been? It's late."

A look of disgust crossed his face. "I didn't know I had a curfew, *Mother*."

Phil flinched. She took a step forward to distract from the involuntary reaction. "Don't say that." Jared had only been fifteen when their parents had died. Phil never intended to step in as a mother figure, but someone had to look after him. He was her baby brother. He meant the world to her.

Her shadow cast across his waistcoat as she stepped between him and the light. "I was worried. I didn't know you intended to go out."

Let alone to such a dangerous place. She bit her tongue.

Jared turned away. "It's none of your business."

What was he hiding from her? She laid her hand on his sleeve. "Of course it's my business! I'm your guardian. I'm your sister."

He didn't meet her gaze. "I went out to meet with a lover. Are you satisfied?"

Her cheeks heated like a furnace. Pickle only compounded on her embarrassment when he lifted his head and squawked, "Lover! Lover!" He took to the air and flapped over to Jared in two broad wing strokes. All the while, the macaw chanted, "Kiss, kiss."

Jared swatted his hand through the air, keeping Pickle at bay. "I am not going to kiss you, you blasted bird!"

Happy for the excuse to delay her response, Phil stretched out her arm. "Come here, Pickle. I'll give you a kiss." The parrot landed on her wrist, his talons digging into her ruffled sleeve as he fought for balance and pinched the skin beneath. She kissed his beak and lifted him to her shoulder. When he settled on his usual perch, he presented his back to Jared. He explored the curve of her ear with his tongue and beak. It tickled.

"Are we done?" Jared asked, his voice short. "Or would you like her name and address?"

Lud, she did not want to be having this conversation with him. It only reminded her that he was nineteen now, no longer a child. He had...

manly urges to satisfy. She did not want to contemplate them.

"Forgive me. Goodnight."

Jared nodded curtly and strode away from her, his footsteps quick.

As he left her in peace, her embarrassment faded. She scooped up the candle, little more than a stub in its holder. Hopefully it would last all the way up to the third story, where her bedchamber resided.

Was he telling her the truth? That had been the one thing he might say to convince her to cease with her questions. Nibbling on her lip, she mounted the stairs as she mulled over his bizarre behavior of late. Avoiding her, sneaking out late at night. She didn't know what to think.

As she reached the third floor, she crossed paths with Meg, who descended from the floor above. Barefoot and dressed in her frilly white nightgown, Meg rubbed at her eyes. Her light brown hair was pulled over her shoulder, contained in a loose braid.

"What's all this ruckus?"

Phil glanced down the corridor, ensuring that her brother wasn't around to hear. "Jared just arrived home. He claimed he was out late...visiting a lover." Color chased onto Phil's cheeks as she repeated the explanation he'd given.

Meg raised her eyebrows. In the wildly guttering light, her brows seemed darker than the pale hair usually reached without the aid of cosmetics. "Let's run on into your room, shall we?" She reached out to guide Phil by the elbow, only to stop short when she noticed the lump of feathers on Phil's shoulder. Warily, she sidled back. "Is he...sleeping?"

Pickle had his head tucked into her hair. His chest rose and fell next to her ear. "I believe so."

Meg shooed her on ahead with her hands. "Carefully, then. Let's not wake the beast."

Pickle didn't stir as Phil strode down the corridor. When she reached her room, she set down the candle on the nearest flat surface and crossed to his perch. She gently eased her hand beneath his feet and transferred him onto the perch. His beak caught in her hair. Despite her frantic gestures, Meg came no farther than the door. Clenching her teeth, Phil twisted her arm awkwardly to guide her hair free of her pet's beak. When she deposited him safely on his perch, he shifted on his feet and tucked his head beneath one wing, still asleep.

"It's safe," Phil whispered.

Skirting the perimeter of the room, Meg found an unlit candle and lit it from the stump of the one near to blowing out. With a whisper of breath, she chased away the flame and carried the new candle over to the stand next to Phil's bed. Phil shut the door and they both perched on the bed, tucking their legs to the side as they faced one another.

"Do you think it might be true?" Phil asked. "Does Jared have a lover?"

Meg looked bewildered. "Why are you asking me?"

"You have brothers. Married brothers. Were they this secretive when they began courting?"

Meg pursed her lips together as she thought. She gave a reluctant nod. "Sean not so much as Pat, but I'm afraid so. Declan is still that way. He won't give up a whisper of who his sweetheart is, even though we're sure she's employed here in the manor, or else at one of the neighbors."

That piqued Phil's curiosity. She would have to keep her eye on Meg's second-to-youngest brother, who she employed as a footman. Perhaps she could guess which maid he had his eye on.

If men were usually secretive when they had sweethearts, then Jared must be telling the truth. Even so, his behavior haunted her. She wanted to be sure. The next time he slipped away, she would follow him and discover exactly who he was meeting with. If she lived in that decrepit part of town, she obviously wasn't among the gentry. Was she using him for his money? Frankly, Phil couldn't give a fig's end about the heritage of the person Jared married...*if* she truly cared for him.

Meg bid her goodnight and stood. Phil reached out, catching her sleeve. "What about...lovers? Did your brothers keep any before they married?"

"Pat? You bet your arse he did. Why do you think he had to marry?" She grinned. She didn't seem as embarrassed by the notion as Phil was about Jared's bedroom activities. "Men will do what pleases them," Meg added. "I wouldn't worry too much, if I were you. Jared seems more the marrying type to me, like Sean."

Phil knew a few things about Sean that his sister, apparently, did not. Her friend's words didn't comfort her at all. Nevertheless, she forced a smile and bid Meg goodnight.

After she'd left, Phil shucked her wrapper and slid into bed. She leaned on one elbow to blow out the candle. Although the flame extinguished, her riotous thoughts did not.

If Jared had ventured into that part of town to meet with a lover...why had the Duke of Tenwick been there? As she squirmed between the sheets, she couldn't help but relive the pressure of his lips on hers, the masterful thrust of his tongue. When her mind conjured his image, it also brought to mind the fact that he slept bare. An ache throbbed between her legs. She resisted.

She clung to the small seed of anger in her chest. He'd kissed her. Right there, in the middle of the alley. If he'd ventured there to meet a lover... A hot, smothering sensation blanketed her chest. It had nothing to do with jealousy. Oh, no. He was a scoundrel, kissing two women in one night. It didn't matter if she was one of them.

As she rolled over onto her stomach, she didn't quite believe herself. Even worse, she would have to see him again tomorrow, knowing what sort of man he was. She'd already accepted his mother's invitation. She couldn't take it back now.

How was she going to face Morgan and pretend he'd never kissed her?

***

"Who is that blond woman batting her eyelashes at my brother?"

A shiver of awareness raced down Morgan's spine at Phil's voice. He thrust his shoulders back, trying to look unaffected before he glanced at her.

She looked stunning. Tonight, she wore a sapphire-blue gown that scooped over the swell of her breasts. The gown boasted detachable sleeves with hints of silver embroidery, mirroring the design along the bodice and down at her hem, over her dainty black half-boots. Her hair was swept up in a simple knot, alluring in its own way as he wondered how she had possibly coaxed all her long hair into that small bunch. Her maid had braided one thin lock into a loop surrounding the bun. Sapphires winked at her ears and the dainty necklace rested at the top of the crevice between her breasts.

Damn. She looked breathtaking in the Tenwick ducal colors. Not to mention the sapphire color brought out the blue in her eyes.

Seeing him struck mute, she cocked an eyebrow. A devilish smirk twisted her lips, as if she knew exactly what the sight of her did to him. Tonight, she smelled like lavender, without a hint of mineral oil. He found himself missing the sharp scent. It gave her a tangibility, something that alerted him to the fact that he wasn't dreaming.

He definitely shouldn't enact one of his dreams about her. Not in the middle of Vauxhall Gardens.

She cleared her throat and flicked her gaze to indicate the group ahead of them. Mother had managed to secure one of the private boxes in the middle of the garden. The front gate opened into a cobblestone walkway that led to an open square. On a raised dais to one side, a quartet of musicians had set up alongside a dance floor. Opposite the dance floor was a long row of boxes, closed on three sides and sharing walls with their neighbors.

At the one on the end, with the crimson curtain secured to the side, his family clustered together with Phil's brother. Mother wore a bit of color today, with yellow beading on her dove-gray dress. Even so, she was eclipsed by Lucy, in a paunchy orange dress, and Miss Vale in pink. Mrs. Vale had declined to attend.

Easily head and shoulders taller than everyone except Mr. St. Gobain, who he topped by no more than a hand or two, Giddy plucked at the cravat at his throat. On the other side of the ladies, and subject to much more attention from the two youngest, Mr. St. Gobain mirrored the nervous fidgeting.

Blast, he should have let Lucy bring her parrot. Perhaps the bloody bird would have taken the opportunity to fly away. The first thing Lucy had done upon being presented with the hyacinth macaw, a large blue bird with a strip of yellow next to her black beak that made her look as devious as his sister, was name her Antonia. Then she'd taught the bird to say 'Giddy.'

It was the only word the parrot knew and she was prodigiously happy to be able to speak at all. Morgan's ears still rang from the assault on his senses.

"The blond?" Phil prompted. Her voice was light, but it had a steely undertone.

He must have offended her in some way. He stifled a sigh. "Her name is Miss Charlotte Vale, but I doubt she's batting her eyelashes at your brother on purpose. Her face is always that way."

Phil harrumphed. She started to cross her arms, but forced them to her sides instead. "Are you sure? She looks awfully flirtatious."

"If so, she flirts with me, my mother, and her morning scones. It's nothing."

Drat, Mother was looking their way. Before she noticed his lack of manners, he offered his arm to Miss St. Gobain. They were, after all, in public. Couples milled, their chaperones trailing them as they navigated the paths or ensconced themselves in the supper room. With so many eyes on them, Morgan and Phil had to pretend to be the polite duke and debutante that Society believed them to be.

Even if they lived dual lives come nightfall.

Even if her light touch on his arm made him burn for more.

He marshalled his concentration and battled for composure. After all, tonight it was his duty to keep her under his eye. The coded missive in his pocket from Strickland sat heavy and gave him information that Gideon had also imparted this morning, after he sifted through the latest spying reports in London, the ones Strickland had finally passed on.

Another spy meeting was set for tonight. Why so soon on the heels of the last, Morgan didn't know, but he was determined to intercept it this time. Philomena would not slip away, that he vowed. Once he confirmed she was meeting with another French spy, he would let Strickland know in no uncertain terms that she was Harker's replacement in the *ton*.

What if she wasn't a French spy?

He tried to tell himself not to be fanciful, but the thought plagued him. If he was wrong and the true spy was someone else, then he would miss this meeting again. Strickland would never welcome him into the field again. He would be stuck filling out paperwork for the rest of his natural born life.

He did enough paperwork to dull even the sharpest of minds. He craved excitement.

He certainly got that from the woman standing next to him. When they were mere feet away from the pavilion, she dug her fingers into his arm and pulled him to a stop.

"How well do you know this Miss Vale?"

He battled the urge to roll his eyes. "Well enough."

"You've bedded her then, have you?"

"*What?!*"

His sharp tone drew the curious gazes not only of his family, but every other peer in eyesight.

Heaven help him, was that Mrs. Biddleford and Miss Maize? Before midnight tonight, this was going to be branded a lover's quarrel. He would read about his own fictitious, doomed engagement in the scandal rag tomorrow.

He lowered his voice. "Of course I haven't."

Phil's eyes twinkled with mischief. "I knew that. You propose to women you accidentally blow a kiss in passing."

He gritted his teeth. "I do not."

"I only wondered if you were attending to the conversation."

"Evidently, I am." He bit off the words.

That alluring smile of hers grew. Zeus, he'd never wanted to kiss her more.

"How do you know Miss Vale?" Phil asked. Her expression made it known under no uncertain terms that she would not forget the topic.

"She is currently residing in my townhouse."

He winced as the words left his lips. Phil's eyebrows soared upward.

Hurriedly, he amended, "She is my sister-in-law."

"Who is she married to?"

"No one." He resisted the urge to rub the white streak in his hair, as he did when he was harried. Mother would know the gesture at once. She, along with the others in his family, now stared in their direction with open suspicion—or, perhaps

144

worse, delight. He shifted to put his back to his family.

Phil braced her hands on her hips. The movement pulled her dress flush against her ample figure, making his mouth water. "If she isn't married, how can she be your sister-in-law?"

"She's the sister of the woman who married my brother earlier this month."

Phil canted her head to the side as she thought. For such an innocent gesture, Morgan got a chilling sensation of foreboding. What was going on in her mind?

"Which brother?"

He fingered the streak in his hair. "Well, it isn't Gideon."

Phil narrowed her eyes. "I could do without your sarcasm. How am I to know which of your brothers was recently married?"

"Have you opened a scandal rag lately? Tristan's marriage is all any of them can talk about."

"I don't read that drivel."

Morgan bit his tongue rather than admit to surprise. Most women—and many men—devoured the weekly gossip sheets.

"Are you satisfied now?" he asked, his voice strained.

Phil inclined her head. She laid her hand on his sleeve and they resumed their approach. He relaxed, believing the topic to have run its course.

How wrong he was.

"What are some of her merits?"

"Well, she doesn't snore."

Phil's hand tightened painfully. "I beg your pardon?"

Thank Zeus he'd mumbled that statement. Louder, he amended, "She doesn't put much in store in gossip."

Somehow, he sensed that it would not bode well if Phil learned that Miss Vale slept in the chambers next to his. The duchess's chambers.

What does she care? They aren't earmarked for her.

No, this was jealousy based on Miss Vale's perceived pursuit of Phil's brother. She couldn't care a whit for Morgan.

But if she did...

Better he not deceive himself.

From the moment he introduced Phil properly to Miss Vale, the evening only grew worse. She constantly tried to insinuate herself between Jared and Miss Vale. This lead to increasingly bizarre excuses to change positions. Each time she changed her seat in the box, her leg or bottom brushed against Morgan and he was reminded of her allure. Mother and Lucy scented his attraction and pounced, concocting elaborate schemes to move Phil back to Morgan's side. It was maddening.

Finally, the table could take it no longer. Mr. St. Gobain thrust himself into a standing position. His hair flopped into his eyes. "Bloody Hell, Phil. Find a place to sit and stay there!"

As all eyes fixed on him, his cheeks turned ruddy. He stepped back, to the curtain of the box shielding them from the public. "Forgive me," he mumbled. "It must be the air in here. I'll take a short walk." He batted aside the heavy curtain, letting in a strengthened gust of renewed chatter, and strode into the crowd.

Mother, who had been seated across from him, on the end of the booth where Morgan sat, also stood. "Oh dear. Perhaps the air in here is a little stuffy." She peeled back the curtain and secured it near the wall.

The lamp inside the box cast an intimate glow on the worn wooden booth and the surrounding box. Tasseled cushions softened the bench. The walls were painted with an elaborate Grecian scene that looked to be a marriage by the seashore, given the focus on a man and woman in the midst of all the scantily-clad revelry. Perhaps he shouldn't look too closely.

Beyond the box, the Vauxhall Gardens were thick with couples and groups, some from the *haute monde*, others workaday families out for the weekend entertainment. Men and women danced in pairs on the dais, laughing as they completed the jaunty steps of the country dance. Lanterns, hung on elaborately-wrought poles, lined the pebbled walkways as they left the square, all save one—the illustrious Dark Walk.

Mother chased everyone at the table out of the box and into the open air. "Perhaps a stroll would be just the thing."

A stroll would not be the thing. Morgan had to keep his eyes peeled for the spy meeting. His mood had soured enough when they'd been isolated in the box for so long, partaking of the cold meats and cheeses that a servant of the Gardens had brought for them. He stuffed his hand into his pocket, fingering that note. Still, if his instincts were right and Phil was the French spy, keeping her occupied would be enough to avert the meeting.

Inclining his head, Morgan offered Mother his arm. "May I escort you?"

"And old woman like me?" She batted her hands through the air, a smirk on her lips. "Of course not. Why don't you take Miss St. Gobain?"

Morgan fought back a groan. Of course that had been her design. She and Lucy had exchanged mischievous looks every time he spoke to Phil. Keeping the irritation from his face, Morgan turned to do his duty and ask Phil for her arm.

"Where has Miss St. Gobain run off to?" Mother sounded worried.

Morgan bit the inside of his cheek. She'd managed to slip the party without any of them being the wiser. The spy meeting was occurring as they spoke.

Chapter Eleven

Jared, you are not going to slip away from me this time. Phil, who had been seated beside Jared when he'd sprung to his feet and left the booth, hurried to stand after him and was the first Lady Graylocke shooed out of the box. As the rest of the party joined her in the open air, she scanned the crowd. Blast! Where had her brother gone? He might have hidden it beneath his aloof, surly demeanor, but he'd been agitated. Phil had tried to minimize that by sitting between him and Miss Vale, though that never seemed to work for long. Lucy wasn't comfortable, or else her mother needed a change of air, and before Phil knew it, she was pressed hip to hip with Morgan once more.

She didn't want to think about *that* distraction. Where had Jared gone? Was he meeting with his lover once more?

He might have lied. Or he might have told the truth. She wouldn't know until she unearthed the truth.

At the mouth of the Dark Walk, she spotted a lanky figure with his topper askew, as if it had been hastily shoved onto his head. The man turned to glance behind him. It was Jared. It had to be.

A gaggle of young women giggled as they strolled past, accentuating their figures for the pleasure of the esteemed Graylocke brothers. Phil insinuated herself in their midst, using them as camouflage until they decided to double back. She skirted the lit promenades until she reached the infamous Dark Walk. Couples used it for illicit meetings. Debutantes found strolling along its length ruined their reputations. Fortunately, Phil didn't give a fig's end for her reputation. She had to know the truth.

While they were ensconced in the box, the twilight had deepened to full night gloom. As she marched away from the lights, the darkness pressed in on her eyes. She fumbled at the bulging reticule on her wrist. Once she found her LEGs, she secured them over her eyes.

This was the pair her father had made, her only working pair. The three-inch-wide, round lenses fitted over her eyes and were held in place by an adjustable strap. Once she buckled it on securely, she adjusted the fittings over the eyes. The lenses themselves might only be three inches wide, but in order to gather the ambient light and amplify it, the contraption jutted out from her head. The LEGs didn't throw the ground in front of her into full light as if it was day. Rather, they enhanced the grayscale of the gloom enough to pick out details that would have been overlooked by her naked eye.

Although it was called the Dark Walk, the path wasn't entirely unlit. Cozy alcoves at long intervals between the trees each held a bench and a mostly-shuttered lantern. The faint trickle of light was enhanced by the LEGs as she walked, and she was able to move without fear of tripping.

The walk, although far from deserted, was populated as sparsely as the lanterns. Couples found unoccupied alcoves and ensconced themselves out of sight of the path, shielded by the long, sweeping branches of the trees and the cultivated high hedges. Others leisurely strolled between alcoves with their arms tucked around each other. Phil strode briskly, examining each pair only long enough to determine that none of them were her brother.

At last, she found him entering an alcove. She quickened her step, hoping to get a glance of the occupant within. Was he alone? Was he meeting a lover or someone more nefarious? As she strolled past, the interior became clear. A woman, seated on a bench wearing a low-cut gown, gestured to him.

Lud, her brother had been telling the truth. Cheeks aflame, Phil turned her face away. She strode back the way she'd come, battling the urge to break into a run. Jared was an adult. He had every right to engage in romance even if she, as a rule, did not. She had her inventions, a passion that Jared didn't share.

Not that she was dispassionate about romance. She'd harbored more than one infatuation, before her parents had died. After that, it had been more and more obvious that she didn't have time to indulge in courtships. Nor did she have the liberty. A man might try to curtail the hours she spent inventing, never mind that it brought in a great deal of money. Surely a husband would make her excursions to the Society for the Advancement of Science meetings as "Phil" a bit inconvenient. She'd fought tooth and nail to win the respect of those at the Society for the Advancement of Science. If she married, she might lose that and become bereft of a space where she was comfortable enough to join in the enthusiasm for technology.

She was better off on her own. If she wanted someone to hang off her sleeve and beg for kisses...well, she had Pickle for that.

Not that bussing the beak of a parrot in any way compared to a man's masterful kiss. Not, for example, the Duke of Tenwick's. Maybe it was the darkened walk, shrouded in silence and intimacy that even the LEGs couldn't banish, but tingles plagued her at the memory of his kiss. A kiss that would have been infinitely more pleasurable if conducted in the privacy of a bedroom. Or, even, one of these private bowers.

She tilted her head down to avoid the gaze of a strolling party as she retraced her steps toward the entrance to the darkened walk. With luck, the Graylockes wouldn't have noticed her absence—or perhaps she could explain it away by her intention to follow her brother. Although the ladies' constant efforts to move her closer to Morgan were both transparent and galling, she could use the distraction from what her brother must be doing at that that moment.

Out here, in the middle of a public walk? No, he couldn't go farther than a kiss. Not that she cared to contemplate that, either.

Her heartbeat stuttered as a tall, broad-shouldered figure separated from the gloom in front of her. She would recognize that gait and manly form anywhere. Morgan. How had he known to follow her here? He'd been speaking with his mother when she'd slipped away, too busy even to notice the abundance of debutantes hoping to catch his eye.

She stumbled. Her toe scuffed against the gravel. *He can't see you,* she assured herself. He couldn't possibly, with the shadows decorating the path. If anything, he would see the form of a young lady, in much less detail than she could see him, thanks to the LEGs. Even so, she didn't want to test that theory should they cross paths. The darkness invited her to succumb to pleasures that were best left to dreams. Especially if a marriage proposal was forthcoming every time Morgan indulged. She had to find a means of escape.

There! The opening between two tall hedges, just wide enough to slip through. She prayed that no one occupied the alcove within, or she was about to interrupt a very private moment. Holding her breath, she slipped between the greenery.

It was empty. The bower stretched no more than four feet wide, ringed by the hedges that soared above her head, trees, and bushes. The middle of the hovel was carpeted in short, tended grass. The bench, its legs made of wrought iron to match the lamp post next to it, beckoned. She sat on the hard, cool surface before her legs gave way. Only a sliver of glass was shown through the shuttered lantern, but the light spilling out was enough for her to spot the individual contours of the leaves on the trees. She pressed her hand onto her chest, over her rapidly thumping heart.

Morgan didn't have LEGs of his own. He couldn't possibly have seen her enter the alcove.

He had. His broad shoulders blocked out the only exit as he shifted sideways to enter the bower. He held his topper in his hand, his hair windswept across his forehead, the white streak at his temple a marked contrast from the rest of his inky black hair, melding with the darkness. His buckskin breeches clung to his muscular thighs and his boots hugged calves that had no need for padding to give them shape. The buttons on his jacket gaped, the halves spreading wide to billow around his waist.

The lantern in here didn't even emit as much light as those in the occupied alcoves she had passed. If she was lucky, maybe he didn't recognize her and she could pretend to be someone else. She rose to her feet. The moment he vacated the exit, she would slip past and hurry back before someone found them alone.

He took a step closer, the strong pine scent of his cologne washing over her, mingled with the starch on his jacket. Heat radiated from his broad, muscular body. He crowded closer to the bench, leaving her no quarter. She was trapped.

Tilting his face down, he ran his tongue along his lower lip. She was entranced by the movement and couldn't help but mimic it. The slow slide of her tongue was torture. The ache in her belly bloomed. She forgot entirely about leaving.

Until he spoke her name. "Philomena. Fancy meeting you here, all alone."

Judging by his tone of voice, he had no intention of letting her leave.

***

Morgan had imagined finding himself alone with Phil too often. With the tall hedges shutting them off from the rest of the world and the darkness providing an even deeper intimacy, he battled the urge to re-enact their kiss in the alley. This time, in a more romantic location, maybe he wouldn't have to cut it short.

You were almost slapped the last time, he reminded himself. In fact, he'd been laughed at.

But she'd also said that she liked it. So had he. Too much. If he gathered her close, would she resist?

He admired her silhouette, the only thing he could see in the dim light. The flare of her hips curved up to her generous breasts. He remembered how soft they'd felt against him. The graceful column of her throat was interrupted by one of the locks of her hair that had fallen free of her coif. And her face... What was wrong with her face? The silhouette was...bizarre.

"What do you have on your face?"

"Oh," she exclaimed. "I forgot to take off my legs!"

"I beg your pardon?" He swept his gaze down her figure once more to the legs concealed beneath her dress. When he'd run his hand along her thigh in the alley, those legs had felt real and very feminine.

She pulled a strange contraption away from her face. "My legs," she said by way of an explanation. "Light-enhancing goggles."

Ever since he'd learned that she was the same Phil who had attended the Society for the Advancement of Science meeting, he had known in the back of his mind that she was an inventor. But for some reason, he hadn't stopped to consider the kinds of inventions she might create. In fact, it had crossed his mind that her attendance at the meeting had been a cover. It seemed that was not the case.

When she offered the goggles to him, he gingerly accepted them. They weighed more than they appeared. What unwieldly things! He lifted one to his face to peer through the lens. The hovel suddenly veered into focus. The silhouettes of the hedges, benches, and tree came into miraculous focus in comparison to only a moment past. When he looked at Phil, he could make out the distinction between her upper chest and the lacy line of her bodice.

He lowered the goggles reluctantly and offered them back. "Masterful."

She stood straighter. A warmth entered her voice as she admitted, "My father made them. I've been trying to replicate them ever since he died."

"My condolences. My father died, too." Morgan rubbed at the streak in his hair. What a buffoon he must seem. "Of course he died, or else I wouldn't be Duke."

She laid her hand on his sleeve. Her soft touch ignited his desire. He wanted to pin her hand beneath his. Somehow, he resisted.

"Were you terribly young?"

"Twenty," he admitted. Little more than a boy who'd fancied himself a man. He'd learned altogether too quickly a man's responsibilities when he'd been forced to grow up overnight.

"I was twenty-one." Her voice was low. He had to strain his ears to hear. Her hand shifted on his sleeve, but she didn't pull it away. "Old enough, at least, to become Jared's regent until he comes of age in a couple years."

Morgan's mother had been his regent for a year, but it had been his stewards that had helped ease the transition the most. His father had been smart enough to surround himself with capable men.

He found and squeezed Phil's hand. He wished for the goggles back, so he could read her expression. "That must have been terribly hard. I had my brothers and sister to think of, but at least I've had Mother all this time to help."

"I do miss Maman. Papa the most, though. We used to spend so much time together, in the invention room." Her voice sounded sad.

Tentatively, he eased closer. He slid his arm around her shoulders and offered her what comfort he could. He expected her to push him away, but to his surprise, she leaned into him, pillowing her cheek on his chest. The goggles jabbed at his stomach between them, but he ignored the irritation. He didn't want to shatter this peaceful moment.

Even though he must. He'd found her alone, but she had to be waiting for someone. Could he convince her to tell him who?

"Are you going to tell me why you snuck away?" His body tensed, bracing for a lie. He forced himself to relax.

Her gusty sigh teased him through his waistcoat and shirt. Gooseflesh raised over his arms and the back of his neck.

"I followed Jared."

Liar.

"And yet I found you alone." He tried to keep his voice soft, but steel edged it. He wanted to shred every lie between them. At least with the truth out in the open, they could deal with it and move on.

What are you thinking? He clenched his jaw. It wasn't as though they had a future, however good she felt in his arms. Desire was intoxicating, but it didn't negate the fact that they were enemies. This truce wouldn't last.

She said, "He's with a...mistress." She spat out the last word as if it was poisonous.

If that were true, it would be bad form for a young man to flaunt such a thing in the middle of a family outing. "He should be more discreet."

She tipped her face up to his. If he only lowered his head, he could kiss her. "Like you and me?"

Blast, but she was right! They'd been away from the gathering long enough to draw attention. His mother and Lucy would leap on this like wolves going for the kill.

"You're right. We should get back."

Hesitantly, she pulled away from him. She fiddled with the goggles, folding them up until they were small enough to fit inside the reticule hanging from her wrist. His gentlemanly instincts bleated for him to move away and offer his arm. He didn't want to put that distance between them. There was too much already.

"You know..." Her voice was light, her face turned away from him. "That glass you have. It's what I need in order to finish my prototype of the goggles."

Curious, he fished out the oddly-shaped lump of glass he carried with him everywhere. He held it between his fingers. "You mean this?"

"Yes." Her voice went gravelly.

When she made a grab for the item, he held it high, out of her reach. The stretch of her arm brought her closer to him again, her breasts brushing the bottom of his ribcage.

His voice was every bit as hoarse when he said, "If you want it back, it will come at a price."

She stepped closer. Her hips brushed against him. Space between them was only an illusion. His head spun. He nearly grabbed her and lowered her onto the soft bed of grass, lest he fall down.

"Fine." Her voice was hard. "I'll kiss you."

His mouth dropped open. He battled with the urge to lower his head and claim her lips then and there. She'd given him permission this time.

Instead, he held himself in check. "I beg your pardon?"

She cocked one hand on her hip. "It's what men want, isn't it?"

Zeus, yes. But not like this. Not with this... complication between them.

He squared his shoulders. It helped that he couldn't see the saucy curve of her lips.

Oh, but he could imagine it. In great detail.

He coughed into his fist to clear his throat. He took care to keep the other hand aloft, the prize out of her reach.

"Actually, what I want right now is the name of the man who gave this to you."

"Oh."

Did she sound disappointed? His heart leaped.

"Why?"

He kept his voice even. "Because it's important to me."

"I highly doubt that." He could hear the roll of her eyes in her sarcastic voice.

His arm was starting to ache. He gritted his teeth, refusing to show weakness by sticking the glass back into his pocket. "Unless you've developed an invention that can read minds, you're going to have to take my word for it."

She leaned closer. Her floral perfume wrapped around him. Where did she like to apply it? Beneath her ears, the hollow of her throat, her delicate wrists? Did she dab some between her thighs? He ached to find out. He breathed through his mouth, shallowly.

"I think you're lying to yourself," she whispered, standing on her tiptoes. Even then, her mouth rose no higher than his collarbone. But if he leaned down...

She added, "What man wouldn't consider a kiss fair trade?" Her voice was low, husky. It did devious things to his body.

"The name of your contact, or I won't give it back." His voice was rough. He battled with himself. This wasn't only his own pleasure he toyed with—he also had the fate of a nation resting on his shoulders. He had to stay strong.

She huffed, then dropped down onto her flat feet and maintained a stubborn silence.

"I guess you don't want it badly enough."

He dropped his arm, tucking the glass into his pocket once more. The relief of no longer having to hold his arm in that position rushed through him, making him giddy. He swayed toward her. If he dipped his head, he could still take that kiss. He could almost taste her on his lips. His blood sang.

No. He turned away, slipping between the narrow gap in the hedges. Without looking in her direction again, he told her, "You know where I am if you change your mind."

Chapter Twelve

Four days. Phil hadn't seen Morgan Graylocke in four days. Which, considering his sister's daily visits and constant invitations, was more difficult than Phil had imagined. She shut herself in her invention room as much as possible.

She'd offered him a kiss—the very thing he'd stolen while they were in the alley a week ago—and he'd declined. Instead, he wanted the name of a smuggler. Why? Did she not kiss well? He couldn't possibly have need for invention parts from France. He wasn't, to her knowledge, an inventor.

But, given his long and upstanding lineage, he might take issue with a smuggler selling French items. No, she couldn't give him the name of her contact, even if the weasel hadn't returned her inquiries after acquiring another prism. She resigned herself to the fact that she wasn't going to be able to complete her LEGs any time soon.

That didn't mean she didn't have plenty of other inventions vying for her attention. She was never devoid of ideas. In fact, she had several pocketbooks devoted to them.

On the perch behind her, her pet parrot squawked, "I want a pickle."

"You are a pickle," she retorted.

He made an indignant sound. When she let down the device she worked on in order to peek over her shoulder, Pickle bobbed his head. "Pickle, pickle, pickle!"

She rolled her eyes. "Go ask Meg."

The macaw launched into the air in a flurry of wings. He soared through the door to the hall, which she left open while she worked in case he wanted to come or leave. Phil returned to her invention. Minutes later, a faint shriek echoed from somewhere else in the manor.

Phil laughed. "I guess he found her."

She pressed her lips together, humming under her breath as she fastened a particularly delicate piece. That done, she consulted her plans to build the remainder of the device. No, that was never going to work. What had she been thinking? She grabbed a sheet of paper and a pencil, sketching out what she had so far. She tilted the sheet toward the afternoon sunlight drifting through the window. As she puzzled out the problem, she tapped the butt of the pencil against the worktable.

After a minute—or maybe five, she often lost track of time while contemplating her inventions—she realized that she wasn't alone. Her brother stood in the doorway, his shoulders hunched and his hands thrust into the pockets of his waistcoat. He wore no cravat, and his shirt was open to bare his throat.

"Jared." She couldn't quite keep the surprise from her voice. She'd been trying to steal a moment with him ever since they'd returned from Vauxhall, to no avail. He seemed determined not to spend a minute in her presence. When she met him in the breakfast room, he exited. When she tried to talk to him, he left the house. The rift between them had grown, seething like a festering wound. At a loss for how to mend it, she'd shut herself up with things she *could* mend.

Her brother stared at his feet. His forelock dripped into his eyes. "Remember when you asked me where I'd gone the other night?"

She dropped the pencil on the worktable and turned toward him. "Yes. Forgive me, Jared. I know you're an adult. I didn't mean to pry. It's just that I was—"

"Worried?" He glanced up through his fringe, his expression sheepish.

He wasn't angry with her. Relief gushed through her. "Yes, exactly. I was afraid you might be in trouble."

His expression turned hard. He swallowed, his Adam's Apple bobbing. "I am in trouble, Phil."

Her knees weakened. She groped for her workbench and sat. "How? What's going on?" Her voice was small. She squared her shoulders and tried to appear strong. No matter what, she would handle this. How much trouble could Jared have found? He was a quiet young man who didn't spend his time carousing, even if he did have a mistress.

Maybe his mistress is with child.

She bit the inside of her cheek. *Maybe you should let him tell you the problem himself instead of speculating.*

Stiffly, he crossed the room to sit next to her. The bench was relatively low to the ground. While it was comfortable to her, his knees jutted up at what looked to be an uncomfortable angle. He didn't complain.

He didn't look at her. The next few moments stretched on in silence as he fidgeted, tugging off his glove one finger at a time and then pulling it back on.

Phil laid her hand on his sleeve. "Jared, tell me. We can handle this."

He dropped his head into his hands. His mournful admission was muffled but it sounded something reminiscent to, "I'm being black-mailed."

Her heart pounded at her ribcage, trying to escape. *Please tell me I heard wrong.* "Blackmail?"

He lifted his head. His eyes were bloodshot and bleary, as though he battled tears. "Yes. By the French."

"The French." Was this an elaborate hoax? "We live in England, now."

"I know." His face scrunched. He raised his gaze to the ceiling, as if seeking guidance. "I don't know how this happened. I don't even remember how to speak French."

Jared had been a toddler when Phil and their parents had fled the revolution in France. At first, England had been a respite to a weary family, but it had soon become clear that their welcome was conditional. If they wanted to make England their home, they had to eradicate all signs of their heritage.

And they had. Phil's father had made a game out of learning English, rewarding her by letting her test his inventions. Within months, English was the only language spoken at home. Soon, she spoke it with such fluency that her accent betrayed no trace that she'd ever lived anywhere except in London.

She hadn't thought about their old home in France for years. This was her home, the only one that mattered.

"Start at the beginning," she told Jared. "What happened?"

"I was approached one night by a woman, Lady Whitewood."

Was she the woman Phil had found Jared meeting with at the Vauxhall Gardens?

"She blackmailed me, forced me to do something for her."

"What did she make you do?"

Phil didn't know this Lady Whitewood, but a name like that didn't sound French. Perhaps she, like Phil's family, had changed her identity. If so, she hadn't also changed her allegiances. Why side with the country that chased you out under threat of death?

Jared shrugged one shoulder, a surly gesture she recognized well. "Small things at first. Listen to a conversation at White's and report back. Bring something here or meet with another person there."

Phil struggled to breathe evenly. She must pretend to be calm, even if she seethed inside. "But now it's worse?"

He gave that one shouldered shrug. "I don't want to do it anymore. If I'm caught, I'll be hanged. But if I don't, she'll..." He dropped his face into his hands, shaking his head. "I didn't want to lie to you anymore."

She squeezed his shoulder. "You did the right thing. I'll take care of this. But *why* is she black-mailing you?"

His shoulders grew even stiffer and Phil recognized the look on his face. She knew it well and it meant he wasn't going to tell her. She knew from experience that if she pressed him on it, he'd withdraw into silence. Maybe even refuse to tell her more or let her help solve the problem. And she needed him to let her help. He was the only family she had, and she couldn't let him get deeper into this mess.

"This will work out fine, I promise," Phil said. She retracted her hand and slipped out of her shoes to mull over the problem. "Here's what you'll do. You'll go to the next meeting as planned. While you have Lady Whitewood occupied, I'll search her home."

With luck, Phil would find something to incriminate Lady Whitewood and Jared could stop this dangerous game. No one ever needed to know, least of all the British government.

Unless they knew already.

Phil's heart skipped as she realized that whenever she had followed Jared to his mysterious meetings, Morgan had interrupted her. She'd thought it an odd coincidence, but now in light of Jared's confession, maybe it wasn't so odd after all.

Was it possible that Morgan was a British spy?

No. It was ludicrous. He was a duke, for heaven's sake!

But if he *was* a spy, it would explain why he'd chosen the name of her smuggler over the chance to kiss her again.

... And it was possible that he thought *she* was the one spying for France.

Had the coincidental meetings—and even the kiss—simply been a ruse to get her to incriminate herself somehow? Yet Phil had sensed real passion in Morgan, a true connection. Then again, maybe he was just a very good spy.

All the more reason to avoid him until she sorted out this problem with Jared.

***

When Morgan stepped into his study, his brother on his heels, he found a young black boy of about ten in front of the desk. Morgan stiffened. Was he a slave? If so, not for much longer. With one abolitionist vote passed in Parliament, forbidding the trafficking of slaves in Britain, it wouldn't be long before the vile trade was eradicated altogether. Morgan studied the boy. If he *was* a slave, perhaps Morgan could buy his freedom.

The boy's round cheeks bespoke of being well-fed and he was dressed in a clean outfit of red-and-cream livery. Morgan didn't recognize the colors or the crest on the breast. The crest looked somewhat similar to a half-dozen noble houses.

As Gideon shut the door, the boy glanced between the two Graylocke brothers. "Your Grace?"

Morgan stepped forward. "What can I do for you?"

The boy bowed, tugging on his forehead. "I'm to give this to you, Your Grace." He held out a thick vellum envelope.

"Thank you." Although thicker than most missives Morgan received, it was surprisingly light. "Are you instructed to wait for a reply?"

"No, Your Grace." The boy bowed. "Good day."

He snaked between Morgan and Gideon too quickly for Morgan to stop him. In the space of a heartbeat, the boy slipped into the hall and shut the door behind him. Morgan turned his attention to the envelope. Its sender would tell him where to direct his inquiries about the boy's freedom.

After he pried off the seal and unfolded the note, he let out a pent-up breath. The note was from Strickland. The boy wasn't a slave—he was a spy. His conscience at ease, Morgan turned his attention to the note. A card remained in the envelope, presumably an invitation.

He groaned. "Strickland believes the next meeting of French spies will be at a soiree tomorrow evening."

Gideon stepped closer, reading over Morgan's shoulder in the afternoon light. "What's wrong with that? Who is Lady Whitewood?"

No one you'd care to meet. "A widow. This isn't the kind of soiree I can bring Lucy to."

Understanding dawned on Gideon's face. "Oh, it's one of *Tristan's* soirees, is it?" His eyes gleamed.

Good God, could he actually be interested in going? Morgan hated those lewd displays. He felt out of place. He wasn't a prude—at least, he didn't think he was—but he didn't fit in with the tawdry crowd as well as Tristan did.

Tristan wasn't in London. Gideon was. And it would make him feel more at ease if he didn't have to attend alone.

He clapped his brother on the shoulder. "How would you like to come with me to ferret out a spy?"

Gideon grinned. "Are we searching for your beguiling Miss St. Gobain?"

Morgan sighed. "We'll find out, won't we?"

A well-bred young gentlewoman like Phil wouldn't attend one of these parties of her own volition. It would ruin her reputation if she was recognized there. If she was in attendance, there could only be one possible reason—because she was the French spy, after all.

He tucked his hand into his pocket, fingering the innocent-looking piece of glass she wanted so badly. He'd examined every inch of it in as close detail as he could. If it held a secret, he couldn't decipher it. Which, given that he was the best codebreaker in Britain, was an ill omen if the glass ring did signify in the French spy efforts.

Like every time he touched the glass, his mind conjured an image of the woman who wanted it back so desperately that she'd offered to kiss him. He should have taken her up on the offer.

No. He hardened himself. If she was the French spy, he couldn't allow himself to be taken in. He had to put the needs of his country above his attraction to this woman.

No matter how she beguiled him.

Chapter Thirteen

This was *not* the sort of ball Phil had expected. Jared flew his colors as he sheepishly ducked his head, plucking at his cravat. Normally she would tell him to stop, but even if he took it off, he wouldn't be as undressed as some of the guests.

Reluctantly, she let the butler take her bonnet and shawl. Jared passed off his topper. She squared her shoulders and resolved not to be embarrassed by the brazen display of skin tonight. After all, she was no prude. If men and women wanted to...indulge, it was no business of hers.

She did wish that she had known before walking in the door, however. She removed her detachable sleeves and gave them to the butler, as well, to stow with her things.

Then she sidled closer to her brother. "Find Lady Whitewood," she instructed. "Keep her occupied."

He nodded, his jaw clenched. She'd already told him what she planned to do tonight—search the townhouse for proof that Lady Whitewood was a French spy, to discreetly pass on to the government. At the very least, she hoped to find whatever Lady Whitewood was using to blackmail

Jared. Once she destroyed it, he would be free to cut his association with the traitor, and their lives could return to normal. Unfortunately, Jared had been very tight-lipped about what that piece of blackmail contained. Phil would have to root it out for herself, for all that Jared was adamant she wouldn't find it in Lady Whitewood's possession.

When it came to her brother's well-being, she would stop at nothing to keep him safe. Lady Whitewood was about to discover exactly how formidable an enemy the St. Gobain family could be.

With a bit of a swagger, Jared entered the nearest sitting room. Phil peeked into the room. The women wore the darker, richer colors that indicated maturity and marriage. Their dresses dipped low across their breasts, showing off their charms. More than half the men had doffed their jackets and cravats, walking around half-dressed and sidling closer than was strictly proper to the women.

Now that her initial shock had worn off, curiosity replaced it. The Society she ventured into now and again upheld such a rigid rectitude that it often grated on her nerves. Perhaps she had been associating with the wrong sort of people all along.

A man pressed his lips to a woman's neck. A brazen gesture in the middle of a room crowded with people, but no one seemed to mind, least of all the woman. She canted her head to allow him greater access. Her eyelashes formed dark crescents against her cheeks as she shut her eyes in ecstasy.

Phil's stomach fluttered as she relived the passion she'd found in Morgan's arms. This wasn't the time or the place to be thinking about him. Until she straightened out this catastrophe around her brother, she had to keep her distance.

And after that? She had always avoided romance, for fear that a man would curtail her independence. That fear still plagued her, but she had to wonder if she was missing out. Once her brother was safe again, would she and Morgan be able to resume their encounters where they had left off? She shook her head. He'd offered her marriage after a single kiss; she doubted she would convince him to let her explore passion with him. Not without a marriage demand. She was not a commodity to be acquired and she refused to treat herself that way. Her body was hers to share with whomever she pleased, whether or not she elected to tie herself to him for life.

To keep herself from being tempted to think more of Morgan and what might never be, she focused on her task. She turned away from the intimately lit room, sweetly perfumed and decorated with provocative works of art. A young woman, no older than Phil, led a man half again her age up the stairs, a promising smile on her face. He, in turn, looked star-struck. Phil checked to ensure no one paid attention to her before she scampered after them.

The couple continued on to the third floor, but Phil stopped on the second. The first door that she tried led to an unlocked study. She left the door wide to allow for light to stream in while she found a candle and tinderbox to light it. The flame flared to life and she set it on the desk just inside the room. She shut the door most of the way, leaving it open so she could hear if someone approached. Then she turned her attention to the room.

The study was tasteful and feminine, the writing desk more delicate than the ones found in men's studies. Above the mantle was a painting of a wild horse galloping across a field. The walls were paneled in oak, a lacy curtain across the window helping to add a delicate touch. Nestled between bookshelves on the far side of the room was a pink settee. Unable to resist, Phil brought the candle to the bookshelves to read the spines. She expected to find lurid novels or poetry, but instead she was surprised to find that she recognized some of the titles. Scientific treatises, the journals of explorers. Lady Whitewood had an interest in science.

Phil clenched her teeth and turned away. She wasn't supposed to like the woman who was forcing her brother to commit treason. She tucked her gloves into her reticule and focused on her task.

A quick search of the shelves and the desk provided no insight on the leverage Lady Whitewood was using to manipulate Jared. Did she have a secret drawer? Phil dropped down to her hands and knees to inspect the underside of the desk.

A man cleared his throat.

Phil bit her tongue as she stifled a yelp. She jerked upright, banging her head on the desk. Wincing, she rubbed her scalp and tried to ignore the sting in her mouth. When she emerged from beneath the desk, she found herself face to face with the last person she wanted to see.

"Morgan." His name escaped her lips without permission.

He was in a state of half-dress, which included a great deal more clothes than when they'd met in the past. Even so, his lack of a cravat and jacket made him all but irresistible. His shirt cuffs were rolled up to his elbow, displaying brawny forearms dusted with dark hair. His shirt was open at the throat. Although his hair was styled neatly, his jaw sported the dark shadow of stubble. He looked dangerous and unrefined.

His gray eyes pierced her. "What are you doing here?"

Did he mean under the desk or in the house? Phil scrambled to her feet, her hackles raised. She crossed the distance to him and jabbed him in the chest. She had to resist the urge to smooth the sting by running her palm over his rough linen waistcoat.

"*I* am here because it pleases me. What are *you* doing here?"

She had to crane her neck back to meet his gaze, but it was worth it to see the arousal flash through his eyes before he hid it behind a mask of hostility.

If they had been in the house under other circumstances, what might their meeting at such a risqué soiree mean for the evening ahead? *But you aren't.* Phil was here to clear her brother of wrongdoing and Morgan had likely followed Phil, hoping to catch her in the act of treason.

So keep his attention. The longer he kept his eye on Phil, the more time her brother would have to meet with Lady Whitewood unnoticed. Phil, after all, wasn't committing treason—Jared was, however unwillingly.

"*I* am here because I was invited." His voice was as cold as stone.

Phil laughed. "So was I." In an indirect way. Her brother had received the invitation, she'd simply joined him.

The rattle of a body colliding with a wall made them both jump. A woman moaned. When Morgan glanced to his right, the color left his cheeks. It returned in abundance. He stepped hastily into the study and shut the door behind him, leaving them very much alone.

Even the door didn't quite muffle the amorous activities going on down the hall. Morgan crowded her away from the door. He trapped her against the desk with one hand on either side of her body. Did *he* have an amorous bent in mind?

Given the steely look in his eye, he didn't. *A pity.*

His cheeks a pale shade of cherry, he muttered, "This isn't the sort of soiree that well-mannered young women attend."

Phil grinned. She leaned her hands behind her on the cool desk to bear her weight, only to brush his bare fingers. The contact scorched her. She didn't pull away.

"When did I ever give you the impression that I was a well-mannered woman?"

A spark flared in his eye. He pressed his lips together as he pulled away. His hand brushed against hers, a slow slide of skin. He took a healthy step back. Cooler air flooded her front, raising gooseflesh on her arms.

"If someone sees you here…"

"I will deal with the outcome, not you." She straightened to her full height. At first, his embarrassment had amused her, but now he treaded too close to telling her what she could and couldn't do.

No one told Philomena St. Gobain what not to do—not unless they planned to see her do it in the next five minutes.

"Thank you for your concern, but I can take care of myself." She turned her face away from his, toward the door. "Now, I'll thank you to leave." She still wanted to check for more secret doors or compartments along the desk or bookshelves.

"No."

Her gaze flew back to his. His pale eyes seethed with challenge.

She glared at him. "I beg your pardon?"

He shrugged. "You heard me. I won't leave. *Now* how will you 'look after yourself?'"

Phil cocked an eyebrow. "I know you wouldn't harm me."

He took a step closer. Not as close as he had been, but enough that she had only to reach out in order to touch him. She fisted her hands by her sides.

"And how do you know that?"

"You're too honorable," she accused.

"Perhaps that's a façade I put on to hide my black heart. Perhaps I leave a trail of wounded women in my wake all across London."

She snorted. "Please. If any woman had been wounded by you, it's because she nurtured hopes that you did nothing to bolster. You forget, you've proposed to me once already."

He gritted his teeth. "I won't make that mistake again, I assure you."

Wouldn't he? He made it sound as though he contemplated kissing her again. A tingle spread over her skin, radiating from her mouth. If he wasn't going to try to tie her to him...

She sidled closer. Her breasts brushed his waistcoat. "Good." Her voice was low and husky. "My body is my own to share with whomever I wish, whether or not he is my husband."

Morgan stilled. If he breathed, it was too shallowly for her to notice. His expression was unreadable. "Aren't you concerned that your husband will expect...certain things?"

The implication that she was held to a tighter standard because of her gender chased away her arousal, replacing it with outrage. "Are you concerned that your wife will expect those same things? Did you save your virginity for her?"

A muscle ticked in his jaw. "No," he admitted, his voice soft. "I did not. Truthfully, I didn't even think of it when I..."

She raised her chin, smug. "Exactly."

"I was scarcely sixteen. I wasn't mature enough to think of anything. If I was given the choice now, perhaps I would choose to."

She raised her eyebrows. "The implication being that because I'm a bit long in the tooth, I ought to confine myself to the shelf forever?"

"What?" He rubbed at the streak in his hair. "No. Of course not."

He looked irresistible when he was frazzled. "I only meant that I—"

"Want to kiss me."

His gaze dropped to her lips. His tongue darted out to caress his lower lip. He didn't even seem to realize that he was doing it.

"That wasn't what I intended to say at all." His voice was deeper than a moment ago, more intimate.

"Do it," she told him. "Kiss me."

"I shouldn't."

Not '*I can't*' or even '*I don't want to*'. Which meant that he did want to kiss her. Perhaps even as much as she did him at that moment.

She stood on her tiptoes and cupped his cheeks with her hands. His stubble scraped against her palm. She loved the rough sensation.

"Should is overrated."

She tugged his head down and melded her mouth to his.

Chapter Fourteen

Phil's touch burned Morgan. Her hands on his cheeks, her lush curves pressed against him, her lips against his. In an instant, he'd walked from a maddening conversation into the re-enactment of an erotic dream. She felt incredible. He raised his hand to cup her hip, holding her closer.

No. She was a French spy. The enemy.

Heaven help him, but she didn't feel like his enemy. She felt like coming home after a long and arduous journey.

Why would she be in Lady Whitewood's study if she wasn't meeting with the French spy? He'd interrupted her, and now she was trying to distract him.

It was working. She tasted divine. He ached to press her closer.

She lightened her kiss, then pulled back entirely. *No*. Every muscle in his body tensed. He encircled her with his arms, keeping her pressed against him as long as possible.

Her breath teased his lips. "Stop thinking. Enjoy the moment."

A weak smile pulled at the corners of his mouth. "I don't know if I can." Something inside him closed off, afraid she would use the admission as leverage. It was just the way he was. He thought everything through.

Even when you kissed her in the alley?

No. That had been instinct, pure and simple, born of the elation of catching her and of the win in Parliament earlier that day.

She brushed her lips against his, a tease that heightened the ache in his loins to a throb. "Try."

When she kissed him again, her mouth moved over his slowly. Her tongue explored the part of his lips. He sank into the kiss, unable to resist. He couldn't get enough. Their kiss turned wild. Her hands slid into his hair. He pressed her even closer, molding her to his body and lifting her until he supported most of her weight. How could this be wrong? She felt so good.

No. She felt better than good. She felt *right*.

He leaned her back against the desk, needing to get closer. He skimmed his hands up the sides of her waist, stopping when his thumbs brushed the undersides of her breasts. Her muslin dress felt as fine as air, and just as easily shredded. How far was she prepared to go?

She arched into his hands, encouraging him to cup her breasts as she broke the kiss. Her cat-in-the-cream smile curled his toes.

"That feels better, doesn't it?"

He made a wordless noise of assent. She had no idea how close he was to throwing propriety out the window. She melded her mouth to his once more in a quick, fiery kiss that left him wanting. Then she wiggled out of his hold and stepped away.

"Let's join the soiree. I think I hear music."

He stared at her. "I beg your pardon?"

Her hair had started to fall free of its pins, the erratic strands caressing her neck. Her neckline—modest, considering the gathering—conformed to the pronounced rise and fall of her chest. Her nipples peaked beneath the fabric. She wasn't as unaffected as she pretended.

Her stormy eyes darkened with desire. "We can't very well make love here, so we might as well enjoy the night."

He glanced at the desk. No, he supposed, they couldn't make love in Lady Whitewood's study. But in his bed...

No. He had more sense than that. As much as he would like to indulge the passion she raised in him, she was a spy...a debutante of good standing...hell, she was fantastic. For a moment, his passion-fevered brain imagined waking up next to her—for life. Perhaps dancing would be the safer option.

She slid her palm into his, tugging him toward the closed door. "Come, it will be fun."

"Dancing." It sounded far more civilized than the scene likely occurring in the salon below.

"Yes. Everyone loves to dance. We'll have a grand time."

The heat of her palm was like a brand. He pulled free. "I need a minute." He dropped his gaze to the fall of his breeches, where his erection strained against the cloth.

Her gaze meandered to the same spot. It didn't help. "Oh. Of course." Her tongue teased her upper lip. Color stained her cheeks, but her eyes didn't show mortification. Blast, was she curious? He put the desk between them.

"Maybe you should go down to the salon ahead of me. I'll be there in a moment."

"Oh." She tore her gaze away. She sounded disappointed. "Are you sure?" She reached for the door.

If she was a French spy and she left, she might meet with her contact before he rejoined her. "No. Wait. Stay with me."

"If you insist." She dropped her hand.

The silence lengthened between them, growing heavy and awkward. Her gaze took a circuit of the room before she landed on him once more.

"So, how long has it been since you..." Her gaze dropped to his fall once more.

Mortification scalded his cheeks. "Phil!"

Her eyes widened with feigned innocent. The candlelight emphasized the blue in her gaze. "What? Is that not appropriate study room conversation?"

"It is not." *As you well know.*

"The door is shut," she pointed out. "We're in private. It certainly doesn't sound like the sort of conversation one would have in public."

"It's the sort of conversation a man would have only with his wife," Morgan bit out. Hopefully that would squash that particular topic of conversation.

Her eyes took on a wicked glint. "Ah. This again. Is this the part where you propose to me?"

Even if he reached his one hundredth birthday, he doubted he would outlive that particular blunder. He gritted his teeth. "It's been too long for comfort. Are you satisfied?"

She canted her head to the side as she thought. "Is that why you have such a vigorous response to me?"

"*Yes.*" There. That should see the end of the topic.

"Oh." She looked disappointed. "I see."

Morgan raised his face to the ceiling as he prayed for patience. He sighed. "It isn't the only reason," he mumbled. If it had been, he would have been scandalizing Society every time he walked into a ballroom.

When he lowered his gaze, she beamed. She took a small step forward, closing the distance between them again. Oh, no. He couldn't have that. He shifted to keep the desk between them before his response to her nearness heightened again.

She perched on the edge of the desk. Leaning one hand on the wood, she leaned forward. The candlelight created an enticing shadow in the valley between her breasts.

"Oh? What are the other reasons?"

"You're a very beautiful woman, Phil."

She glowed at the praise. "And?"

"And...passionate." What did she want him to say?

"And?"

"Stubborn."

The corners of her mouth twitched, but she didn't drop the subject. "And?"

Was he going to have to name every damn adjective in the English language? "Beguiling, maddening, and too clever by half. Shall we dance?"

She hopped off the edge of the desk. "I thought you'd never ask."

Cheeky. He should have added cheeky.

He checked the corridor before they emerged. Whoever had paused there during their midnight tryst had long since moved above stairs. The second floor was deserted. He offered Phil his arm.

"Are you certain you wouldn't like to go down before me? Your reputation…"

"Is in question just from my attendance at this soiree, remember?"

True. But he didn't want to be trapped into marriage with her because of an ill-timed rumor.

Did he?

He shook his head. Clearly, he'd left his sanity at home tonight.

When they descended to the first floor, he expected to cause a stir. The Duke of Tenwick always did upon walking into a room. Instead, he found the guests too wrapped up in each other to care a whit for who else was in attendance. He straightened his shoulders. This anonymity was kind of…nice. He scanned the interior of the room for Gideon, picking him out easily from the other guests. His brother, the tallest man in attendance, danced with a widow almost twice his age. If it could, indeed, be called dancing. To Morgan, it looked more like turning in time to music. As Gideon completed a revolution, the widow pressed indecently against him, Morgan caught his expression. His brother looked harried. Morgan bit back a laugh.

Phil turned her face up to his. "What's so funny?"

"Gideon's here. It's nothing."

"Is he?" Phil glanced over her shoulder, but Morgan wasn't in the mood to speak about his brother. He swept Phil into his arms, making like the other dancers.

He savored the excuse to hold her close. Unlike the polite dances, there was no space between them, no tantalizing touches of the hand or coy looks. Instead, he pressed Phil flush against him. He willed his body not to react to the tease of hers. The fact that they were in public helped.

Even if the lighting here was lacking. The room was dim, the couples crowding into the shadows left by strategically placed lights. The quartet played a soft, elegant beat that allowed for a slow dance that even the most inept man could perform admirably.

Phil pressed her cheek to his chest as she looked around the room. She didn't protest their closeness. In fact, she capitalized on it by swaying her hips in time with his.

He glanced again around the room to remind himself that they were very much in public. Anyone would see his reaction. That knowledge helped to temper his ardor somewhat.

"This doesn't seem like the sort of evening Gideon would enjoy."

Morgan laughed. His brother now signaled him with frantic jerks of his head, begging to be interrupted. Morgan shook his head. "He asked to join me."

Somehow, he sensed that Gideon wouldn't be making that mistake twice.

"Perhaps he's getting more adventurous," Phil said. She settled against him, no longer trying to peer at the other guests, seeming content to stay in the circle of his arms and spin with him.

Most women would be scandalized. They would act brazen or modest. Phil did neither. She accepted their closeness and acted just as she normally did, teasing him with conversation as they danced. Her self-assurance was refreshing. He found himself looking forward to spending the rest of the night with her.

And he did, save for two short stints. Once when Gideon snagged her for a dance in order to lose the persistent widow trying to entice him into bed. The second time when Phil escaped into the ladies' withdrawing room. Was she meeting with the French spy? Morgan stared after her. He couldn't follow her there.

Giddy sidled up to him. "Do we have to stay here much longer?"

Morgan smirked. "Is it not everything that you imagined?"

"Very funny. I keep getting pinched in uncomfortable places."

Morgan lost the battle of composure. He bent double, clapping his hand over his mouth to stifle his laughter. His brother, surly, shoved at his shoulder, toppling Morgan into the wall. He leaned against it as he caught his breath.

"It isn't funny."

"It is." Morgan wiped at his eyes.

Gideon glared. "No one is bothering *you*."

"That's because I've already staked a claim on the beautiful Miss St. Gobain. I'm keeping an eye on her."

"And a fine job you're doing of it." Giddy's tone was sour.

It sobered Morgan somewhat. He stared toward the corridor, only to find her re-emerging into the room with a bright smile. She'd returned already? That wasn't near long enough to meet with a contact. Morgan took an involuntary step toward her.

"Can we leave?"

"Not yet," he told his brother. "I can't leave before Phil. But if you're in such agony, you can leave first. Send the carriage back after you're done with it."

Gideon clapped him on the shoulder. "You don't have to ask me twice." He bolted for the door. Two women slipped out after him, trying to catch him. Morgan hid a smirk.

His smile grew as Phil approached. He would keep an eye on her for the rest of the night, for the good of the nation. Not to mention for his own good. He hadn't felt so light and free in years. He constantly had to remind himself that he was watching her for a reason. If she had a message or a missive to pass on to a contact, he had to be there to intercept it.

And if she didn't approach her contact while he was nearby? Well, then, by the end of the night, she must still have the missive on her. Which meant that if he visited her at the St. Gobain townhouse tomorrow morning, he might be able to find it there.

Chapter Fifteen

"You're remarkably cheerful this morning," Mother remarked, seated across from Morgan with her back turned toward the carriage driver.

Lucy, seated beside him, leaned closer, staring at him as if he was a specimen in a museum. "Are you humming?"

The large, blue bird squawked from her perch on Lucy's arm, tethered to her wrist by a cord to keep her from flying out of the open carriage. "Giddy!"

Lucy nodded. "Quite right, Antonia. I think he is a bit giddy this morning."

Squashed in the corner with his knees drawn up to his chest, Gideon rolled his eyes. By now, they'd all prayed for the bird to learn another word. Any other word. Personally, Morgan was trying to teach the parrot to say, 'Let's go for a walk.' At least that way, he could buy himself a few moments of peace and quiet.

Lucy leaned closer once more, as did the bird. The yellow streak around Antonia's beak made her look as though she smiled mischievously. He raised a hand to ward her away, in case she decided to peck out his eye or something equally sinister.

The parrot canted her head this way and that as she examined him. She made an odd, purring coo. "Giddy," she pronounced. She made it sound as if he was on his deathbed.

Lucy sat back, taking the blasted bird with her. Why had he ever bought the parrot for her? Antonia had been nothing but a headache from the moment he'd brought her into the house.

His sister added, "It's odd for you to be so cheerful after such a late night. I think I heard you come home around three of the morning."

Morgan raised his eyebrows. "And what were you doing awake at that hour?"

She gave him a dazzling smile, the kind even brighter than her sunny yellow dress. "I had an idea for a story. I had to write it down, of course."

"Of course."

He leaned back against the leather squabs.

Unfortunately, Lucy didn't drop the topic. "You never offer to join Mother and I when we visit Phil."

"Neither does Gideon."

Giddy raised his hands. "Don't bring me into this."

Lucy ignored them both. With a sly smile, she asked, "After such a late night yesterday, should we hope that today is an especially happy occasion? The kind with a proposal, perhaps?"

Morgan choked on his own tongue. "I beg your pardon?" he spluttered.

Diagonal from him, Gideon grinned. "Yes, Morgan, is there a proposal in your future?"

He glared at them both. Although Mother said nothing, he noticed that she attended to the conversation a little too closely for his liking. "Don't be daft. I'm only joining you as a courtesy, to thank her for joining us at Vauxhall Gardens the other day."

"That was nearly a week ago, dear," Mother pointed out helpfully.

Lucy added, "And you were off with her on your own for a particularly long stretch then, as well."

Do not blush. Whatever you do, do not blush. He felt the heat plague his cheeks nonetheless.

Thankfully, the carriage pulled to a stop in front of the lofty St. Gobain townhouse. He jumped out the moment the driver laid down the steps. Unfortunately, it would be the height of rudeness if he tried to escape their company. He stepped to the side and offered his hand to help his mother out of the carriage.

She held the bonnet to her head with one hand as she grasped his with the other. On the top step, she was only a touch taller than him. She leaned closer. "I think Phil will make you a splendid wife."

He stifled a groan. "Miss St. Gobain will not make me a splendid wife. She will not make me any wife at all. And please, by Jove, don't suggest any such thing to her."

Mother brightened. "You don't think she needs encouragement in order to settle her preference on you? That's a tad arrogant, wouldn't you say, dear? For all that you are a duke, women like to be wooed, you know."

"I will not be wooing Miss St. Gobain. There is nothing between us."

He handed Mother to the cobblestones and reached up to accept Lucy's hand—the hand not currently occupied as a perch for Antonia. Lucy said, "You might as well stop lying to us. We can see that there is a great deal going on between you and Phil. We have eyes, you know."

Morgan glanced to Giddy for help.

His brother grinned impishly. "I think we should have a proper wedding this time, not that rushed affair that Tristan and Freddie insisted on."

Morgan gritted his teeth. *I am going to skin you in your sleep.*

Gideon's eyes danced. He was taking revenge for Morgan's lack of help at the lewd soiree last night.

Clearly and concisely, Morgan bit out, "There will be no wedding between me and Miss St. Gobain. Perhaps I ought not to visit her, if I will be raising false hopes."

Mother latched onto his arm, preventing him from climbing into the carriage once more. "Don't be ridiculous. You're already here. If she's seen you from one of the windows, it will be the worst insult for you to leave without saying hello."

Not to mention, if he left he wouldn't have any chance to search the manor for whatever she had intended to pass along to the French last night.

Clenching his teeth, he inclined his head. "Very well. Let's get this over with."

He escorted Mother to the front door, where they were greeted by a staid butler no older than Mother. He stepped aside to let them in. To his credit, he didn't mention the fact that Lucy had brought her pet. Giddy, the last in the line, inclined his head and offered the man his hat. Morgan did the same and passed along Mother's bonnet.

As he took it from her, she whispered, "Do you prefer someone else?"

Lud, would he never put an end to this conversation?

"No. I don't intend to marry this Season."

There. Perhaps that would mollify her. He hadn't turned down the possibility of marrying entirely, just not this year.

She whispered, "You aren't getting any younger, my dear. If you want to be fit enough to run after your children as they play, the way your father—"

"Mother." He refused to have this conversation in Phil's house, with her servants looking on in curiosity. "Can we speak of this later?"

"I still think Phil—"

He coughed into his fist, drowning out her words.

The butler hung back, looking from one to another as if he hoped the conversation would continue. With a broad smile, Lucy stepped forward.

"Your hair looks a fright, Morgan. Phil won't be impressed with that." She reached up with her free hand to comb his fringe into place.

His groan was cut off by Antonia's shriek.

"Lucy, shut your gob!"

Lucy gasped. "Antonia! What did you say?"

Giddy pumped his fist in the air. "Aha! My hard work paid off."

With a glower that could have peeled paint, Lucy rounded on him. "*You* taught her to say that?"

"Shut your gob, shut your gob."

Morgan bit the inside of his cheek to contain a smile. He should have thought of trying that. He winked at Giddy behind Lucy's back.

Mother turned to the butler. "Our apologies. Antonia is usually a much more polite bird."

The man shook his head ruefully. "Think nothing of it, Your Grace. We're used to it around here. Why don't you and Lady Lucy settle into the sitting room? I'll send Lady Philomena down in a moment." He bowed to Morgan. "Gentlemen, if you'll follow me, I'll show you to the study."

"Wait," Mother said. She reached out to snag Morgan's arm, but he sidestepped her. "Wouldn't you rather all be together?"

"The study sounds like just the thing," Morgan answered the butler. He turned his back, pretending not to notice his mother's glare. Anything for a few moments' respite.

The butler led him and Giddy to the second floor and ensconced them into a sparse room. It was clear from the lack of decorations and clutter that the study was rarely used, if ever. The chestnut-brown drapes were secured to one side with a faded gold tie. The wide, masculine desk was bare. The sideboard, where one might usually find decanters of brandy or whiskey, was bereft. The bookshelves lining the wall opposite the sideboard was the only part of the room that showed signs of use. Books crammed the space, stacked on top of one another in haphazard fashion, volumes put back out of order, even a couple books left open to a particular page and nestled on top. Seeing them, Morgan couldn't help but smile. He was willing to bet that all of these books were Phil's.

"Can I offer you some refreshment?" the butler asked.

Giddy answered. "Yes, thank you. Will the master of the house be long?"

Morgan shot his brother a quizzical look.

The butler bowed. "I will send him along shortly."

The moment the man vacated the doorway, Morgan turned to his brother. Gideon shrugged. "I wanted to know how long we have to search."

Search. Right. He hadn't come here to learn what sort of books Phil enjoyed reading, or what she found so important that she couldn't possibly shut the book. They had to find the French secrets.

"I'll start here," Gideon volunteered. "You check the floor above."

Morgan nodded. "Right. We don't have much time."

As he stepped out the door, Giddy called after him, "If you're found out, just say you were looking to say hello to your ladylove."

Pity Morgan didn't carry anything he could throw at him. He shut the door decisively instead, muting his brother's chuckle.

True to his word, he loped up the steps to the next floor. With his luck, he expected to find the bedchamber. Instead, he found two freckle-faced toddlers, a boy and a girl judging by the length of their hair and their clothing.

The girl brandished a feather duster. "The big bad giant is coming to steal Aunt Phil. Get him!"

With a shrieking war cry, the children launched themselves at Morgan. He caught them, one arm each, though he nearly got a feather in the eye for his troubles. He grinned. There was something charming about children. They couldn't give a fart whether he was a duke or a beggar. From the moment he'd stepped onto the landing, he'd become a part of their game. He held them high as they shrieked with glee.

"The giant has us!" The girl writhed, trying to stick him with her feather duster. It knocked him in the head a couple times. He readjusted his hold so he didn't accidently drop her.

"Stop that, tiny knight," he told her. "I've got you so I've won. I can have my prize."

The boy giggled. "Aunt Phil! He's come for Aunt Phil!"

"Exactly," Morgan boomed. He bounced the two children on either hip. "Now that I've defeated her brave knights, what other obstacles will I face in the perilous journey ahead?"

"You'll have to climb a really tall tower," the boy said. He spoke so fast, with a bit of a slur, that Morgan took a moment to puzzle out his words.

Once he did, he answered in mock surprise, "But I'm a giant! I can step to the top."

The girl shrieked happily and kicked him in the side. "Then you have to kiss the princess."

"If the princess is Phil, that won't be any trouble."

"Of course it's Phil. You're going to keep her, aren't you?"

The children stared up at him with wide, guileless blue eyes.

"Of course I am," he said. The words stuck in his throat. Was this still a game?

The children grinned. The girl wiggled to be put down. "Come, come, I'll lead you to her."

The moment he set her on the ground, she took him by the hand and tugged him along. The boy helped, pushing Morgan to a greater speed.

They were intercepted in the hall not by Phil, but by a thin wisp of a young woman, a year or two younger than Giddy. She had light brown hair and freckles to match the children. Her complexion was milk-white.

"Your Grace! I'm terribly sorry. This is my niece and nephew. They didn't mean anything."

His smile slipped. Game time was over, it seemed. He was back to being the Duke of Tenwick. He'd enjoyed the respite.

"It's fine. They were no trouble."

The young woman didn't appear to be listening to him. She held out her hand to each of the children. "Bonny, Brandon. Phil has guests. What do we do when Phil has guests?"

Glumly, Bonny answered, "We play in the attic."

"Or in the kitchen, if you'd like. I hear Grandmam is making tarts."

The boy perked up at this. Even Morgan cocked half an ear. What kind of tarts?

The girl couldn't be bribed with food. "Aunt Meg, can I play with Pickle?"

Meg, who had begun to regain some of her color, turned almost transparent as she blanched. "No," she croaked. "He's napping."

"Oh." The girl looked glum. It tugged at Morgan's heart.

"There's another bird down in the sitting room. If you tell my mother and sister that I gave permission, I'm sure they'd let you play with her."

The children tugged on Meg's arms with repeals of, "Can I? Can I?"

"Heaven help me, don't say there's two of them now." Her voice was so muffled, he couldn't be sure he'd heard correctly.

She mustered a wan smile. "Thank you, Your Grace. That's a very generous offer." She whisked the children past him, though she didn't look enthused. When she reached the stairs, she called, "Phil is in the invention room. Just pull on the bracket on the wall in front of you."

He wasn't looking for Phil. In fact, he should be looking to avoid her. But when he stepped abreast of the bracket on the wall, a decorative metal protrusion that might comfortably seat a candle, he couldn't help himself. He tugged on it.

A section of the wall separated next to the bracket and pushed inward. When Morgan splayed his hand against it, it rolled easily to the right.

Inside, the steady glow of a lantern lit a square room that stunk of mineral oil. The occupants didn't appear to notice the stench. Along the wall to the right was a thick work table littered with papers, odds and ends, and half-finished devices that Morgan couldn't begin to imagine the use for. The walls, lined with shelves upon shelves, were stuffed with yet more strange devices. In the center of the room, seated atop a perch with a wide basin beneath to catch his droppings, the green-winged macaw ruffled his feathers.

He stopped preening himself and twisted his neck to stare at Morgan with one eye. "You're in a pickle."

For opening a door? Morgan sincerely doubted that. He ignored the bird and stepped into the room.

The other occupant was Phil. Dressed in a simple black smock that scooped low across her breasts and clung to her hips, she consulted a diagram. The paper was weighed down at the corners with what looked to be two mirrors smaller than his palm, an inch-long screw, and a glass tube. Phil craned her neck as she examined the diagram from various angles, her hands cupping her current invention to keep it from falling apart. She plucked the screw from one corner and inserted it into the device. That corner of the paper curled. Morgan stepped closer, peering at the paper. Was that a woman's breast? He took a healthy step back. Perhaps he didn't want to know what she was creating.

He coughed into his fist, alerting her to his presence.

She jumped. Whirling, she pressed a hand to her heart. "Morgan! How long have you been there?"

Apparently, she hadn't heard him come in. "Only a few minutes. Please, don't let me distract you from your work."

She glanced down at the contraption, then met his gaze once more. "It's to help Lady Westlake. Her infant is finicky and she experiences great

214

discomfort if she can't feed him at certain times of the day. This will help her pump milk for him to drink when he's ready."

Morgan eyed the contraption. "It looks... uncomfortable." He suppressed a shudder. Thank God he wasn't a woman and didn't have to go through *that*.

Phil frowned. She lifted the device and held it in front of her chest. "Humph. You're right. I need to start over."

"What?" He held up his hands in surrender. "No, I didn't mean that at all. What do I know? I'm just a man, and not even an inventor, at that."

Phil wasn't listening to him. She crumpled the schematics for the breast pump and pulled a blank sheet of paper toward her. She leaned over the desk as she sketched in wide, vigorous strokes of her hand. The position deepened the shadow between her breasts. A lock of her hair escaped to tease the curve of her neck. She muttered under her breath. "Maybe buckles instead of screws to hold the straps in place. Yes! Buckles. That way, it's adjustable." She worried her lower lip between her teeth as she sketched.

Morgan was forgotten. That suited him just fine. He backed up to stand beside the parrot perch, afraid that he might disturb her again with an ill-considered comment. In fact, he shouldn't even be in here with her. He had intended to search her house for proof of treason, but for some reason, he wanted to stand here and watch Phil work instead.

To his left, Pickle squawked. He reached out, gently grabbing one of Morgan's fingers and tracing it with his beak and tongue. He seemed to like the taste of Morgan's leather glove because once he finished, he pulled away and said, "Pudding house."

Then again, that might be an insult to a bird. Morgan chose to take it as a compliment.

"Um. Thank you."

The parrot squawked and felt along another of his fingers. The sensation was muted due to his gloves, but it still tickled a bit.

Beaming with triumph, Phil finished her sketch and turned. "Done. That should work better. Did you seek me out for any particular reason, Your Grace?"

Morgan fought a grimace. He was back to being the Duke of Tenwick again. He much preferred to be himself with her, sans title.

No. I'm sorry to bother you. The words rose to the tip of his tongue and he almost made his excuse to leave.

Pickle shrieked, flapping his wings as he balanced on the stand. "Kiss, kiss."

She waved her hand in dismissal. "Not now, Pickle."

Yes, now. Morgan crossed the space between them in two steps and bent to slant his lips across hers. A reminder that he was more than a duke. He was a man. Her mouth softened beneath his, welcoming the brief caress of his lips. The moment he lifted his head, he took a step back, not trusting himself. The press of her lips was intoxicating like fine brandy—spicy and sweet and she made him burn.

Her eyelids fluttered open. She batted her thick eyelashes. Her irises were dark. With the color in her cheeks and the parted bow of her lips, she'd never looked lovelier. "What was that for?"

Not quite the reception he'd hoped for. He swallowed against the lump forming in his throat. "You wanted me to stop thinking. It was impulse."

Her mouth curled into a sensual smile that made every part of him burn. Including some parts best left unnamed. Parts that had best behave, considering that his mother and sister were in the house and bent upon him marrying this Season.

"I'm glad you're taking my advice to heart." Her gaze slowly traveled down his torso. He clasped his hands in front of his groin. Her smile grew.

He cleared his throat. "This... this room is impressive. You made all of this?" He couldn't keep the awe from his voice. When she'd confessed to being an inventor, he hadn't imagined a scope like this. She was brilliant.

She tore her gaze from his to examine the room, as if seeing it again after a long absence. Her gaze lingered on a shelf over his left shoulder. "I made most of it. Some were my father's inventions. He didn't care for writing out plans, so I still haven't puzzled out how a lot of it was made."

He turned, following her gaze. The goggles she'd worn in the Vauxhall Gardens rested on the second shelf from the top, above a short ladder. "Like your father's..." Did he have to say it? "... legs."

The corners of her lips twitched. "The light-enhancing goggles, yes." Her eyes twinkled.

Zeus, he'd never wanted to kiss her more. Instead, he tucked his hand into his waistcoat pocket. The peculiar piece of glass met his fingers. He drew it out, studying the way it reflected the light of the lantern on the work bench.

Phil's expression turned guarded. Her chest swelled as she held her breath. She didn't take her eyes off of him.

Pickle tried to climb onto his arm and snatch the glass out of his hand. He shook off the bird. "This isn't for you. It's for Phil."

Her lips parted as her face lit up. She started to reach out for it, but stopped short.

Put it away. She's an enemy spy. You don't know what she'll use it for. But he already knew, from the hopeful look on her face, that he was going to hand it over. Strickland should assign someone else to the field, because in her hands, he was like clay. He wanted to be a part of something bigger, a part of something that *she* made.

"Do you mean it?"

"I do." His voice was hoarse. He held out the ring of glass. Her bare hand hovered over it, and him. He'd never wished more that he hadn't worn gloves.

"I won't tell you the name of my contact." Her eyes were hard, steely.

"I didn't ask it of you this time."

He was a bloody fool.

She narrowed her eyes. Her fingers traced circles over the glass in his palm. Was she trying to drive him insane?

"What's the cost?"

"No cost." His voice was hoarse. "I only want to watch you work." The strength of that desire surprised him. He clamped his lips shut before he spilled more of his secrets.

"I accept." She snatched the piece from his hand and rose onto her tiptoes to press her lips against his cheek. His skin tingled from the contact as she turned to her work table.

On the end was a brown, paper-wrapped parcel very similar to the one she'd carried two weeks ago when he'd caught her in a tête-à-tête at the Society for the Advancement of Science meeting. She unwrapped it, revealing a replica of the goggles he'd already seen, though these were slightly different. For one thing, they weren't assembled. Morgan stepped closer, peering over her shoulder as she expertly fitted the pieces together, including the glass he'd given her.

Bored, Pickle soared from the room. Morgan thought about asking whether or not the bird was allowed to stray from his perch, but thought better of it. Phil seemed so consumed by her task that he didn't want to interrupt her.

After she fitted the last piece into place, she lifted the device and thrust it into Morgan's hands. "Here. Hold this. We'll need to shut the door." She brushed his arm as she circled around him to push the sliding wall shut. "And shutter the lantern, too."

The fabric of her dress pulled tight across her rump as she stretched across the work table to slide the shutter on the glass-encased lantern closed. A crack of light seeped from between and beneath the panes, but darkness descended on the room. He blinked, barely able to make out her silhouette as he waited for his eyes to adjust.

"So?" Phil's voice held notes of impatience and excitement. "Do they work?"

"Oh." He was supposed to test the goggles? "Let me check."

He raised the contraption to his face, peering through it the way he had the other pair at Vauxhall. He expected the details of the room to jump into detail, but they did not. In fact, they looked even more warped than they had previously. And...was it his imagination or was Phil's silhouette upside down? He lowered the goggles.

"They don't work." He hated forcing out the words. Would she be disappointed? Would she resent him for damaging her glass piece in some way that he hadn't realized?

Light flooded the room as she opened the shutter on the lantern once more. "Oh, bother." Resignation seethed in her voice, but nothing more sinister.

"I'm terribly sorry."

When she turned, her expression turned baffled. "Why?"

He'd wanted to see her face light up as she accomplished her goal. He'd wanted to be the person to make that happen. Instead, the encounter fell flat. Disappointing.

He shrugged. "It didn't work."

She crossed to him and gently pried the goggles out of his hand. She laid them on the table. "Not everything works. I'm not disappointed."

"Why aren't you? I am. That was the part you needed."

She shrugged. "I thought so, too. As it turns out, I was wrong. That happens sometimes." Her mouth curved in that secretive smile, as if she knew something she couldn't wait to impart. She leaned closer and he caught a whiff of her floral perfume. "If I achieved everything I wanted, what would I strive for?"

Me. The notion came upon him so suddenly and with such strength that he nearly kissed her again. He stepped back a pace instead.

"Perhaps we should adjourn to the sitting room. My mother and sister are waiting to see you."

"Are they?" She patted down her hair, which didn't help to tame it in the slightest. If it had once been part of a coiffure, it was no longer. Nearly half the strands had escaped. "You should have told me sooner."

And relinquish his time with her? A pox would take him before he'd do that.

"Pic—" She stopped short as she turned to the vacant stand. "Where did Pickle go?"

"He flew off before we shut the door."

"Oh dear." She nibbled her lower lip as she bolted for the door. She pulled it open with ease.

"Should he have stayed in the room? I didn't realize..."

"No," she said, flapping her hand as she trotted off down the hall.

He paused to slide the door shut before he loped after her.

"It's just that when he finds himself without something to do, he—"

A shriek echoed from somewhere else in the townhouse. Phil winced.

Morgan cocked an eyebrow. "He terrorizes the household?" Perhaps he should have thought twice before acquiring a bird for Lucy.

Phil smiled, rueful. "Mostly Meg, actually. She's afraid of birds, you see."

"Ah. Then perhaps it was bad form of me to suggest that she introduce her niece and nephew to my sister's new parrot."

Phil's face lit up. "You bought Lucy a parrot? Oh, how delightful!"

"Not to Meg, no doubt."

She giggled. "No, I doubt Meg approves at all. It's a good thing she doesn't live with you."

"It sounds as though she has her hands quite full here," he agreed.

They descended quickly to the parlor. Meg stood in the doorway, her arms raised to ward away any aviary attacks. She stepped aside with a grateful look as Phil and Morgan reached her.

"Come now, children. The duke has returned. Let's go to the kitchen."

"Awww," Brandon whined. "I wanted to play some more."

As Morgan stepped into the doorway, he found his mother seated on the settee next to Lucy. She was looking at something that the young girl was showing her. The boy stood by the perch next to the window that both parrots currently shared, trying to grab a fistful of Pickle's long tail. The parrot wisely kept his tail elevated.

Bonny, the girl, squealed as she saw Morgan. "You found Aunt Phil! Did you kiss her, Mr. Duke?" When she said 'Duke,' it sounded more like 'duck.'

Don't look at Phil. If he did, his family was sure to see the truth in his face. The heat climbing up his neck likely gave him away.

Across the room, Brandon turned away from the parrots. "'Course he did. She's awake, isn't she?"

"I was already awake," Phil informed him, her tone matter-of-fact. "I was working."

Meg came to their rescue. She held out both her hands for the children, though she didn't step into the room. "Come along, let's see what Grandmam's made for us."

Brandon scampered into his aunt's embrace. Bonny followed more slowly. She stopped in front of him and offered a wobbly curtsey. He bowed to her from the waist. He hadn't done that since he'd been introduced to King George shortly after attaining the dukedom.

The moment the children whisked out of sight, Mother sighed. "They are so dear. I had thought that I would have grandchildren by now." She gave Morgan a pointed look.

Beads of sweat formed around his hairline. He offered his best smile and said glibly, "Given Tristan's adamancy to have a hurried wedding, I doubt you'll have to wait long."

"He isn't the heir."

Actually, until Morgan begot a son, Tristan *was* his heir. He held his tongue and glanced around the room for allies. Lucy was no help, her sly gaze moving from Phil to Morgan and back. Morgan could practically hear the wedding bells chiming in her head. In the leather armchair next to her, Phil's brother looked bored. He leaned his chin on his fist. Gideon stood at the sideboard, pouring himself another tumbler. When Morgan caught his eye, he shook his head. When he raised his eyebrow quizzically, Morgan returned the signal. He hadn't found any sign of treason, either.

Granted, he hadn't looked very hard.

He changed the subject. "The birds seem to be getting along well."

His tactic worked. Lucy preened. "It's a shame you missed it! They're such good friends. He flew in and called her his Pickle. She said he made her giddy. It was love at first sight."

Morgan and Phil exchanged an amused glance. Her mouth curved in that alluring, mischievous smile that never failed to get under his skin.

When he returned his gaze to his relatives, Mother regarded them with a sly expression. Not this again.

Antonia called, "Lucy, shut your gob."

Lucy balled her fists. "Shut *your* gob, you rude bird."

Gideon snorted. She rounded on him.

"Giddy, this is all your fault!"

Antonia swiveled her head, repeating, "Giddy. Giddy, giddy, giddy."

Pickle took up the cry, too.

Gideon wiped tears from the corners of his eyes as he laughed. "I have never been more proud of any decision that I've ever made."

"I am going to get you back for this."

Pickle got bored and started preening Antonia. Startled, Antonia examined her suitor. When she cocked her head, she looked like she was smiling.

She burst, "Let's take a walk."

Lucy's mouth dropped open. "Who taught her *that?*"

Laughter rumbled in his chest. Before he gave in, he said quickly, "That sounds like a splendid idea. We should go at once."

He dragged Phil out of the room with him. He didn't care if anyone followed. The moment they reached the front door, she clapped her hand over her mouth to suppress her giggles. He leaned against the door as he lost the battle with his amusement. He hadn't laughed like that in a long time.

In fact, his chest felt lighter because Phil was there, sharing it with him.

Chapter Sixteen

Phil felt light enough to fly. She grabbed Morgan by the hand and towed him through the door before the others caught up to them. The sun beamed down at them, infusing her with energy as they stumbled onto the street.

He laughed. "Shouldn't we wait for the others?"

She grinned, leaning closer. "Do we always do what we *should* do?"

His gray eyes darkened. His gaze dropped to her mouth. A tingle swept through her as she wondered if he would kiss her, right there on the street. She ran her tongue across her lower lip in anticipation.

The front door burst open. "Phil, wait! Don't you want your bonnet?" Lucy leaned out the door, waving her arm to get Phil's attention. Curiously, she didn't scamper down the steps to catch up to them.

Reluctantly, Phil stepped away from Morgan. "Thank you, but I like the sun. I'll be fine without one."

Lucy ducked back into the house. Didn't she intend to come with them? The door gaped wide, showing the shadowed entryway and the harried Mr. O'Neill as he fussed after the guests. The irritable squawk inside the house didn't bode well. Phil exchanged a look with Morgan, who shrugged.

A moment later, Lucy returned to the doorway and lobbed a hat in his direction. It spun through the air and whacked him in the shoulder, narrowly missing Phil's head. Morgan fumbled to catch it before it toppled to the ground. He mashed it onto his head.

Somehow, the end result was just as sinfully sexy as he was without a hat. There was something debonair and forbidden about him in full formal dress. Something—dare she say it—ducal. The black topper cast shadows onto his chiseled cheeks. As his sister stepped through the doorway, a sigh escaped his lips.

The blue macaw perched on her glove. The area around her eyes and beak was a blazing yellow grin.

"Not the bird," Morgan muttered under his breath.

Phil shrugged. "It could be worse. She might have brought mine. Lucy's parrot at least seems willing to endure a leash." A thin cord, tied to the bird's ankle, ended at a bracelet around Lucy's wrist.

On her heels, Lady Graylocke, Lord Gideon, and Jared exited the house. Phil's brother didn't look happy about joining the expedition, but to his credit, he smoothed the expression upon reaching the bottom of the stairs.

He offered his arm to Lady Graylocke. "May I have the honor of escorting you, my lady?"

With a smile, the dowager duchess waved him off. "Thank you, but you don't want to be stuck with an old lady like me. Why don't you escort my daughter?" There was a twinkle in her gray eyes, a darker shade than Morgan's. Was she hoping that Lucy and Jared would make a good match?

Lucy would drive him out of his mind. He was a quiet sort of young man, the kind who observed more than he spoke and made friends with difficulty. Then again, maybe Lucy would be the perfect wife for him. Phil didn't know enough about matchmaking and marriage to make an informed decision. She resolved to stay out of it.

Jared didn't seem particularly thrilled at the idea. He eyed Lucy warily, then offered, "She seems to be busy escorting her bird."

Lucy nodded. "Quite right. I'm afraid I need both hands in case Antonia decides to take flight."

Which, at some point, the bird undoubtedly would. Phil had tried to take Pickle for a walk a time or two. Open spaces only encouraged him to wander and terrorize young ladies. Within the first week, he'd managed to become an expert at chewing off his leash.

Lady Graylocke looked disappointed, but she accepted Jared's arm nonetheless. She started speaking to him in a quiet voice that didn't carry. A look of alarm crossed his face.

Phil exchanged a glance with Morgan. Should she interfere? He didn't seem concerned.

Adjusting his hat, Gideon stepped up next to her. He offered his arm. "May I offer you my escort, Miss St. Gobain?"

"Oh." She'd expected to find herself on Morgan's arm. Judging by the twin glares his mother and sister were leveling at him, everyone else had expected that as well. If Gideon noticed the murderous looks, he ignored them.

Seeing no other choice, Phil slid her hand onto his arm. "Thank you."

She gave Morgan an apologetic look. His face was impassive. If she hadn't known better, she would have thought that he didn't care who escorted her.

Wait. *Did* she know better? He'd kissed her. They'd shared her enthusiasm for her inventions. He'd even given back the prism. But did that mean as much to him as it did to her?

"To Hyde Park?" Gideon asked, his voice light.

Phil shrugged. "Why not? It isn't terribly far a walk."

Gideon needed no further encouragement. He set off at a loping pace down the street, lined with townhouses five or six stories tall, each with a neatly-groomed lawn and enough space between the buildings to walk two abreast into a larger space out back. Phil scrambled to keep up with his long-legged stride. She fisted her skirt in one hand and drew it up over her ankles.

"Would you mind slowing down? Unlike you, I don't have legs like a stork."

He grinned, but slowed his pace. "Forgive me, Miss St. Gobain."

She glared at him. "Call me Phil. You've done so before."

He raised his eyebrows. "I don't believe, at the time, I knew you were female."

"And now seems like the perfect moment for you to stand on ceremony?"

"You and my brother seem to be getting close."

We are.

We aren't.

Truth warred with instinct. She bit the inside of her cheek. She didn't know what answer to give him. Were she and Morgan getting close? If so, she didn't know whether to welcome it or discourage him.

She still had to save her brother from his predicament with Lady Whitewood, and she couldn't have Morgan looking at her too closely until she did so.

Gideon bent nearly double to mutter near her ear. "Or is it all an act to fool him, Lady Spy?"

Phil bit back a groan. She counted ten steps before she hissed back, "I am *not* a spy."

"Of course you would say that."

"I thought Morgan was the only spy in the family."

Gideon laughed. "You're joking, right? Did he tell you that?"

Phil chanced a glance over her shoulder. Lucy battled to restrain her parrot, who wanted nothing more than to fly into a sky several shades lighter than she was. In the rear, Lady Graylocke still engaged in an awkward conversation with Jared, given the look on his face. Morgan was the closest, mere paces behind, his eyes narrowed as he stared at Phil and Gideon.

She faced forward once more. "He didn't tell me a thing. I deduced it from his behavior."

Gideon straightened. "Well, think of it as a family business."

Phil raised her eyebrows. "Are Lucy and Lady Graylocke in on the business as well?"

His face blanched. "Lawks, no! And I trust you won't tell them, or I'll have to expose you as well."

Phil rolled her eyes. "I told you, I'm not a spy for anyone."

Though Jared was, however unwillingly. She clamped her lips shut, refusing to say another word.

Fortunately, they soon reached the looming gates of Hyde Park. The tall, wrought iron bars were pushed wide to admit visitors. Gideon and Phil strode in without encumbrance. They paused on the soft grass next to the gate to wait for the others.

Within moments, Phil found herself snagged out of Gideon's grasp by Lucy. She demanded to know more about Phil's inventions and picked her mind on the art of parrot training at the same time. Phil wished that she had more pearls of wisdom to offer, but Pickle was, for the most part, ungovernable. If he behaved, it was because he wanted to, not because she told him to.

Lucy squawked rather reminiscent of her parrot as Antonia leaped from her arm to perch on a tree branch above them. Still attached, Lucy's arm was wrenched up over her head. She glared at Antonia's iridescent blue tail-feathers. "If you decorate me with your droppings, I'll put you in Giddy's room. Don't think I won't."

Phil wasn't entirely sure how this would be a punishment for the bird, but Lucy seemed convinced that it was something to be avoided. For Gideon to avoid, perhaps.

With her hand still dangling in the air, Lucy turned to Phil. She leaned in closer. About a hand taller than Phil, she had to crouch a bit to put their faces on an equal level.

"Tell me the truth. Do you have any feelings for Morgan?"

Phil's breath seized. Her chest ached as she risked a glance over her shoulder. Morgan and Gideon, several inches apart in height, were ensconced in conversation with their mother and Jared. Jared had dropped Lady Graylocke's arm and now stood a bit to the side, on the edge of the circle. Every now and again, he cast an uncomfortable glance around him and fiddled with the ties on his shirt. He'd already managed to lose his cravat.

Morgan glanced in Phil's direction. Ten or more feet separated them, but as he settled his gaze on her, her breath caught as if he was pressed up against her again. His gray eyes pierced her, as if he searched her mind for their topic of conversation.

I doubt you'd approve.

Phil turned her gaze back to Lucy, who looked smug. Considering her arm still hung above her head, it looked comical.

"I feel that Morgan needs to learn to live life rather than think about it."

Come to think about it, he'd already started to take her advice on that front. His impulsive kiss earlier in her invention room had proven that. Most lords—hell, most *men*—would have laughed in her face and continued to live their upright, prudish lives. Deep down, Morgan must battle against the same sensation she did. The rigid confines of Society pressed too tight sometimes, demanded too much. She didn't want to conform. She much preferred to be herself.

Lucy smiled. "You're just the woman to teach him about life."

Phil cocked her eyebrow. She pressed her lips together to keep from laughing. "Perhaps. But please don't entertain any hopes that I'll marry him."

Lucy's expression fell. "Why not? Don't you think he'll make a good husband? He's kind and considerate, if a bit of a boor about some of my more reckless activities. But I'm sure you could bring him around. He seems smitten with you."

Shaking her head, Phil muttered, "Whatever Morgan is, he isn't smitten with me." Bent on uncovering her French connections, perhaps. Eager to keep an eye on her. Perhaps even consumed by lust when they found themselves alone. But certainly not smitten.

"I beg your pardon?"

Phil forced a smile. "I said he'll make some woman a fine husband, I'm sure. But that woman won't be me."

"Why not?"

She fought the urge to rub her temple, where a throb had started in time to her pulse. "I don't intend to marry, Lucy."

Her dark brown eyes grew as wide as saucepans. "Ever?"

"Ever. I like my life the way it is."

She didn't want a man to stop her from inventing, or from doing anything else she pleased. *Morgan didn't stop you earlier.* In fact, he'd encouraged her efforts. He'd seemed disappointed when his contribution to her LEGs hadn't resulted in a working prototype. *Could* she consider marrying him?

No. It would be mad.

Lucy looked a bit sad as she whispered, "Maybe you should consider living life instead of thinking about it, too."

Phil glanced at Morgan again. He stared at her with an unreadable expression in his eyes. For all that he was a spy, and likely only staying close to her in order to catch her in an act of treason, he couldn't be a blackguard. He'd given back her prism, after all. He'd genuinely wanted it to work.

Wait. Maybe she could make something else out of the prism. A sketch already formed in her mind's eye. She turned to Lucy, determined to jot it down before it slipped away.

"You carry a pocket book, don't you?"

"Yes," Lucy said, her voice wary. "In my reticule. Why?"

"Drat." That reticule dangled from the wrist currently suspended in the air. "I just got struck by inspiration. I have to write it down. I'll have to go home."

She turned away as Lucy called, "Wait a moment! I'll go with you. Come here, Antonia." The parrot squawked. Given the vigorous wing flapping and repetition of, "Giddy, giddy, giddy," Antonia didn't plan on emerging from the tree any time soon.

"No time," Phil called over her shoulder. "I can't let this idea slip away. I have to jot it down now!" She hiked her skirts to her knees and bolted from the park.

If anyone followed, she didn't notice. Her mind was already ensconced on the second floor of her townhouse, in the invention room. She breezed into her house, panting for breath.

"Miss Phil—"

She waved at Mr. O'Neill and dashed for the stairs, taking them two at time. Mutters pooled like eddies in her wake as she passed other servants. She slid to a stop in front of her invention room and yanked on the bracket, pushing aside the door with impatience. The lantern still burned. Her hands shook as she found a scrap of paper. It had a blueprint for a musical instrument that played itself on one side. She flipped it over, found a pencil, and scribbled down her idea, tracing the lines in her mind's eye.

Feverishly, she hunted for the parts she would need to complete the device. It was simple, similar to one or two mechanical toys that she'd made before. It shouldn't take her long. Once it was complete, she would send it to Morgan and he could delight in the knowledge that he *had* helped to build something, after all. Her body hummed as she considered the way he would smile when he saw it.

She hunched over her desk, frantic to complete the project. If anyone came to interrupt her, she didn't notice for a long, long time.

Chapter Seventeen

Phil had been insensible to the world when Morgan and his family had caught up to her at the townhouse. Jared had apologized and explained that she got that way sometimes, when consumed by an idea. Even so, Morgan had expected to see her that night, at the soiree Jared had confirmed that they had been invited to. She hadn't been there.

Was she ill? Had she not wanted to see him?

Giddy clapped him on the shoulder as they marched up the stairs of the Tenwick townhouse. "Cheer up, old chap. If you don't chase away that sour look, all those lovely debutantes Mother and Lucy threw at you tonight will run screaming."

Morgan glared at him. "I thought I asked you to help mitigate that."

"I did!" Gideon pressed his hand to his heart in mock injury. "There are only so many debutantes I can dance with at once."

Morgan rolled his eyes. "I'm glad you're amused. Wait until Mother turns her attentions on you. You won't be as apt to joke, then."

Truthfully, Morgan wouldn't have found the night quite so excruciating if any of the debutantes had been able to hold a candle to Phil's vivacious personality. But no, Mother and Lucy seemed bent on throwing insipid, pale, proper young ladies into his path. All were interchangeable. In fact, he doubted if she set them in front of him at that moment, he would be able to recall their names. And he had an impeccable memory.

He could remember in vivid detail, for instance, the way Phil ran her tongue along the edge of her upper lip as she assembled one of her inventions. She hummed under her breath, too, a chaotic, nonsensical tune that it was a miracle her parrot hadn't yet learned. It was an assault on the ears.

He'd loved every second of it. It, like her, had been unique, unpredictable. He rubbed at the streak in his hair, afraid to admit that he might be falling for an enemy spy. Unlike Freddie, his brother's bride, it didn't appear as if Phil was being coerced into spying. Sooner or later, he would have to escort her to Newgate Prison and the gallows.

At the landing, he turned away from his brother. "I'm heading to my study for a bit."

Giddy hesitated. "Do you want some company?"

"No." Morgan's voice was curt. He forced himself to soften it. "I'd prefer to be alone."

"Would you...like me to talk to Mother? Perhaps I can convince her to let you alone for a bit."

Morgan smirked. The only way Gideon would be likely to do that would be if he confessed to their mother that he hoped to find a bride instead. Morgan shook his head. "I wouldn't ask that of you. Thank you, but I'll speak to her myself."

Or maybe he wouldn't. If he admitted why he hated all the vapid young debutantes she tossed in his path, she would only redouble her efforts to match him with Phil. That, he couldn't have.

He bid his brother goodnight and shut himself in his study. The room was cool and quiet, a blessing after the night he'd had. He crossed to the mantle, knowing the way by rote, and lit a candle. Once it flared to life, he scanned the study, a force of habit. Everything was in its place. He relaxed.

Wait—what was that on his desk? It looked a bit like a little mechanical duck with a ribbon tied around its neck. No, not a duck. A parrot. He smiled as he plucked it off the desk.

The contraption had been weighing down a note. Morgan lifted it.

Even if something doesn't work out as intended, it can still create something wonderful. -P.

Had Phil...*made* this for him? He peered at it closer. Sure enough, the piece of glass he'd given her, or one very similar to it, was set in the very heart of the parrot. At the back, a little winding key stuck out between the metal wings. Morgan twisted it. He held his palm flat and set the toy in the center. The little parrot danced, flapping its wings. As it did, the glass in the middle caught the light of the candle and transferred a rainbow of colors onto the metal, making it look as though the bird was as colorful as Pickle.

His breath caught in a thick, aching lump in his throat. Phil had made this for *him*. It was the most unique, thoughtful, bizarre gift anyone had given to him. It embodied everything he loved about her. No other woman would think to give him a gift like that. In fact, aside from his family, no woman had ever given him a gift at all. Then again, he felt closer to Phil than he had any other woman of his acquaintance. She was more than an acquaintance, more than a friend. Heaven help him, but he might have fallen in love with her.

His eyes burned. He set the toy down on the edge of the desk. What was he going to do? He turned toward the window, even though night had blanketed London and all he could see was his reflection thrown back at him in the glass.

A figure appeared in the doorway. Morgan turned to face Lord Strickland.

The spymaster did not look pleased. The steely gleam in his eyes matched his stiff gait as he entered the room and shut the door. Like Morgan, he was dressed in eveningwear. The candlelight glinted off beads of sweat on his bald pate.

"It's been two weeks."

I know. Morgan bit his tongue. He straightened his shoulders. He refused to cower before Strickland, even if he was Morgan's superior.

Strickland stalked closer. "Tristan could have done this in one." He offered the statement with a blasé shrug, as if it was a fact, not a motivator.

Morgan narrowed his eyes. Was Strickland trying to stir the rivalry between him and his brother? Apparently, he'd never been told that the rivalry was all one-sided. Morgan didn't much care if Tristan could do it faster.

You might have at the beginning of this mad mission. Back then, he had yearned for fieldwork, for the glory and the danger. There was a danger, all right, but thus far his heart had been the only casualty.

He couldn't give Phil up, even if it seemed to be what Strickland wanted.

"I'm working as fast as I can," Morgan answered, his voice even. "I have a few more suspicions I need to check out."

That didn't seem to be the answer for which Strickland hoped. The stocky man bristled. "What sort of suspicions?"

Morgan stepped closer, using his height to his advantage. "You want the new commander of the

French spies in London, right? Not a minor member."

Strickland made a face. "I could have a dozen minor members if I wanted. I want to know who Harker's replacement is."

"Then I need a bit more time." His fingers curled into his palm. The bite of pain steadied him. He couldn't give Phil up. Not yet. Even if she was a part of this spy network, she couldn't be the leader.

For his sake and hers, she couldn't.

"Don't take too much time. This is a war, Tenwick, and don't you forget it."

When Strickland turned, Morgan's knees weakened. What could he do? Soon he was going to have to make a choice—his duty to his country or Phil. Strickland paused at the edge of Morgan's desk. Morgan's breath caught. Did he suspect that Morgan had been taken in by an enemy spy? If he assigned another man to this job, that man wouldn't hesitate to hand Phil to the hangman's noose. He couldn't let that happen. He couldn't let Strickland lose faith in him.

The spymaster paused to run his fingers over the gift Phil had sent him. Every muscle in Morgan's body stiffened. *Don't touch that*. It was Morgan's, not Strickland's.

"Cute toy. Is there a happy event on the horizon that might be splitting your interests?"

Every breath shredded Morgan's throat as though he inhaled a vat of needles. He fought for composure. If he leaked even a shadow of the turmoil gripping him, Strickland would know the truth.

"No. This mission has my full attention, I assure you." His voice was cold. He infused it with dismissal, as he might if he faced a thieving servant. Strickland held his gaze for a moment more, his eyes hard and measuring.

Morgan didn't back down.

Strickland nodded. "I'll expect a progress report from you tomorrow, then."

"Monday." Any sooner and Morgan wouldn't have time to concoct something plausible. He'd have to give up Phil. He couldn't.

The spymaster's eyebrows twitched, falling down across his eyes. "Monday," he repeated between gritted teeth. "But it had best be there with the morning post."

Morgan nodded stiffly. "It will be."

His heart stopped beating as Strickland's gaze bored into him, searching out his secrets. With a nod, the spymaster turned on his heel and exited the study. He left the door wide open behind him.

Morgan planted his palm on the desk beside the toy parrot. His knees gave way and he dropped into his chair. His heart made up for missing a beat by pounding three times as fast.

Zeus, Phil. What have you gotten yourself into? His eyes ached as he shut his heavy eyelids.

He didn't know what to do. Did he turn his back on his country in order to warn her? Or did he turn her in?

The decision burned like salt in an open wound as he scooped up the little parrot toy and the candle. His footsteps were heavy as he trudged up the stairs to the family wing. As he reached the top steps, a gray-haired maid juggled a tray laden with a cup of chocolate and some biscuits as she attempted to open the door to his mother's room.

Mother must have still been awake. Desperate to confide in someone, he loped forward to take the tray from the maid. "Allow me." He deposited his candle and the parrot on the tray before he gripped the handles.

The maid curtseyed. "Thank you, Your Grace. I was just bringing that to the dowager. Will you have some vittles before bed?"

"Thank you, no. In fact, if you'll just open the door, I'll bring this to her. You can go to bed."

She curtseyed again. "Of course, Your Grace. Thank you."

Morgan gritted his teeth. He hated being bowed and scraped to. It was why he usually surrounded himself with those servants in his household who were also spies. At least they knew he was put to better use than sitting like a lump in a Parliament chair for half the year.

The maid claimed one of the two candles perched on the tray and left as he backed into his mother's room, carefully balancing the tray. He found his mother abed. In the candlelight, her room looked as though it was swathed in dark colors, burgundy and chestnut, charcoal and sapphire. Nestled against a heap of pillows with a book in her lap, Mother perked up the moment she saw him.

"Morgan! What are you doing here?"

He carefully set the tray in her lap before he spilled the contents of the cup. "I noticed you were awake. Do you have a few moments to talk?"

"For you, always."

He turned on his heel, shutting the door and dragging a surprisingly heavy, spindly chair from between the armoire and the vanity. He lowered himself into it next to her.

"Oh, bother. I would have asked for two cups of chocolate, had I known you wanted to join me."

Morgan smiled. "Thank you, but I'm not thirsty."

"Why don't you have a biscuit?"

When Mother thrust the tray at him, he took one, if only to keep her from calling the servants to bring something else. He opened his mouth, but he didn't know how to broach the subject of

Phil. He couldn't confess the full extent of his troubles. Thus far, he and Tristan—and now Gideon—had managed to keep Mother from worrying about their extracurricular activities by the simple method of hiding the fact that they were Crown spies. He couldn't expose her to more distress for their well-being by confessing his role in the war. As it was, she worried herself near to death over his brother, Anthony's, involvement.

With a little frown, Mother picked up the parrot toy. "What's this?"

"Forgive me. That's mine." He reached forward to retrieve it from her. Although his hackles didn't rise the way they had when Strickland had touched the device, Morgan didn't want anyone to touch it. It was his. Phil had made it for *him*.

Mother held it out of reach. "Wait a moment. What is it exactly?"

"It's a toy. It winds up through a key on its back."

Mother flipped it over and wound up the toy. It danced as she set it down. She smiled, one of the purest, most genuine smiles that he'd seen in years. He felt like a heel for wanting to take away the toy, but it didn't belong to her.

"It's darling."

She cast him a coy glance as he snatched the parrot from her side of the tray. He put it back closer to him, within easy reach.

"Why did you buy it? Will it be needed in, oh, about nine months' time?"

Heat scalded his cheeks. "Don't look at me that way, Mother. I've gotten no woman with child. It was a gift."

"A pity."

He stuffed the biscuit into his mouth to save himself from having to answer.

Mother pressed, "Who gave it to you?"

He swallowed, his mouth suddenly dry. "Phi—Miss St. Gobain sent it to me. She made it, actually."

"Did she?" Mother brightened. "Oh, how delightful!"

He rubbed his hand over his chin. The bristles of his stubble, beginning to grow in again, roughened his skin. "I think so. Can I...can I ask your honest opinion of her?"

Mother reached over to squeeze his hand. Her skin was warm. "I've already given you my blessing."

"Yes, but I know how desperate you are to see me married."

"Not so desperate," Mother said. "Not if she wouldn't make you a fine wife."

He cocked an eyebrow. "You must have sent twenty such women in my path tonight. None of them would have made good duchesses."

Mother grinned. "That was to remind you how wonderful Phil is. She is a singular woman, Morgan. She cannot be replaced."

He ducked his head and picked up the parrot, tracing the intricacies with his finger. "I feel the same way."

"I knew it!"

He raised a weary glance toward his mother. "I don't want to make a mistake and lose her. But first, I need to know if she is a good woman, a loyal woman."

"She strikes me as the sort of woman who wouldn't turn her back on you once she's welcomed you into the fold. Morgan, dear, stop worrying so much. That's my domain. It's your domain to live life and be happy. Does Phil make you happy?"

"Yes." His voice was hoarse, the word soft, as if he didn't want to admit it to himself.

When he raised his gaze, he found tears in his mother's eyes. She smiled. "Then that's all that matters."

Not quite. Morgan still had to find a way to keep Phil from the hangman's noose. He didn't want to—couldn't lose her. He laid the parrot toy on the tray again.

"Can you look after this for me tonight? I have to go out."

"Of course."

Morgan leaned over to press a kiss to his mother's cheek. "Thank you." When he straightened, he strode for the door.

He'd almost shut it behind him when Mother called out. "Give my regards to Phil."

He shook his head as he shut the door. Not a chance. What he had to discuss with Phil tonight was far beyond his mother. He only hoped that once he confessed his feelings for her, it would be enough to sway her from spying for the French. He didn't know what else he could do.

No, that wasn't quite true. At that moment, he didn't know what he *wouldn't* do to convince Phil to join him, in war and in life. His chest tightened. He had never been so frightened of a conversation.

He knew with searing, earth-shattering clarity how Tristan had felt upon being confronted with Freddie's treason. Morgan could only hope that his and Phil's predicament would end just as happily.

Chapter Eighteen

As Phil licked her fingers and dabbed the plate to catch as many crumbs of the seedcake as she could, Meg stepped into the kitchen. She propped her hands on her hips.

"Phil, what're you doing?"

The kitchen was dark and cold, the servants having long since cleaned and retired to bed. The sole light came from the candle Phil had carried downstairs with her, set now on the stained and pockmarked table likely used for chopping. The pantry door stood open, a testament to how she had found the seedcake.

Phil brushed off her hands as she answered, "I was hungry. I believe I missed supper."

"And lunch," Meg answered. "Which is why I set aside some food to be reheated." The kitchen staff, by now, were experts at reheating food.

With a sheepish smile, Phil stood. "Oh, good. That seedcake didn't go terribly far." She stepped up to the stove, examining it. Under her breath, she muttered, "Now, how do you turn this thing on?" Considering that she could probably construct a stove from the parts she had in her invention room, her cooking skills were woefully inadequate.

Fortunately, she had Meg. Her friend shooed her back onto the stool by the pockmarked table. "I'll do it. It won't do for you to set the kitchen on fire."

Phil pursed her lips. She considered arguing, but if she did, she would have to reheat her own meal. She sat on the stool to wait.

"Where's that blighted bird of yours?" Meg asked conversationally as she lit the stove. Once she stoked the coals, she shut the grate and found a long-handled iron pan. She set it atop the stove as she waited for it to heat up.

"Pickle wasn't in the invention room. I thought he was with you."

Meg scrunched her nose with disgust. Her freckles pinched together. "Not if I can help it."

Phil shrugged. "He must be in the house somewhere. I can whistle, if you want."

"No, thank you. I think we'll do fine in the kitchen without that overgrown canary trying to filch the food."

Phil tucked away a smile. She picked a few more crumbs from her plate. "Did you have my invention delivered to the Tenwick townhouse?"

Meg cast her a speaking look. "My brother delivered it personally, as I told you three hours ago."

"Did you? Forgive me. I must have been pre-occupied."

The maid rolled her eyes. "Yes, you were fiddling with those goggles again."

"LEGs," Phil corrected.

Meg found and scooped some butter into the pan, scarcely waiting for it to start melting before she added the contents of a covered plate—cubed potatoes, turnip, ham and diced onion. Absently, she said, "I refuse to call them legs unless they start walking."

Phil grinned. "If I did that, I doubt they would be of much use as light-enhancing goggles."

When Meg didn't answer, Phil drummed her fingers on the table. "Was the gift well received?"

"I don't know." Meg tilted the pan to pour the contents onto the plate once more. She then crouched to spread the heated coals across the inside of the stove, to encourage them to cool.

Phil shifted on the stool. "Which brother delivered it? I'll ask him just as soon as I finish eating."

As her friend deposited the dish in front of her and found her a fork, she said, "It won't do you much good. The duke wasn't at home. Here." She shoved the fork into Phil's hand. "Eat your hash."

A determined glint lit Meg's eye. Phil dug into the food, shoveling a forkful into her mouth. "It's very tasty. Why wasn't Morgan at home?"

"He was probably out at the ball you missed." Meg nudged the plate closer, glaring until Phil took another bite.

Once she swallowed, she asked, "Three hours ago? What time is it?"

"After midnight. Eat some more."

A knock sounded from the front door. Meg frowned. "Who can be calling at this hour? Stay here," she told Phil. "I'll answer the door."

Phil shrugged. She applied herself to the meal as her friend left. She hadn't lied, it was delicious. Before she knew it, she'd devoured everything on her plate. She was a bit thirsty, though. She rooted around until she found a jug of milk. She poured herself a glass.

Meg returned, an odd look in her eye and seeming a bit frazzled. "Pickle is up in the servants' quarters this evening," she informed.

Ah. That explained her frazzled look.

Phil polished off the milk in her glass and set it down. "I'll fetch him out again."

"No." Meg waved her hands, trying to banish away the idea. She put the dishes in the sink and scooped up the candle on the table. "The children love him. Let him stay the night."

Phil frowned. Although Pickle might be quiet when it was dark, come dawn he would put up a racket. "Are you sure? He can be disruptive."

With brusque little touches to Phil's shoulders and back, Meg herded her out of the kitchen. "Nonsense, the twins will love some extra time with him." She turned Phil toward the stairs. "It's late. Off to bed now."

Phil shrugged. Given the long day at her worktable, perhaps sleep wasn't the worst suggestion. However, Meg's enthusiasm to hurry Phil up the stairs surprised her—especially when, on the third floor, Meg said goodnight and moved to continue up.

"Wait. Aren't you coming to my room with me?" Meg usually helped Phil to undress. In fact, she usually insisted upon it.

Meg yawned, hiding the expression behind her hand. "I'm dreadfully tired. Do you think you can get on without me tonight?"

"Of course." Phil had done so before, usually after insisting vehemently that Meg not wait up for her.

"Wonderful." Meg grinned. A sparkle lit her eye from the candle she held. "I won't wake you early tomorrow. It's been a late night, and all."

"Thank you." Phil's voice held a questioning note. She usually preferred to rise early no matter how late she stayed up the night before. Then again, she didn't need Meg to rouse her most days —in fact, Meg spent a lot of her time trying to keep up with Phil's schedule.

"Have a good sleep."

Wait, did she just wink at Phil? Maybe it was a trick of the light. A moment later, she whirled and continued up the stairs. Shaking her head, Phil trudged down the hall on her own, wondering at her friend's odd behavior.

When she reached her bedchamber, she discovered the reason. The door was left wide, a candle on the vanity beckoning her forward. But, to her surprise, the room was not empty. Morgan perched on the edge of her bed, waiting for her.

Of all the ways she'd pictured the Duke of Tenwick awaiting her in her bedchamber, seated at the foot with his elbows braced against his knees was not one of them. At least, not while he was clothed in full eveningwear. His royal blue jacket gaped open, the gold buttons gleaming, to reveal a cream-colored waistcoat and snowy white shirt. His cravat hung loose, the color a stark contrast to the dark stubble along his jaw. He wore blue knee breeches and tall Hessian boots. A sight to behold in a ballroom, no doubt, but in her bedchamber she would have preferred to see him without a stitch. It would, at the very least, have made the night infinitely more fun.

And, in her fantasies, he certainly didn't wear a brooding expression. A lazy smile perhaps, his mouth red from kissing and his hair mussed. Alas, it was not to be.

Upon recovering from her shock, Phil turned and shut the door. Meg must have seen him—perhaps she'd even let him in. But Phil highly doubted that a man as sensitive to reputation as him would care to have his presence in the manor bandied about, if only among her staff.

The bed creaked as he stood. Phil mustered her composure and turned to face him. Why had he come here so late? Had he received her gift? His gray eyes were sharp, but she couldn't tell from their expression whether he'd loved the gift or hated it. Her stomach twisted. As did her hands in her dark skirts, the same she'd worn earlier in the day when she'd seen him. She forced her fidgeting hands to stop.

As she opened her mouth, she found herself cut off as he blurted, "You have to stop spying for the French."

Phil slowly closed her mouth. She would have preferred to hear a confession of his undying love —or at the very least, his esteem for her—but, admittedly, pretty words best belonged with the rest of her fantasy. This, it seemed, was business.

But why was he here if he still believed her a French spy?

She stepped closer. The shadows beneath his eyes weren't only due to the flickering light of the candle. He looked worried. Distraught, even. When she reached up to touch his cheek, he turned his face to kiss her palm. The bristles of his growing beard scraped her wrist.

He stood and cupped her face. His gaze was haunted. He kissed her forehead, then the tip of her nose, then her lips. He lingered there, a soft but urgent pressure. He pulled away only enough to look her in the eye.

"Please, Phil." His voice was a rasp. "I know you were born in France. Obviously, you have some lingering loyalties, and I can't blame you for them, but you must cut ties. I can't stand by and watch the woman I love throw her life away."

Her breath caught. Maybe this was exactly like her fantasy, after all. She swallowed hard before she found her voice. "You love me?"

"With every corner of my wretched heart."

She smiled, reaching up to lay her hand atop his, still cupping her cheek. "I love you, too."

The admission set loose a torrent that had been dammed between them since they'd met. Morgan crushed her to him. His lips found hers, hard and hungry as he pressed her against his body. She clutched at his broad shoulders, her head spinning. His hands roved over her back and hips and rear as if trying to memorize her shape. That wasn't a bad idea. She ached to explore him, too.

But perhaps she should explain a few things first.

Reluctantly, she broke the kiss. As he rested his forehead against hers, breathing hard, she whispered, "Would you love me even if I wasn't a French spy?"

"God, yes." His voice induced a shiver over her skin. "That's what I'm trying to convince you to do."

She smiled. "Your wish is my command. I don't spy for the French. I never have."

He pulled away, his expression baffled. "If not the French, then who?"

She met his gaze, willing him to believe her. "I'm not a spy at all."

His expression closed off. "Don't lie to me, Phil. I'm a Crown spy. I know the signs. Every time I've followed a tip to interrupt a secret meeting, you've been there."

She backed away, wrapping her arms around her torso. This was the difficult part. Could she trust him?

Of course she could. This was Morgan, the man who loved her. The man she loved, as well. In fact, if any man had been made for her to marry, it would have been him. He didn't try to belittle or stifle her intelligence, her inventions, her freedom. He respected her. Perhaps he even admired her. If she would trust him with the rest of her life, she could damn well trust him with this.

She caught and held his gaze. "It wasn't me. The spy is..." She took a deep, steadying breath. "The spy is my brother. But it isn't his intention."

***

Morgan's ears rang. Relief warred with dismay in his chest. Phil wasn't the spy he was looking for.

Her brother was. And if Morgan turned *him* in to the crown...he was sure he would lose Phil. He sat heavily on the bed. The mattress swayed a bit on its ropes but quickly settled into place again.

"What do you mean, it isn't his intention?" Morgan's voice was gruff. More so than he'd intended. Guilt stabbed him as a shadow crossed over Phil's face.

He held out his hand to her. He gentled his voice. "Please, come here. Tell me everything."

His heart pounded a chaotic racket in his chest, so loud it nearly drowned out his thoughts. Phil took a hesitant step forward, lifting her skirt above her ankles as she did. When she slipped her hand into his, he clutched her. Her skin was a bit clammy. She was afraid.

Of him? Or of the news she intended to impart?

Tentatively, she perched on the edge of the bed next to him. He didn't release her hand. He needed that connection between them. Her leg bounced with nervousness.

"He doesn't want to spy," she whispered. "He told me so."

"And you believed him?"

Morgan tightened his hold on her hand as she tried to pull away.

"Of course I did! He's my brother."

Morgan lifted their joined hands to press his lips to her skin. "I have brothers, too, remember? They've lied to me on occasion. This is important. I want to know if you're sure."

"I am."

Her eyes were dark and stormy with the temper she kept a tight rein on. Given the purse of her lips, she would unleash that tempest on him if he said another word against her brother.

"Jared can't even remember our home in France. His home and allegiance is here, in England."

Morgan searched her face, trying to detect any hint of doubt. There was none. She believed her brother to be innocent. Perhaps not of wrongdoing, but of the intent. He released a slow breath and adjusted his hold on her hand.

"I believe you."

She relaxed.

"If he doesn't want to spy, then why is he doing so? This isn't the sort of thing you can do by accident."

Phil raised her eyebrows, as if reminding him of how he'd erroneously thought she was a spy. He winced and added, "Usually."

Her mouth thinned again. Her eyes glittered like shards of glass. "Lady Whitewood is blackmailing him into doing her bidding."

"Lady Whitewood?" Morgan frowned. He'd read her name on one of the reports recently, hadn't he? Maybe the crown already knew about her. If so, she wasn't the spy he was sent to catch.

Wait. The invitation. He hadn't read her name on a report, it had been from one of Strickland's missives.

"She was the woman who held the...soiree."

Phil nodded. "She was. When you found me in the study I was looking for whatever she had on Jared."

Morgan winced. And he'd stopped her from finding it. "Forgive me."

Phil gave a one-shouldered shrug. "I would have been surprised to find anything so easily accessible, in any case."

Adjusting his hold on her so he could slip his arm around her, Morgan battled with his emotions. If what she said was true and Lady Whitewood was, in fact, the French spy he was looking for, then he could turn her in. Elation sang through his veins at the prospect as he contemplated it. Phil wouldn't be in danger anymore. And his days as a field spy would be over.

He didn't know if he was disappointed or glad that he would no longer be putting himself in direct danger. He would be relegated to paperwork again, a make-work job. But he would also have much more time to spend with Phil.

His stomach sank. *If* she wanted to spend time with him. If he delivered Lady Whitewood to Strickland while Jared was still being blackmailed, Strickland would find every leg of her enterprise—including Jared. His life might still be at stake. Against his will or not, providing sensitive information to the enemy was a hanging offense. If Jared wound up dangling from the business end of a noose, Phil would never speak to Morgan again. She probably wouldn't even be able to look at him.

Lud, what was he going to do?

You'll have to stop it. It was the only way he and Phil could have a future.

Withholding information from Strickland might also be considered a hanging offense. Morgan gritted his teeth. He would have to take his chances and keep wind of this from Strickland for as long as possible. Even so, he would have hours, maybe a day or two at most to sort this out. Would it be enough time?

Phil shifted in the circle of his arms to look at him. Her eyes were dark. The candlelight deepened the color of her lips. He wanted nothing more than to dip his head to capture her mouth again and forget their troubles, at least temporarily.

He couldn't. He had to fix this first. Maybe then...

Definitely then. This time, he wouldn't let Phil laugh off his marriage proposal. He bloody well wasn't going to let her slip out of his life.

"Do you still love me, even though I kept this from you?"

Zeus, yes. He gave in to temptation and swooped in to press his mouth to hers, infusing the kiss with all the strength of his love for her. When he raised his head, she panted. Her chest rose and fell, drawing his eye to the enticing curve. It wouldn't take much effort to pull down her bodice...

He shouldn't. He was trying to convince her of his love, not his lust. Even if he ached to join them together in every way possible.

He cupped her cheek. "Of course I love you. If anything, the fact that you would put yourself in danger to save your brother makes me love you even more."

That secretive smile he adored so much crossed her lips. She rose from the circle of his arms, leaving him feeling empty. When he reached for her, she came willingly, hiking up her skirts as she straddled his lap.

Ah, God. She had to feel his erection pressing against her. He couldn't help it. She was five-feet-two-inches of temptation.

Her smile widening, she whispered, "Good." She brushed her lips against his, an achingly light touch. "Because I do love you, Morgan Graylocke."

When her lips returned to his, he encircled her with his arms, cupping the back of her head with his palm to keep her from breaking the kiss. He savored every second, the feel of her body in his arms. He trailed his free hand down her back, splaying his palm and urging her closer. He never wanted to let her go. If he couldn't fix this issue with her brother, he might not get the chance to kiss her again.

She broke the kiss, gulping for air. He brushed the stray locks of hair away from her neck and pressed his lips to the tender skin. As he darted his tongue out to taste her, she moaned. Her fingers tangled in his hair, clutching him to her. Lud, could he have fallen in love with a better woman? Not bloody likely.

Her hands slipped free of his hair to trail over his shoulders. He groaned with desire. There were too many layers between them. He wanted to feel her bare skin on his.

As if she heard his thoughts, she plucked at the loose knot of his cravat, easily undoing it. He lifted his mouth from her neck. She kissed him hungrily as she pulled the cravat away and let the strip of fabric flutter to the floor. She slipped her fingers beneath his collar, undoing the fastenings.

He broke away. "What are you doing?"

She cocked an eyebrow. "I'm seducing you. If you have to ask, maybe I'm not doing it right."

He caught her hands, stilling her. He couldn't think while she was undressing him. In fact, he could barely keep from helping her.

"This isn't the place." His voice was hoarse. Lud, he wanted nothing more than to surrender to her. *She might hate you in a few days.*

Maybe, but she loved him now and he could barely think straight. Her skirts were hiked up to her hips, leaving her stocking-clad legs to frame his and her hot core flush against the erection that strained his breeches. He could feel her heat even through the thick fabric.

The corners of her lips twitched. "Morgan, we're in a bedroom. On a bed. I gather that seduction is exactly the sort of thing that occurs in such a place."

She shifted against him, brushing over his aching cock. He dropped his hands to her hips to keep her still. "It isn't the time, then."

She leaned closer. Her breath brushed the shell of his ear as she whispered, "Doesn't it feel like the right time to you? It does to me." Dipping her head, she tongued the hollow just beneath his ear. His entire body ached, centered on that one tiny spot. Zeus, it felt fantastic. He moaned. He wanted to give in, wanted...

No. He couldn't. He grasped her by the shoulders and eased her back. Was he trembling? He didn't know how he found the willpower. He wanted her more desperately than he wanted his next breath.

"We have to make a plan. To save your brother." He could barely think straight.

She cocked an eyebrow. "I don't know about you, but my mind is in no shape to tackle that problem right now."

As she shifted her hips against him, her lips parted and her eyes darkened. His hold on her shoulders prevented her from pressing against him. This...this was torture. His gaze dropped to her bodice. Her nipples had hardened, tenting the fabric even through her undergarments. He licked his lips, trying to stave off the urge to dip his head and capture one of her nipples in his mouth.

She noticed his waning attention. Breathless, she added, "The plan can wait. My brother won't get caught between now and an hour from now."

He lifted his gaze to hers, his arousal reflected in her expression. "It'll be a lot longer than an hour," he promised. "Two or three hours at least. Maybe all night."

She squirmed against his erection. "We'll discuss it over breakfast tomorrow, then."

When she leaned forward to reclaim his lips, he couldn't think of any reason why he shouldn't surrender to the passion between them. He wanted her. She wanted him. If tonight might be the only night he had, he was going to damn well make the most of it.

Chapter Nineteen

Morgan kissed Phil as if he would never see her again, and she loved every second. The urgency, the way his hands roamed across her back, traced the curve of her waist, and finally rose to cup her heavy, aching breasts. She'd never wanted him more than she did at that moment. Knowing that he loved her as much as she did him...this union was right.

She pushed his jacket off his shoulders, battling to expose all the skin that she'd dreamed about since seeing him naked. How would that skin feel against hers? She'd never done this before, fearing the complications that might arise, not the least of which that she might be trapped into marriage with the man she indulged with. That was still a possibility—more than possible, given that he had already asked her to marry him once. But, this time, Phil wasn't afraid. She loved him. He didn't try to control her. She trusted him. Not to mention she craved his presence when they were apart. Marriage to Morgan didn't sound as frightening as it used to.

And she was curious, too. She'd battled her attraction to him ever since they'd met. How would it feel to finally appease that ache?

The moment she wrestled off his jacket, his hands returned to her. He cupped her breast, kneading it as he swiped his thumb across her sensitive nipple through the fabric. She arched against him with a gasp. The muted sensation increased the ache between her thighs. She squirmed against him as she tried to appease it.

With a groan, he cupped the back of her head. The hand at her breast slipped around to her back, undoing her buttons. Thank goodness she didn't bother with stays when she was working. By the time he slipped her buttons free, the back of her dress gaped and he was able to pool it down around her waist, taking her chemise with it.

When her breasts were bare to the air, he broke the kiss to admire her. His hot gaze swept over her skin. Her nipples pebbled as he trailed the pads of his fingers over her skin. He started at her collarbone and slowly, reverently, lowered his fingers to trace the curve of her breasts. It was torture. She leaned closer, hoping he would take the silent hint and touch her more firmly.

"Morgan."

A smile turned up one corner of his mouth. "Yes?" His voice was every bit as gravelly as hers. His gaze was rapt on the slow circles his fingers were drawing over her breast. Every revolution tightened the ache inside her.

She panted. "What are you waiting for?"

His smile grew. "I warned you. This is going to last all night."

"You didn't tell me it would be tort—oh!"

His fingers circled her areola before he rolled her nipple between his thumb and forefinger. "Forgive me, I didn't quite catch that."

Phil lost the ability to form words. Instead, she leaned forward to capture his mouth. She kissed him voraciously as she rocked against the ridge beneath her bottom. His chest swelled. He liked that just as much as she did.

When she broke the kiss, she whispered across his mouth. "Don't torture me."

"It seems only fair when you—"

He reached blindly in the air as she slipped off his lap.

"Phil—"

She pushed her dress over her hips until it pooled on the floor. Next came her drawers and stockings. Her shoes were most likely in her invention room, shucked when she tried to solve her problem with the LEGs.

The moment she straightened, all thought of her invention flew from her mind. Morgan stared at her with promise, with urgency. He didn't say a word, but she knew he desired her. She'd never been naked in front of a man before. The bald admiration in his expression encouraged her. He liked her. No, he loved her. She shivered in anticipation. She couldn't wait for him to show her.

Naked, she knelt at his feet to help him remove his boots. She set them next to the bed and ran her hands up his calves as she found the tops of his stockings beneath the hem of his knee breeches. He reached for her, cupping the back of her head as he tried to urge her back onto the bed.

She grinned. "Not interested in making it last anymore, are you?"

"Maybe next time."

She pulled off the second stocking before she rose. The moment she straightened to her full height, he cupped her jaw and drew her closer for a kiss. As the kiss grew frantic, she leaned closer to him. Her sensitive breasts rubbed against the stiff fabric of his waistcoat. She gasped at the sensation. Desperate to feel his skin against hers, she fumbled for the buttons.

The moment she slipped one free, his muscles surged beneath her. He flipped her onto her back on the soft mattress, pressing her into it with his weight. His hands traveled over her arms, legs, belly, chest. Everywhere, as if he tried to memorize her figure. She returned his attentions in kind, reveling over his broad shoulders, the muscles bunching beneath the cloth. She needed it off.

So did he. He performed the task for her, wrestling off his waistcoat and pulling the shirt over his head. He left her briefly to remove his breeches and drawers. Phil rolled onto her side, propping her head up with one hand as her gaze feasted on his masculine form. Surely no one could be closer to perfection. He was as perfect as a Grecian statue. His muscular torso, dotted with hair, trailed down to a lean waist and thick erection. It bobbed as he stepped forward to rejoin her in bed.

The moment he pressed his body to hers, Phil sank into his warmth. She threaded her hands through his hair and met his kiss halfway. She'd never felt closer to anyone. Even so, she wasn't close enough.

She broke away, gasping for air as Morgan trailed hot, open-mouthed kisses over her neck. Her pins had lost their battle with her hair and the locks tumbled around her. Morgan muttered under his breath as he brushed them away to press his lips against the skin hidden beneath.

Every muscle in her body felt attuned to him. The press of his waist and torso against hers, the tangle of their legs, his rigid manhood trapped between them. She arched against him, desperate to feel more of him.

"Closer."

She whimpered when, instead of moving closer, he lifted himself away. He leaned to one side next to her as his hand followed the curve of her hip and pulled around to dip between her thighs. When she opened her mouth—to protest or to encourage him, she didn't know—he captured her mouth, tangling his tongue with hers as he explored with his hands. He must have liked what he found because he groaned into her mouth. A second later, he rose above her.

"Closer," she whispered, clutching at his broad shoulders. She pulled him down against her, so they were skin to skin as he spread her thighs and plunged between them.

The pain of joining was fleeting, and far outweighed by the pleasure. Though he stilled, groaning his pleasure as he pressed his face into the pillow next to her temple, she urged him on. She kissed his shoulder, flicking out her tongue to taste his skin. She dug her hands into his back as she canted her hips, urging him on.

He whispered praises, most of them indecipherable as he savored their joining. Soon, the tide of pleasure overwhelmed them both and they found themselves writhing against one another, searching for an elusive peak. Phil reached it first, arching into him as he nibbled on her earlobe. She shattered, pulling him close as her body convulsed around him. His breath and his strokes quickened. At the last moment, he pulled out, spilling his seed onto her belly instead.

Right. They weren't married yet. She'd been so caught up in the moment that she'd forgotten. Luckily, he hadn't, or there might have been a few eyebrows raised in nine months.

His arms trembled as he kept himself from collapsing on her. She reached up, rubbing her palm along the stubble that had roughened her skin in the most delightful way. He turned his face to kiss her palm.

With visible effort, he moved away from her. She pushed herself onto her elbows even though the satisfaction rippling through her lulled her toward sleep.

"Come back to bed."

"I will, in a moment." He bent, giving her a good view of his taut behind as he fished something out of his pocket. Her eyes drifted lazily closed as she relaxed. The bed dipped as he returned to her.

He nestled himself behind her, pressing against her left side from shoulder to thigh. As he reached across her to gently wipe the semen off her stomach, it was the most tender act anyone had ever done toward her. He shifted to press a kiss to her shoulder before he wrestled the sheets out from under them and covered her. With her limbs heavy with satisfaction, she wasn't much help. He didn't seem to mind. When he slid beneath the sheets, curling on his side and snaking an arm around her stomach to keep her near, she'd never felt so protected or safe. As an adult, it had never been much of a concern for her, but she realized that the nights between now and the wedding, when he wasn't at her side, she would miss this intimacy.

If there was a wedding. Morgan hadn't asked. His proposal had seemed such a knee-jerk reaction the first time they'd kissed that she'd expected he would spout another the moment they finished. Instead, his breath fanned the back of her neck, relaxed and even.

"Morgan?"

His chest vibrated as he made a sleepy noise.

She opened her mouth, intending to ask him to marry her if he wouldn't perform the task, but instead all she said was, "I love you." She did. What if he didn't want to be trapped into marriage any more than she had when they'd first met?

"I love you, too. More than anything." His voice faded and shortly after he spoke the last word, the arm around her waist grew even heavier. He was asleep.

Exhaustion pulled at her, but her mind was awhirl. She wouldn't be his mistress...or would she? She loved him. She wanted to be near him. She shouldn't overanalyze the situation.

And yet...

What if he didn't want her in his life forever? The strong beat of his heart behind her, the arm around her waist, she loved every reminder of his nearness. She never wanted to be parted. Was it all one-sided?

It can't be. Her head warred with her heart as she lay next to him, waiting for sleep to overcome her and end the torture of her thoughts.

Chapter Twenty

Sunlight streamed through the window, warming the sheets over Morgan's legs. The naked woman next to him murmured in her sleep and nestled closer. Her cheek was like silk as she nuzzled his chest just beneath his collar bone, as though trying to find a more comfortable position. He breathed slowly, evenly, afraid to wake her.

He should go. He'd known it when he'd woken briefly at the crack of dawn. But Phil had stirred then, welcoming him back to her, and he hadn't been able to tear himself away. He was a selfish man. Every time she touched him, he surrendered to her, even when he knew he shouldn't.

The urge to propose to her, to make her his in every way, rose to the surface, nearly overwhelming. He tightened his hold around her. His palm slid over her smooth skin to the small of her back. Her breathing quickened. She moaned a bit, a small sound that made him ache.

Leave before someone finds you here. He didn't want to. But he had her reputation to think about. Even if her maid kept her lips shut, the other servants in the house might not be so kind. He couldn't tarnish Phil's reputation, not when he didn't dare offer for her. At least not until they solved this problem with her brother. He didn't want to tie her to him when there was a very real possibility that she would soon loathe him.

Stifling a sigh, he shifted beneath her, trying to slide to the edge of the bed. It woke her instead.

She blinked her eyes, her eyelashes tickling his skin. Her mouth was soft and plump from sleep. Her eyes were a deep, vibrant blue with nary a trace of gray in them today. Her hair tumbled around them in disarray, conspiring to keep him near her. He didn't mind one bit.

"Morgan?"

Her voice was gravelly with sleep. Zeus, she was beautiful. No one, in art or in life, could possibly compare.

He mustered a smile. "Good morning." His voice was rough from sleep.

Her mouth curved in the secretive smile he'd grown to love so much. She squirmed until she could kiss his mouth, a soft little peck that had him instinctively tightening his arm on her and pulling her closer. He never wanted to let her go.

When she lifted her head again, her breath came in pants. Her chest rose and fell against his. "Good morning to you, too." Her voice was breathless.

"Shall we see if we can make it better?" He leaned forward to recapture her mouth.

With a groan, she rolled away. "It's morning."

He tucked one arm beneath his head as he leaned back in bed. "I didn't know I turned into a pumpkin after midnight."

She cast him a sarcastic look. "The household will be awake. And we have much to discuss."

He sighed. "I don't suppose you'd be able to help me leave without detection?"

Her mouth dropped open. "Why?"

"Why?" He lifted his eyebrows. "Phil, surely you know that the servants talk."

She shrugged. "So what if they do? I don't care."

"Your reputation—"

"Is mine to worry about."

As she slipped from beneath the covers, baring her lovely body to the air, all thoughts of leaving slipped from his mind. Staying seemed an infinitely better choice. In fact, he would rather not leave the room.

Sadly, she plucked a chemise from her wardrobe and covered all that beautiful skin. The thin white fabric flirted with her knees, leaving her calves and ankles bare.

She glanced over her shoulder. "You promised to discuss how best to approach this problem with Lady Whitewood and my brother, remember?"

Ah. Treason. Guaranteed to kill the mood. He stifled a groan as he got out of bed, too. Without Phil with him, it didn't hold much appeal.

Instead of searching for his clothes, Morgan crossed the room to Phil. He caught her around the middle as she was bending to don her stockings, hopping on one foot. She yelped as she collapsed against him. He ran his hand down her side from breasts to hip, savoring the smooth feeling of her chemise. He tipped her head up, bending to kiss her.

"Are you sure?" he whispered against her mouth. "I can leave, if you want."

She fisted her hand in his hair, pulling him down for another kiss. He lingered, loving the feel of her mouth and body against him.

"I don't say anything I don't mean," she told him.

He tried to remember if she'd insulted him at some point, but couldn't concentrate with her lush curves pressed up against him.

"I want you to stay. Have breakfast with me. You did promise to solve this problem with me, didn't you?"

"I did," he answered. He didn't hesitate.

Her mouth firmed, her eyes turning hard as she fought to maintain eye contact at that awkward angle. Her fingers tightened on his hair.

"Then you must stay. I won't let you do this without me."

Something approaching a laugh slipped from his throat. "My dear, I wouldn't dream of it. I'm no fool, and you're more intelligent than I am. Together, we will solve this." He infused his voice with every shred of confidence he had. He voiced none of the fears.

"Yes, we will." Her hand slipped from his hair to trail along the side of his face. Tingles erupted in her wake. She grinned. "My, your beard grows fast. In a day or two, you'd be as hairy as a bear."

He rolled his eyes as he stepped away. When he passed his hand along his jaw, rough stubble met his palm. "Don't remind me." Shaving twice a day was deuced annoying. But the beard, as it grew, was also quite itchy.

Phil pulled on a plain brown dress as he found his drawers and breeches. A bit formal for breakfast, but he couldn't very well go down without. He didn't even have a banyan here, for heaven's sake. Briefly, he considered rectifying this.

No, he didn't need one. If he made a habit of spending his nights with Phil, it would be because they had solved the issue of her brother's treason and she had become his wife. She would accept his proposal this time, wouldn't she? Butterflies erupted in his stomach.

"Can I have your help with the buttons?" Phil pulled her long, wavy hair over her shoulder and presented her back to him.

He ran his finger along her spine, tracing the curve and resultant shiver.

"I want your help doing them up, not undoing them," she said, her voice halfway between a laugh and a groan.

He bent and pressed a kiss to the back of her neck. He snaked out his tongue to tease the bare flesh. "I'm getting around to it."

"Breakfast will be cold, at this rate."

"Eating is overrated."

The moment he finished the last button, she danced out of reach. She must have sensed his intentions. With a grin, she turned to face him. "I might be willing to forego breakfast, if I thought there was any chance of conversation in here. You know I can't think straight when you touch me."

Neither can I. Morgan wanted nothing more than to touch her again. She must have sensed it, too, because she backed to the door and laid her hand on the latch.

"Put on a shirt. You'll scandalize the staff."

He laughed. "That would be a first. Usually, it's my brother scandalizing the household."

"Gideon or Tristan?"

"Anthony," he answered, just to be ornery. Though, to be sure, when Anthony was home, he spent more time carousing than Tristan, and he wasn't half as careful about hiding it from Mother as Tristan tried to be. Anthony had once confessed to Morgan that he had to make up for the rigid way he held himself out at sea, as an example to the officers beneath him.

Welcome to my life, Morgan had answered. Certainly, if he had any sense at all, he wouldn't have spent the night here with Phil.

Sense was overrated.

He found and donned a shirt, but Phil didn't give him time to pull on his stockings or boots before she slipped her hand into his and tugged him out the door. He grinned as she led him down the hall, eager. He must have made her famished.

The servants in the corridor hid their smiles behind their hands but didn't otherwise look surprised to see him. Morgan's cheeks heated. Apparently, even if he had tried to sneak out, it would have been no use. He ducked his head, fingering the streak in his hair with his free hand. He'd never spent the night at a woman's place before. Never before had he met a woman he'd like to wake up next to in the morning.

Phil, on the other hand, didn't seem concerned that the moment they trotted past, the maids giggled and whispered. What were they saying about him? What would they tell others?

He might want to make an effort to take the London reports back from Gideon over the next few weeks, until his name didn't pop up with quite so much frequency. Unfortunately, since he was a duke, that might not be for months. He was always a favorite topic on everyone's lips.

Until now, that hadn't included scandal.

The scandal won't last long, he assured himself. They would free Jared from whatever blackmail Lady Whitewood had on him, and then Morgan would be free to marry Phil. He refused to consider any other alternative.

The breakfast room seemed unusually crowded to Morgan. Not only was a footman waiting to ladle their food onto plates from the row of dishes on the sideboard, but a maid held a steaming pot of tea and another carried a carafe of coffee. As he and Phil stepped into the room, hands still joined, the maids grinned and exchanged glances.

Morgan glared. *Don't you dare make her feel uncomfortable.* He didn't care if they were her servants, he wouldn't allow anyone to make Phil regret the passion they'd shared last night. She was too precious to him.

One more reason why he had to solve this problem as soon as possible, so she could become his wife. No one gave the cut direct to a duchess.

Fortunately, Phil didn't seem to notice her servants' behavior, let alone get offended by it. She took the head of the table and Morgan dropped into the chair next to her. She continued to hold his hand as the food was placed before him. That posed more of a problem; he needed his right hand to eat. Unwilling to relinquish a moment of touching her, he tried his best not to embarrass himself with his left hand.

"My first thought was to retrieve the black... hat," Phil said, casting a look at the staff. She reached out to sip her tea, which the maid had fixed for her with milk and sugar.

He nodded. "That seems like a solid idea. Do you know what kind of hat the lady in question has taken? Perhaps she took it to appease a gambling debt? Or from a lover?" He could think of a dozen other things a young man might get into trouble doing—in fact, his younger brothers had probably explored them all. Those, however, seemed the likely two for a bored man of Jared's station.

Phil sighed. Her face fell. "I have no idea. Jared refuses to tell me. He seems bent on the fact that we won't find anything."

"Leave that to me," Morgan said.

She raised her eyebrows. "Us." Her voice was as sharp as steel.

He should have considered that she would want to accompany him out into the field as well as concoct the plan. He took a deep breath. Given the look on her face, even if he tried to talk her out of going with him, she would undoubtedly sneak off and follow him. He would have a better chance of keeping her safe if she was at his side.

He nodded. "Very well."

The tense, determined look on her face faded into one of surprise, which she soon covered with satisfaction, as if she'd expected him to agree with her all along. He bit his tongue to keep from snorting. He knew what most men in his position would do. Fortunately for him, he was more intelligent than most men.

When he had his amusement under control, he added, "That won't solve the problem entirely, but it will remove Jared from...the situation. If we want to keep him away, we'll have to arrest the lady who stole the hat."

Phil nodded. "That sounds simple enough."

He held his tongue. Nothing about this mission had proven simple so far. Even talking in circles so the staff didn't catch on had his head throbbing.

They continued to eat. Phil rubbed her thumb over his hand idly, seemingly unaware that she did so. The servants slowed as they passed by the room, craning their necks to see inside. Morgan offered them his coldest ducal stare. The maids twittered again next to the sideboard, their words too high pitched to decipher. He turned his glare on them.

Abruptly, they silenced. Because of him? Not bloody likely. They hadn't taken his wordless admonishments to heart yet.

Phil glanced up, toward the door. "Jared."

Reflexively, Morgan tightened his hand. He turned, standing as he did. Jared, half-dressed in his shirt sleeves and breeches, stared at him and Phil, appalled.

Morgan slipped his hand from Phil's. He stepped forward. *This isn't what it looks like.* Well, perhaps it was, but Morgan wanted to impress that he had the best of intentions toward Phil. *After* they solved Jared's problem, of course. A throb started in Morgan's temple.

Phil scurried around him, herding Jared into a chair. "I've asked for Morgan's help with your little problem. He's...in a position to help."

Morgan released a breath when she didn't announce him a British spy in the middle of the breakfast room. *That* piece of gossip certainly wouldn't help the situation if it circulated London.

Rather than sit, Jared backed away from his sister. "Obviously, you have everything under control." Disgust laced his voice. He backed out of the room, shooting daggers at Morgan.

Every muscle in Morgan's body stiffened. That hadn't gone according to plan. Did Jared not like him? He'd seemed a perfectly affable fellow when they'd met previously. And he must have seen the way Morgan's mother and sister had been pushing him and Phil together. It was inevitable that he and Phil should succumb eventually.

Lud, he'd made a mess of this, hadn't he?

He slipped past Phil. "I should go after him, talk to him." Tell him that he meant Phil no disrespect. Just the opposite, he loved and esteemed her more than any other.

Phil caught his sleeve. "I don't think it would do much good when he's in a mood like this."

Morgan frowned. When he turned to study Phil's face, he found her pensive. Her eyes were stormy. "Then he's usually like this?" Perhaps it wasn't due to his presence, then. Or was there something else afoot with the young man?

"Not with guests."

Morgan smiled tightly. "Perhaps it was the shock of seeing me here at such an early hour."

She pointed to the grandmother clock in the corner. "Not so early. It's nearly half ten of the morning."

When had it gotten so late? Morgan's stomach clenched. "I should return home."

"Wait—" Her hand tightened on his forearm. "We still have the particulars to discuss."

Stay a few minutes longer. The urge to give in to her was almost overwhelming. But if he stayed for a few minutes, it would be an hour or more before he left. Better he leave now.

"I like your initial instinct to search her home. I assume I interrupted you before you got far?"

She nodded.

He laid his hand over hers. "Then that's what we'll do. I'll ask around and see if she has any other properties in or around London that warrant a search. I'll meet you here tonight."

She smiled. He marveled at how a simple curve of her lips could instantly brighten the room. "You'd better," she warned, amusement lacing her voice.

He leaned down, the urge to kiss her mounting. The shift of bodies at his peripheral vision reminded him that they were not alone. He pressed his lips to her cheek instead.

"Until tonight, my dear."

He slipped out of the room and returned upstairs to collect the rest of his clothes.

***

Phil caught Jared an instant before he left the house, fully dressed. "Wait. We need to talk."

"Do we?" His mouth twisted with distaste. Color infused his cheeks as he turned away. He didn't look her in the eye.

She brushed her hand across his sleeve. He jerked away. She bit the inside of her cheek. *Like Morgan said, it was a shock for him.* "I know you must have been startled this morning, but you shouldn't worry. Morgan is a good man. He's helping us."

The muscle in Jared's jaw clenched. "I don't need your help anymore. I'll handle it on my own."

Her mouth fell open. "Why not? Jared, this is a family matter. I want to fix this."

He lifted his hands halfway to his hair before he dropped them with an exasperated breath. When he turned to her, his eyes snapped. "By God, Phil, I didn't want you to prostitute yourself to a duke in exchange for his influence!"

The words rang through the house. The patter and hum of voices as the servants went about their chores went silent. Phil's cheeks heated.

"It isn't like that at all," she said, raising her voice for the others to hear. In a lower tone, she added, "We love each other."

Jared scoffed. "Is that what he told you? He only wanted to get between your thighs."

She flinched at his scathing tone. "What is *wrong* with you this morning?"

She regretted the words the instant they left her mouth. The rift between them widened, almost an audible rip in the air as his face hardened.

"I'm a man, remember. Not a boy. I know what men are like."

Maybe he did, but Morgan wasn't that sort of man. For heaven's sake, he'd proposed to her the first time they'd kissed!

Jared jutted out his chin. At that moment, he reminded her so much of their mother. Grief swamped her, so hot and thick she could barely pull herself out to see him in front of her. She blinked away tears.

"Did he propose to you?" Her brother's voice was hard.

She swallowed, but she couldn't answer one way or another. It had been weeks since that first proposal. He hadn't mentioned marriage since. She'd hoped, once they woke up...

After they attended this business with Jared, he would propose, wouldn't he? If not, Phil would propose to him. Perhaps he was still afraid she would laugh in his face.

In a soft voice, she said, "He agreed to help before he spent the night. Before I...seduced him." Good God, did she have to have this conversation with him? If he insisted he was a grown man, surely he could see that she was a grown woman, more than capable of making her own decisions on who warmed her bed. "He's a good man, Jared."

Her brother's expression didn't soften. "We'll see. If he doesn't marry you, I'll call him out myself."

Because finding herself trapped in a forced marriage was always the right answer.

She balled her fists. "You can't duel a duke."

He lifted his eyebrows, his expression cold. "I'm a grown man. I can do whatever I please. And right now, it pleases me to go out."

Her stomach turned somersaults as he walked away from her, storming through the door and slamming it shut behind him, to the shock of Mr. O'Neill, their butler. Phil swallowed heavily, choking back the tide of tears that threatened to overwhelm her.

Jared didn't understand the truth. Maybe he didn't want to. At least, between Phil and Morgan, he would soon be free of this spying business, free to return to the carefree young man he'd used to be.

In the meantime, she had work to do.

***

The moment Morgan entered his townhouse, he found himself faced with three sly-faced family members. Thank Zeus it was before noon and the two newest additions to his family were still abed.

Mother beamed, clasping her hands over her chest and pressing her lips together as if she waited for an announcement. Lud, he'd love to give her one, but he couldn't. He hadn't asked Phil to marry him yet.

Lucy, arms akimbo, fought a losing battle to contain her grin as she tried to appear stern. "Where have you been? You weren't down to breakfast."

"I was at the club." From time to time, his work necessitated that he lie to his family, and he'd started to become quite good at it. Even if Mother, for one, likely knew the truth.

Judging by his grin as he folded his arms across his chest, so did Giddy. "You were at the club all night?"

Morgan gritted his teeth. He glared at his brother, who didn't seem the least bit perturbed. *You are not helping.* Gideon's grin widened.

"Yes." His voice was stiff.

Lucy harrumphed. "Is that so? It must be a new club, then. I don't believe White's remains open 'round the clock."

Not quite, but she would be surprised at the hours the club sometimes kept, depending on the patron. Given that he was a duke, they would likely keep it open for him if he desired. It was one of the few benefits to his station.

He raised an eyebrow. "Since when did you become my keeper?"

She stuck out her tongue. "Since you lost all sense mooning after Phil. Don't think we haven't noticed."

Morgan looked to his brother for help, not that he found any. Mother beamed with delight. He couldn't stand there in the entryway, under the weight of all this pressure. *Don't you think I would have proposed to her if I could have?* His only hope was to absolve her brother of treason, and then they might stand a chance.

Brusquely, he shoved his way between his sister and Giddy. "I need to change out of these clothes."

"Not sleep?" His sister's voice was sly. "You must have gotten *some* sleep last night, after all."

"Not much," he muttered under his breath. He smiled as he remembered the night, even if the cold reality of the situation soon chased away his good mood. Thankfully, his back was turned to his family, so he couldn't see their faces.

"Wait," Mother called as he reached the stairs. The click of her footsteps on the floor punctured him like needles.

He paused with his hand on the banister, but didn't turn around.

"Do you have any news you'd like to share with us?" Her voice was light and effusive.

He gritted his teeth. "No."

He managed four steps before his mother's voice rang again. "She said no?"

Guilt bowed his shoulders inward. He ducked his head. "I didn't ask." Obviously, she meant a proposal.

She gasped. "Morgan Arthur Benedict Graylocke, what sort of man did I raise?"

He cringed at the use of his full name, with all the middle names. Nevertheless, he didn't say a word. He didn't trust himself. If he did, the truth might pour out, and he couldn't get his mother involved. He continued up the stairs.

"Don't walk away from me," she called. Her footsteps on the stairs heralded the fact that this conversation was far from over.

Abruptly, they stopped. "Let me speak with him," Gideon said. Although his voice was pitched low, it carried to Morgan's ears.

He shook his head. What could Giddy possibly say that he hadn't said to himself? He hurried to his room.

By the time he reached it, his brother was one step behind. Morgan stepped through the door to find his room neatly cleaned, everything put in its place, the bed made—not that it had been used— and the drapes pulled apart to let in the wan sunlight. His valet—the man he was borrowing from Tristan—must have found a spare moment in between his spying duties.

Giddy shut the door behind them. Rubbing the streak at his temple, Morgan turned. He didn't want to have this conversation with anyone, not even the brother he was closest to.

"Don't get me started. I would have proposed to Phil, if I'd been at liberty."

Gideon raised his eyebrows. He crossed his arms, leaning back against the door. "At liberty? I didn't know you were suddenly engaged to someone else."

Morgan didn't bother answering something so obviously ridiculous. Instead, he crossed his room to his wardrobe and searched for clean clothes.

Giddy stepped away from the door. "Is this about...our mutual business?"

Morgan sighed. He dropped down onto the chair to remove his boots. "In a peripheral way. I have a problem I need to solve."

"Can I help?"

Giddy looked earnest, his eyes bright and his expression open. Morgan shook his head, hating to disappoint his brother.

"Not this time." As Gideon's face fell, Morgan blurted, "The moment I need your help, I promise I will come to you."

Giddy's mouth thinned, but he nodded. "As long as you know that I'm here when you need me." His voice was a bit surly, but resigned.

Standing in his stocking feet, Morgan crossed to clap him on the shoulder. "I know, and I'm grateful for the support. I daresay I'll need it, if what I plan tonight goes poorly."

His brother smiled, mollified for the moment.

With a fond smile, Morgan added, "Now, get out of my room. I need to dress."

Chapter Twenty-One

"Leave the carriage here," Phil instructed as she rapped on the roof.

Morgan nodded. Although her carriage, unlike his, didn't have a crest on the side, approaching Lady Whitewood's townhouse on foot would likely draw less attention, especially considering that they hoped for the lady in question to be out. His sources had produced no other holdings in London; aside from the townhouse, Lord Whitewood had bequeathed her a small estate in the country, over a day's drive from Town. Reports claimed that Lady Whitewood had been in London since Christmas, so she couldn't have stashed her blackmail at the country estate.

Morgan preceded Phil into the open air. He reached up to hand her down. Tonight, she'd opted to wear men's clothes for mobility. He didn't know how he'd ever believed her to be male. Although she'd bound her chest flat, there was still a slight curve to her torso. Her unruly hair didn't quite fit under her hat. Stray strands sprung up to frame her cheeks and neck. Her breeches clung to her shapely legs, and her bottom filled out the rear to advantage. He admired the view as she joined him on the cobblestones. Her form was undoubtedly feminine. Every muscle in his body attuned to her when she was near.

Fortunately, her head seemed to be clearer of lust than his. She turned away from him the moment they set foot on the street. "Let me collect my bag out of the boot and we'll be on our way."

With a frown, Morgan followed on her heels. "Your bag?"

Sure enough, she hefted a bulging sack that looked to have been fashioned out of a pillow case. The silhouettes of various shapes crossed each other through the linen.

Nonchalant, she answered, "I fashioned a few inventions in case we needed them to infiltrate the house."

If Lucy or Gideon had announced such a thing to him, he would have groaned. But, even though the sack drew more attention to them than he would like, he was curious about the wonders she hid inside it. "What sort of inventions?"

She smiled. "You'll have to wait and see, won't you?"

They meandered down the street toward Lady Whitewood's residence. As luck would have it, they came into view just in time to watch her carriage drive off. She rode in an open carriage today, not a coach like they'd arrived in, and so Morgan was able to identify her in the seat along with a gentleman he didn't look too closely at.

The moment they passed, he turned to Phil. "I suppose it's time to put your inventions to the test."

He waited to ensure the street was clear before he hurried Phil across with a hand at the small of her back. Even through their clothes, her heat seared him.

Her inventions did come in handy, beginning with a small device that helped to unlatch the servant entrance on the side. Phil listened, placing another gadget to her ear that she claimed enhanced her hearing. She charitably gave him the light-enhancing goggles to wear, not that he needed them. Once they slipped into the house, they found a candle burning in the kitchen and snatched it.

The kitchen staff were abed and the stove was cold. Given the rustling above stairs, the servants were on their way to sleep now that the sun had set.

"Let's begin with the ground floor," Morgan suggested. "By the time we finish, we should be able to sneak up to the second floor without interference."

Phil nodded. "Shall we split up and search different rooms?"

He hesitated. He didn't want to be parted from her. He shook his head. "We'll finish the rooms faster if we work together, and we'll be less likely to be caught if we only occupy one room at a time."

She nodded. "Lead on."

They agreed that Lady Whitewood wouldn't have left the blackmail where the servants would easily find it. That ruled out the kitchen, pantry, and linen closet. They started their search in one of the drawing rooms, each taking half the room and checking it thoroughly.

In the study, Morgan found a hidden compartment in the underside of the desk and pulled out several sheets of correspondence. A quick glance showed it was all in code.

"What's that?" Phil asked, meandering from her end of the room, with the bookshelves.

"Code," he answered. He skimmed his finger along the first message, deciphering it in his head. "This must be old. I think it's from Elias Harker."

"Didn't he die recently?"

"Yes," Morgan said absently. "At my estate. Mrs. Vale shot him."

Phil said nothing. The silence grew, heavy and laden with disapproval.

Morgan raised his eyebrow as he glanced at her. "Harker *was* a French spy."

"Yes. Of course. He most likely deserved it." Doubt lingered in her voice, as if she didn't condone anyone's murder no matter the circumstances. Truthfully, he didn't either. Let the magistrates decide who deserved to die. He wanted no part in deciding such a fate.

"He was aiming a gun at her daughter at the time."

"Charlie?"

Morgan shook his head. "No. Freddie. Tristan's new wife."

"Then I'm surprised Tristan didn't kill him."

Morgan chuckled. "He might have, if he had been close enough. Then again, by that time his sense was so muddled that he might have thrown himself in front of the bullet instead."

"Then perhaps it's for the best that it worked out this way."

Morgan nodded. His lips thinned. If Harker had still been alive, and Mrs. Vale still keeping an eye on him, he wouldn't have been sent into the field. Perhaps Lady Whitewood wouldn't have taken it upon herself to blackmail Phil's brother into committing treason. Of course, then Morgan might never have met Phil. He would like to think himself above such insensibility as he described of his brother, but the truth was, if he was in the same situation with Phil in danger, he would do everything he possibly could to keep her safe.

Even if it meant throwing himself into danger in her place.

He pushed the thought away. "Can you find me some foolscap? I need to decode some of these others."

A curious look overcame her features. She found paper while he dug out a pen, ink, and sand to blot the page. He pulled the first sheet toward him, copying out the translation as he deciphered it. The moment it referenced a code book, the same book he and his brother had passed along a month ago, Morgan switched to the next message. It also contained old news. The third mentioned a meeting between Lady Whitewood and a gentleman who signed his name as "Monsieur V." The message didn't indicate the date of the meeting, only the place and time, so Morgan copied the information to send to Strickland later.

"How are you doing that so fast?" Phil breathed. When he turned to her, he found her expression in awe. A strange, warm feeling expanded in his chest.

He shrugged. "It's only a code. Once you memorize the cipher, it isn't terribly hard to crack. These are using outdated codes."

She squinted, comparing two of the missives beneath the light of the candle. "But they're different codes, surely. They look nothing alike."

He nodded. "They are. With two different people. But, like I said, once you memorize the cipher, you don't even need the book anymore."

"Brilliant." She pulled out another page, squinting at it. "And this one? It seems like a normal letter to me."

He looked over her shoulder. The missive was written in French, but there were accents on letters that didn't need them. He pointed those out. "See these? It's more than poor spelling. This is certainly a code."

"Oh?" She stood straighter, looking at him expectantly. "What does it say?"

The words burned in his throat as he admitted, "I don't know. I've never seen this cipher before."

"Oh. Then you can't read it?"

"Not yet." He slipped a clean sheet onto the top of the pile of papers and carefully copied down the missive, including the exact slant of the letters and every mark on the page. As he did, he murmured, "I'll have to take it to my study and look it over."

"But you don't have the key to the code."

He gave a one-shouldered shrug as he compared the two pages. Satisfied they were identical, he sprinkled sand on his copy to blot the letters. "It doesn't matter. I've cracked more than one French code. In fact," he thrust back his shoulders with pride, "Strickland has confessed that I do so more quickly than he can. He sends all new codes directly to me, now."

"Strickland?"

He winced. He shouldn't have given away his superior's name, not even to Phil. "Britain's spymaster, but that stays between you and me."

"Certainly," she said with a nod. "If he relies on you so much, how can he afford to send you into the field?"

He shrugged. "It's only paperwork. It isn't that glorious."

She raised her eyebrows. "You forget, I invent things from thin air. I know the value of a brilliant mind. This field work?" She waved a hand in dismissal. "Anyone can search a room. Not everyone can do what you can."

He'd never felt that way. Sitting behind a desk had felt stifling, as though he was being given work simply to occupy him and make him feel important due to his status as Duke. However, the confidence in her voice was infectious.

"You really believe that?"

She slipped between him and the desk, her body brushing against his as she reached up to cup his face. "Of course I do. I love that brilliant mind of yours. I can't wait to see you in action." Her voice dropped to a purr. "It's very attractive."

"Is it?" His smile grew. He leaned forward to whisper in her ear. "Shall I start writing you love letters in code?"

"Only if you leave them in our bed." She threaded her fingers through his hair.

Our bed. The word tingled through him like a touch. He melded his mouth to hers, not caring that they were in enemy territory. She wanted him. When this was all over, they would have a life together, and he'd get to see her and touch her for many years to come. Decades, even.

God, he loved her. His chest ached.

He ended the kiss entirely too soon for his liking. In his passion, he'd leaned her back against the desk. She turned, noticing the splotched words on the missive that she'd sat on.

"Bollocks," she said, rubbing at her rear. "I've ruined it."

He chuckled. "It was worth it. I'll copy it again."

She left him to it, continuing to search the room while he copied down the few missives in the new code. Her enthusiasm filled him and he couldn't wait to return home to see what he could make of them.

In the end, unless it was contained in one of the letters he couldn't decipher, they found no indication of blackmail. Indeed, no mention of Jared's name at all. As they ended in Lady Whitewood's bedroom, Morgan sighed. He patted his pocket. "I'll get started on these right away. With luck, I'll be able to decipher them within a week and we'll know what she has against Jared." If, indeed, the letters mentioned the blackmail at all.

Morgan refused to meet Phil's gaze. Even if she didn't, he knew a week was too long. Strickland wouldn't wait that long to learn the truth behind Morgan's hunch, and Morgan couldn't offer him Lady Whitewood. If he did, she might lead Strickland back to Jared. As a small player, Jared was expendable—meaning that Strickland could opt to bring him in for questioning or even execution.

He couldn't let that happen. His and Phil's future was on the line.

Dimly, from deep in the manor, he heard a door slam shut. His heartbeat quickened. He met Phil's fearful gaze. "What was that?"

He rushed to the window even as she whispered the words. A carriage turned onto the street, the seats empty. It was the same that had delivered Lady Whitewood from the premises. How long ago had that been? He hadn't expected her return for hours.

"We have to get out of here," he said, his voice terse.

"How?" Phil's expression was tense. Her gaze snapped to the door as they heard footsteps up the stairs.

"The window."

"We're three stories up!"

It didn't matter. The window was their only way out. "Do you have anything in that bag of yours that will help?"

She frowned. "I don't think—"

He yanked the sheet off the bed.

Phil gasped. "Morgan, she'll know we—"

"She'll know we were here if she catches us, too." He whipped the sheet, turning it into a makeshift rope as she unlatched and opened the window. He tied the end to the leg of the vanity, situated beside the window. One tug proved that the table was solid. It would hold Phil's weight, for sure. He tossed the end out the window. "Go," he ordered.

"What about you?"

"I'll be right behind you. We'll meet at the carriage. Now, go." He helped as she started to climb onto the sill, lifting her rump until she dangled out the side. "Hurry," he hissed.

He kept an eye on the closed door. The footsteps were louder, now. She must be in the corridor. Was she armed? He was not sure what he would encounter here, but he didn't want to kill anyone, least of all a woman. Killing a French spy was what had gotten him into this mess to begin with.

He glanced out the window. The sheet didn't reach the bottom of the house. The strain on the makeshift rope let up as she released it, dropping to the ground. Her silhouette jumped upright a moment later. He let out a breath. She must not have hurt herself.

He climbed onto the sill just as Lady Whitewood entered the room. For a moment, they stared mute at each other. Then she fiddled in her reticule. Morgan jumped out the window. The rope sheet burned against his palms as he slid down its length. He caught himself on the end, slowing his progression before he let go, falling the last story to the ground. He landed heavily, jolting his knees.

He glanced up in time to see Lady Whitewood stick her head out the window. He dashed into the night before she wasted her shot or worse, hit him dead on. His heartbeat didn't slow even after he reached the carriage and Phil. She'd already stowed her bag in the boot again.

He wrapped her in his arms, holding her to his chest as his heartbeat quivered. Her arms encircled his back and she clutched him just as fiercely.

She didn't know. Lady Whitewood had seen his face. She knew now that he was a spy. Even a fool could deduce that he was her enemy. Now that she knew he worked for the Crown, she would retaliate against him. If she did that, Phil would be in danger, collateral damage.

Every minute during his service, he'd longed to be out in the field. Not anymore. Now, he wished he'd never come out from behind his desk. If he hadn't, the woman he loved wouldn't be put in even greater danger.

One way or another, he had to fix this, and soon.

Chapter Twenty-Two

Morgan's hand on the small of Phil's back burned her even through her clothes as he herded her up the steps to the Tenwick townhouse. He hadn't stopped touching her since the moment they'd reunited by the carriage. His hand on her arm, on her knee, on her back—he'd made certain she couldn't forget that he was nearby. He hadn't said a word about their close call, but evidently it was making him a touch overprotective. For the moment, she didn't mind.

The butler opened the door and Morgan ushered her into the house. He'd insisted on returning to his home in order to decipher the letters he'd copied. The moment she stepped past the butler and into the house, she stopped short. Morgan bumped into her. He shifted his hands to her shoulders.

Jared stood in the middle of the entry way. His collar was askew, his cravat nowhere to be found, and his hair stuck up at all ends. His eyes were wild, his expression livid, as he rounded on them.

"Phil, where the devil have you been? I returned home to find you gone, and no one had the faintest clue where you'd run off to except that you'd left with *him*." With the last word, Jared leveled a vicious glare at the duke.

Phil felt Morgan's chest and abdomen stiffen behind her. He tightened his hands on her shoulders. "I beg your pardon?" His voice was as cold as a winter gale.

Stepping another foot inside so the butler could shut the door, Phil risked a glance at Morgan's face. The candlelight illuminating the entryway cast hard shadows across his chiseled face and clean-shaven jaw. She returned her gaze to Jared, keeping herself between him and the duke as her brother stepped forward, one fist balled and the other hand jabbing through the air in accusation.

"You heard me. Release her this instant. We don't have need of your services."

If anything, the cutting demand only made Morgan hold onto her tighter. He ran one hand down her arm to thread their fingers together. Something indescribable filled Phil's chest. He didn't act like he wanted to hide her and keep her from breaking like she was a glass figurine. He acted as though she was his partner, and he garnered strength from her presence and support. She squeezed his hand, giving him everything he asked and more. The lump in her throat prevented her from speaking.

Morgan's voice was calm, concise, but far from warm as he answered her brother. "Considering the predicament you've gotten yourself into, I wouldn't be so hasty to eschew my support, if I were you."

Jared sneered. "So you're a duke, what can you do?"

"I am a British spy and right now I am the only thing keeping you from dangling at the end of a noose outside Newgate."

Phil flinched. She reflexively clenched Morgan's hand as she screwed her eyes shut to avoid the image. It wouldn't happen. They would stop it. They were working together now—they had a chance.

In a softer voice, Morgan added, "We made progress on that tonight when we searched Lady Whitewood's home. I have some letters to decode, if you wouldn't mind moving."

Jared stubbornly continued to block Morgan's path. His jaw was set. His eyes snapped. "You put her in danger? I don't care if you're Prinny himself, I'm not going to stand idly by and let you use my sister and make free with her safety!"

She flew her colors at the accusation. She'd already told Jared that Morgan wasn't using her. That he would confront the duke with such a claim...

Morgan's hold on her didn't alter. He rubbed his thumb across her skin. "Your sister is a strong, capable woman able to make her own decisions. In any case, she wasn't the one caught—I was."

A chill traveled down Phil's spine. When Morgan had met up with her, safe and whole, she had assumed they'd both managed to elude Lady Whitewood. She twisted in his arms to look at his face. His jaw was clenched as he met Jared's gaze.

She pressed her lips together to keep from voicing her fears. Morgan was a grown man, and a spy. He had undoubtedly been in dangerous situations before. But couldn't he contribute to the spy effort without being in the thick of danger? He had a gift with the way he was able to decode those messages. He would be a valuable asset from the sidelines, out of harm's way. She lowered her gaze to their joined hands. Was it wrong of her that she wanted to keep him safe with her, at home?

She cleared her throat and informed her brother, "We didn't find whatever she is using to blackmail you tonight. At least, not that we know of. Morgan did copy a few letters to decode and whatever it is might be in there. If you would tell us what we are looking for, it would be most helpful."

Jared held his rigid stance a moment more before his strength flagged. He deflated. He stared at the floor as he admitted, "You won't find it, Phil. I told you that already."

She thrust her shoulders back and opened her mouth to reassure her brother that she would, no matter the cost. Lady Whitewood couldn't be allowed to continue.

To her surprise, Morgan dropped his hand from her shoulder and extricated himself from her hold. He stepped around her, tentatively reaching out to pat Jared's shoulder. "Why don't you come into the parlor to sit down while you tell us why we just wasted an evening?"

Morgan's voice was kind, but Jared flinched all the same. His mouth set into a sullen line, but he heeded the duke's suggestion. Phil trailed behind as they entered the sitting room.

The room was dark, swathed in shadow, but the butler followed them and solved the situation by lighting a branch of candles for them. He lingered over the task, as if waiting to hear the story himself. Jared slumped in an armchair. Morgan sat near him on the corner of a settee. Feeling odd and secluded, Phil trudged after him and sat.

The butler finished his task, throwing light into the room. He stepped closer to the men. "Would you care for a stiff drink, sir?"

Jared hesitated, then nodded. Morgan did the same. The butler retreated to the sideboard to procure the drinks. Silence reigned all around, growing uncomfortably tight. After the butler returned with two tumblers of amber whiskey, he turned to Phil. "And you, miss?"

"I'll have the same."

The butler didn't bat an eyelash. He turned to follow her edict. Likely, he relished the excuse to remain in the room. Come to think of it, he hadn't reacted to her attire, either. She still wore men's clothes. Her estimation of the man rose.

Morgan waited for the butler to bring her drink before he said another word. When the old man lingered near the doorway, that word was directed to his staff. The duke raised an eyebrow. "You may leave."

"I'll hear it somewhere else, sir."

"Shut the door behind you. This is a family matter."

Phil's stomach warmed as he said *family*. It was as though he was already accepting Jared as his brother—and her as his wife. She sent her brother a look that said, *See?*

Jared rolled his eyes. If the duke noticed, he didn't make any response. He trained his gaze on the butler until the man bowed and left.

Morgan turned to her brother. "Don't mind him. He's also a spy, as are a good number of my staff. I'd advise you not to speak freely in front of them until I can point out which are trustworthy."

Instead of replying, Jared sipped on his drink. He didn't meet Morgan's gaze or Phil's.

After a moment, Morgan prodded, "You seem dreadfully certain that we won't find the blackmail being used against you. Why is that?"

Jared sighed. He drained his tumbler and set it on the table haphazardly. It clinked as it made contact and wobbled, nearly falling over. Her brother stared into his hands for a moment before he confessed. "There is no item being held against me. It is a person."

Phil's stomach tightened. She shifted on the settee, holding her drink on her lap. "What do you mean?" Surely Lady Whitewood couldn't be threatening a member of their family...threatening *her,* could she? Jared would be just fool enough to think he could keep her safe.

He ran his fingers through his hair and admitted, "I do have a lover. At least, I did."

Although he hadn't finished with his drink, Morgan set the glass neatly on the table next to Jared's. "Perhaps you should start at the beginning."

Jared let out a gusty breath, but he nodded. He stared across the room, as though reliving the past. "Her name is Claire. Her family had a falling out that ended with her father shut up in debtor's prison. I met her..." He shook his head. "It doesn't matter where I met her. We fell in love."

Phil tightened her hands on the tumbler in her lap. Why hadn't Jared told her this? She was his sister. If there was someone important in his life, she wanted to know. How long had this been going on for?

"The night she confessed that she was with child—my child—Lady Whitewood approached me. She knew about the affair, the child, everything. She told me if I didn't aid her, she would not only expose Claire, but she alluded that she had people watching her. People who could hurt her." Jared swallowed audibly. "Claire was reduced, you see. Living in a bad part of London without protection. Now that she was with child, she'd finally accepted my proposal. I was on my way home to talk to Phil, but..." He thrust himself back in the chair, blinking rapidly.

Was he crying? Phil hadn't seen him cry since he was a child. Her stomach twisted in knots.

She spoke around the lump in her throat, her voice hoarse. "You could have come to me. If you love her...then so would I."

"It didn't matter," Jared said, his voice sharp. He flicked his forelock out of his eyes. "The moment Lady Whitewood approached me, I knew we couldn't be together. I got up all the money I could in a morning and told her to change her name and leave England. Go anywhere, overseas, to the continent, as long as she didn't tell me where."

Phil opened her mouth but didn't know what to say.

Morgan spoke instead, his voice soft. "So you wouldn't be able to give away her location if you were tortured. Smart. I assume you instructed her never to contact you?"

Jared nodded. "I did. I tried not to look for her, but I couldn't help myself. I didn't look hard, but I couldn't find her when I tried, so it must have worked. And now...I've been giving her time to get as far away as possible, pretending that Lady Whitewood has a hold on me."

Phil licked her lips. "But she doesn't. I mean, Claire is safe, isn't she? That means that you don't have to do what Lady Whitewood says anymore."

Neither of the men looked her in the eye. Morgan ran his finger along the white streak in his hair, by his temple. "It isn't that simple," he said after a tense silence. "No doubt Lady Whitewood has proof that he has been spying for her, which even if it was done to protect another is still treason." He shook his head. "No, we'll have to get to the root of the problem. We must discover how many others know about this. If it is only Lady Whitewood and whatever men she assigned to watch Claire, then we may have a chance of putting this to rest."

"How?" Phil asked, her voice small.

"We'll take her out of the game. We'll need—"

A rap sounded on the door. Morgan fell silent at once, sitting straighter as the butler opened the door to reveal a stocky, balding man with a bit of a paunch. He looked harmless enough.

Turning as white as the streak in his hair, Morgan jumped to his feet. "Strickland."

Phil's stomach dropped into the soles of her shoes as she pinned her gaze on the newcomer once more. On Britain's spymaster.

***

Morgan swallowed around a painful lump in his throat as he entered the study behind Strickland. He dismissed his butler as the man set down a branch of candles to light the room.

Strickland wasted no time with small talk. His eyebrows inched down over his eyes as he turned, his expression hard. "Someone saw you jump out of Lady Whitewood's window tonight."

His words stabbed their way down Morgan's back like cat's claws. For Strickland to have heard such a rumor so quickly, it could only have been a Crown spy who had seen him. "Are you assigning men to watch me or Lady Whitewood?"

Strickland dropped into the chair in front of Morgan's desk, leaning his elbow against the arm in a deceptively casual pose. He couldn't be so calm, not if he was accusing Morgan of keeping secrets from him. Morgan clasped his hands behind his back. His hands tightened to the point that pins and needles poked the tips of his fingers. If Strickland had a man on Morgan that he hadn't realized, then he might already know...everything. The duke clenched his teeth, trying not to betray his anxiety.

The spymaster raised his eyebrows. "It shouldn't surprise you that I've been acting on suspicions of my own."

"I haven't committed any wrongs."

"No, but you have been keeping something from me." Strickland leaned forward, bracing his elbows on his knees. Somehow, he seemed more commanding seated than Morgan felt while standing.

You are a duke, he reminded himself. Tonight, that knowledge didn't help a whit. If someone other than a Crown spy had recognized him as he escaped out Lady Whitewood's window, rumors would flood the gossip mill. Those rumors might hurt Phil. He couldn't let that happen.

Strickland asked, "Have you been recruiting without telling me?"

"You know I recruited my brother to help me while Tristan is away."

"And yet it was a very different young man who accompanied you to Lady Whitewood's tonight."

Morgan stiffened at the fact that Strickland knew Phil was involved. *Right now, he thinks she's a man.* Morgan wanted to keep it that way.

He fished the copied letters out of his pocket, the only evidence he had against Lady Whitewood, and the only way to distract Strickland. "I found these in Lady Whitewood's house, along with other coded correspondence indicating that she was in contact with Harker and with an unknown man known as Monsieur V. She is certainly a French spy."

If Strickland had someone inside Lady Whitewood's home, he would already have known that. Which meant he had to have been keeping an eye on Morgan, instead. Did Strickland have agents inside Phil's home? Her maid seemed loyal, but Morgan hadn't examined the rest of the staff too closely. It might already be too late for Jared.

Morgan's stomach flipped. He couldn't give up. If he sat idly by while Phil's brother was arrested, she would never speak to him again.

He handed the correspondence to Strickland. "These had a code I wasn't familiar with. I haven't had a chance yet to look at them." How much did Strickland distrust him?

The spymaster waved his hand. "Send over copies in your report and let me know the minute you decode them. The information might be time sensitive."

He still trusted Morgan enough to let him do his job. Perhaps that didn't extend to field work, but Morgan found himself wishing he wasn't embroiled in this kind of danger anymore. It had seemed terribly exciting while he'd been barred from it, but now that his slip-ups put Phil in danger as well...he wanted his safe job, decoding messages from his desk, creating ciphers, and training new recruits.

"I'll send a runner when I'm finished with deciphering the letters."

Strickland nodded. "Good." He passed a hand over his face. "We suspected Lady Whitewood while Harker was still alive, but we could never place her at any of the information exchanges we caught wind of."

Quietly, Morgan admitted, "I know why she's never there."

Strickland didn't say a word, but the way he straightened in the chair spoke for him. Morgan had his full attention.

"She blackmails men into spying for her."

The spymaster leaned back in his chair, waiting for more. He fiddled with the cravat at his neck, an idle gesture. When Morgan provided no more information, Strickland asked, "Do you have proof of this?"

"I do. I have contact with one of the men she has been coercing."

"This hasn't made it into any of your reports."

Morgan straightened his spine. "You said you wanted the puppet master. I knew that wasn't the man in question. To be honest, after reading her correspondence, I'm more inclined to believe the spy you're looking for is Monsieur V."

Strickland said nothing. His gaze bored into Morgan, as if the spymaster tried to read his secrets from nothing more than his expression. By will alone, Morgan didn't look away. Sweat beaded along his neckline, not only from the stagnant air in the study. He ignored it as his comfort plummeted.

When the itch grew too great, Morgan swiped the back of his neck, wiping away the line of sweat. He met his superior's gaze as he confessed, "I am freeing my source from her influence, along with any other patriot she'd sunk her claws into. This can't be allowed to continue."

Strickland's eyebrows climbed. Morgan was stating an intention—he wasn't asking permission. What was the point of winning a war if the people they were tasked to protect became collateral damage, anyway?

"Are you going to tell me who this source is?"

Morgan clenched his jaw. "I will not."

You either trust me in this, or you don't. Considering that Strickland had assigned a spy to follow Morgan's movements, it seemed more likely that the spymaster didn't trust him.

"I could hazard a guess," Strickland warned.

The duke clasped his hands together again. "It would be just that, a guess, until such a time as I rectify the situation. Then I will, of course, report to you in full."

With a harrumph, Strickland stood. He paced to the sideboard and poured himself a drink. Morgan never took his eyes off of the spymaster, though the set of the man's shoulders remained as casual as if they spoke of the weather instead of the weight of the war.

His back still turned, Strickland swirled the liquid in his glass. He sipped before he asked, "This unnamed source. Will he agree to become a double agent for us, to pass us information and give Lady Whitewood only what we tell him?"

Morgan hesitated. There it was, a solution that spared Jared the hangman's noose. But in so doing, it kept him in a dangerous position. Morgan couldn't answer for him, not without speaking to the young man—and likely to Phil, as well. "I don't know," he answered softly.

The door smacked into his shoulder as it opened behind him. Jared, not seeming to realize that he'd marched in on a private conversation, let alone walloped a duke in so doing, stormed abreast of Morgan and announced, "I do. I'll do it."

Chapter Twenty-Three

Phil watched the spymaster, Strickland, enter the dark, humid London air. The front door swung shut behind him with a note of finality. Her ears rang.

She looked to Morgan for confirmation. Surely she couldn't have heard right. Jared was supposed to be set free of spying, not drawn even deeper into the web as a double agent. His face was set, his jaw determined.

Her chin wobbled. "How did this happen?"

With aching clarity, she recalled the day Mr. O'Neill had come into the invention room. At first, she'd thought Papa had returned from the fair where he'd gone to display his inventions. Instead, their butler stood in the doorway, his face drawn as if he carried a great weight. God, she'd thought she'd split in two from the grief of the news. Jared hadn't been any better. She'd clung to him, her only living family, and they'd somehow survived that troublesome time. If someone were to come to her door and tell her that *he* had passed on... She didn't think she could bear it. Not her baby brother.

She pressed her hand to her mouth to contain a sob. "Jared, how could you? Don't you realize how dangerous this will be? We were going to get you out of this devilish business."

His face hardened. He drew away from her. "I'm not a child."

The pain in her chest gained a sharp edge. She felt as though she was drowning beneath the weight. "I know, but—"

Morgan stepped in, cutting off the light from the candles beside the door. He steered Jared past the staircase and into the parlor. "She's worried about you. Let me speak with her alone a moment. It won't help anyone if you get into a row."

Jared's chin turned mulish. Phil recognized that look. He was about to argue with Morgan instead. Although they stood the same height, Morgan had ten years' experience on Jared and didn't look concerned.

"I'm going to do this," Jared warned.

"Did I speak a word otherwise? I want a moment alone with your sister."

The younger man's mouth eased from its stubborn line, but he still looked surly.

Morgan leaned his head closer and lowered his voice. Phil strained her ears to hear.

"It's been a long night. We're all tired. Why don't you make yourself comfortable in the sitting room? I'll bring Phil in to join you once she's cooled off."

Phil bristled. What did he mean by that?

Her brother nodded and slipped into the parlor without further argument. He must be wrung out after the day. Come to think of it, so was she.

When Morgan turned to her, she lost all desire to fight with him. He looked just as concerned as she felt. He held out his hand and she slipped hers into it, letting herself be led to the staircase. They sat on the hard steps, their thighs and sides pressed together in the narrow space. When he lifted his arm to encircle her shoulders, she laid her head against his chest.

"I know how you feel, Phil, but arguing won't help."

His words rumbled through his chest, vibrating against the side of her face before they emerged softly into the air. She sighed, burrowing her face deeper into his waistcoat.

He laid a kiss on the top of her head before he added, "My younger brother is a spy as well."

"Gideon? Is he in the thick of danger the way my brother will be?"

Morgan lifted his head. She turned her face up to meet his gaze. The angle of the shadows made his face unreadable. "Gideon, no. At least, not yet. But Tristan is always doing fieldwork. In fact, if he wasn't on his honeymoon, you would have met him and not me. I usually contribute from behind a desk."

Her brother was going to be looking the enemy in the eye every time he went on an assignment and that scared her to death. But knowing that Morgan wouldn't be doing the same made her giddy. He'd come to mean so much to her. She couldn't stand to lose him any more than she could her brother.

"Is it wrong that I'm relieved to hear that? You have so much to offer. You don't need to put yourself in harm's way."

He kissed her forehead. As he pulled away, their eyes met. The air between them charged with energy and promise. His gaze dropped to her mouth. Phil didn't so much as breathe, for fear that she would spoil the moment.

Despite the longing on his face, Morgan pulled away again. He loosened his arm around her shoulders as he shifted marginally, as far as the steps allowed. The shoulder opposite her was pressed against the wall.

He cleared his throat. "I believe you now, but believe it or not, I used to be jealous of my brother's forays into the field."

"Why?"

With a sheepish look, he shrugged. "I felt like he was contributing more than I was."

"How can you say that?" She shook her head. "You have so much to contribute! Just look at the speed with which you decoded those messages tonight. I can't imagine being able to do so as fast."

A smile played across his lips as he ducked his head. The light shifted across his cheeks, showing them a bit more pink than usual. "We all have our place. I can't stop my brothers from spying, but I can be there to support them as they need it." His smile turned rueful. "At this point, I'm going to have a full head of gray hair by the time I turn forty. I can't help but worry about them, and I'm not asking you to stop, either."

"But I can't keep Jared from doing this." She'd known it the moment he'd confessed what had happened. He wasn't the sweet, heartbroken fifteen-year-old who had leaned on her when their parents died. Hell, he would be a father soon, if they were able to reunite him with Claire.

Morgan squeezed her shoulders. "You can't. I intend to have a long talk with Jared about his future and the dangers involved, but ultimately, it will be his decision."

She sighed. "Do you think there's a chance it won't be necessary? If we arrest Lady Whitewood..."

"A double agent would be an immeasurable help to Britain."

She turned away. "I don't care a whit about Britain. I care about keeping my family in one piece! He's all I have left." Tears sprung to her eyes, and she wasn't quick enough to blink them away this time.

When she tried to rise out of Morgan's embrace, he tucked her into his side once more. He rubbed her back as she wept into his collar.

"I know. Believe me, I know." His voice was tight with worry, but warm with understanding.

He did know. He had to face it every day. How could he be so strong when he watched his brothers dive into danger? She didn't know how she was going to be able to stand aside and let Jared do it all by himself. She fixed things. That was the sort of person she was. But this couldn't be fixed.

Morgan whispered, "You have me now, too. And my family. They're no substitute for yours, but I'm sure you'll come to love them just as much."

He spoke as if they were married, or would be soon. Was he proposing to her? With her eyes swollen from crying and her face no doubt blotchy, it wasn't precisely the proposal she had envisioned. She didn't say a word, but relaxed into his embrace.

After a while, Morgan's chest stirred beneath her cheek. He urged her to her feet. "Come, my dear. Let's find your brother and mine. We still need to formulate a plan to deal with Lady Whitewood and her blackmail. Let's not think on the problems of the future until we've solved this one."

She nodded and slipped her hand into his as they rose. When she started to toe off her boots to leave them beside the front door, he looked at her askance.

She shrugged. "I think better without shoes."

With a smile, he swooped in to press his mouth against hers. She indulged him for the moment, while they could. After all, they weren't likely to find much time alone for the next long while.

Chapter Twenty-Four

Morgan and Phil went over the details one more time of their carefully crafted plan to release Jared's lover and baby but still allow him to work as a double agent. Satisfied, they headed toward the drop site. Morgan's stomach had shrunk into a tight, hard knot. He stood next to Phil and Jared as they prepared to lay their trap. The tall buildings in the alley muffled the sounds of London's nightlife. Although they were outside of the clean, safe streets of Mayfair, they hadn't strayed too far. Morgan didn't want the night to turn to disaster through the interference of London's cutthroats and ne'er-do-wells.

A thick fog blanketed the alley this evening. Between the mist of the fog and the drizzle sprinkling from the sky, his exposed skin had a film over it and the outer layer of his clothes was damp.

Catching his hand, Phil gave him a small smile. What small measure of light filled the alley came from the lantern at her feet. Ahead loomed the junction of two alleys where they would execute their plan. The spies he'd dispatched had spent the last two days leaving various rumors, each with the same kernel at the heart: that an inventor was working for the Crown to create a device that would change the tide of the war against Napoleon. By this time, Lady Whitewood's spies should have intercepted one or more variations of that rumor and deduced where the location of the meet was from the scraps of knowledge circulating. He hadn't wanted to make it too obvious, or else the French spy might smell a trap. In order for this to work, it had to be her who arrived to intercept Phil, no one else. He had reached out to as many spies as could be spared in order to keep Lady Whitewood's known associates—and possible spies—occupied so that she would have no choice but to come herself.

"I'll be fine," Phil murmured.

She was to be the bait in this plan, and Morgan couldn't even stand beside her in case she needed him. He'd argued with her on that point, it was too risky. But her stubbornness and independence—the very things he loved most about her—won in the end. Though their rumors hadn't named precisely who the inventor was, it was well known that Phil—or cousin Phil—sold inventions. Morgan wasn't sure if Lady Whitewood knew Phil was really cousin Phil, but since most of London did and, since most of London knew that Phil would trust her designs to no one, they figured it would be in their best interest to have Phil meet with the "spy" from the Crown and hand over the designs. Putting Morgan in that role might have raised Lady Whitewood's suspicions.

In the end he'd had to settle for taking a secondary role. He would be hidden here, further down the alley, with the blasted fog obscuring his view of the proceedings. Gideon had reluctantly agreed to be the lookout. At first he'd proven resistant to the idea of remaining out of sight on the sidelines, but once Morgan had pressed upon him the importance of the role, he had agreed. Not only was Giddy given the light-enhancing goggles and tasked with ensuring that no one sneak up on the meeting, but only he and Morgan were able to make the sound indicating danger. Morgan had settled on the bird-whistle his family had used when playing in the woods as children. Innocuous enough, but distinctive to his ear.

Jared, as the go-between, was less than pleased—but, to Morgan's surprise, his chafing at his role stemmed not from desiring the glory but from the fact that his sister played the bait. Not that, in this instance, there was any glory to be had. Jared knew he had to stay out of sight. If Lady Whitewood saw him where she was expecting to intercept a meeting between English spies she might guess that he had become a double agent and flee before they could capture her.

Once Lady Whitewood arrived and tried to snatch the plans Phil carried, she could be arrested for treason and interrogated. Morgan would satisfy himself with knowing the names of anyone else who knew about Jared's lover and child and then he could see to it that no one else would threaten them. Once he was finished with her, he would send her to Strickland for further questioning. The plan seemed straightforward enough.

Unfortunately, he'd often found that even the simplest of plans tended to turn awry.

"Gideon is in place," Jared announced, his voice soft.

Phil squeezed Morgan's hand and let it drop. "I suppose it's time."

He clenched his hand, wishing he still had hold of her as she strode away from him to the center of the intersection. She carried the lantern with her and placed it at her feet, illuminating her silhouette. She wore a dress tonight, despite her protests. His spies had spread the rumor that Miss St. Gobain, not her "cousin Phil," was the Crown inventor. Morgan wanted to ensure that Lady Whitewood recognized her.

Phil turned, craning her neck as she looked at the building, on the roof of which Giddy laid in wait. What was she doing? She would give away his position. Morgan hadn't had time to train her before they put the plan into play, but he'd thought that not looking at her backup would be common sense. She ran her hand over the rolled up parchment that held their fake invention design, and stepped toward the building where Giddy rested.

Morgan headed her off. "What are you doing?"

She tore her gaze away from the roof to tell him, "Gideon is wearing my LEGs wrong. He won't be able to see anything."

He caught her by the arm as she started to move past him. They'd laid a ladder against the side of the building, where the light of the lantern didn't reach, in order for Jared to reach Giddy easily and relay messages.

"Let Jared do it. You have to wait for Lady Whitewood."

Phil shook her head. Her mouth was mulish. "Jared doesn't use my LEGs. He won't know how to fix it." She thrust the parchment into his hand. "Hold this a minute. I won't be long."

"Phil..." Her name faded into the fog as she did the same. Morgan gritted his teeth. They didn't have time for this.

He chafed as the seconds lengthened. How long did it take to scamper up a ladder and fix a pair of goggles? At this rate, he might have to pretend to deliver the plans in her place.

A crow's caw penetrated the air, making his blood run cold. He and Giddy had settled on two separate signals in case of emergency. A warbler if someone approached, and a crow if someone was in imminent danger.

Phil. Morgan bolted for the ladder, needing to assure himself that she was safe. He palmed the pistol in his pocket with his free hand. The metal handle imprinted itself against his skin.

Jared, instructed to keep out of sight lest Lady Whitewood recognize him, met him at the base of the ladder. Morgan scanned the shadows, but the fog was too thick. He saw nothing. Where was Phil?

"What's wrong?" Jared asked.

Morgan couldn't formulate the words to answer him.

Giddy whistled and slid down the ladder in a long leap as they made room for him at the bottom.

"What's going on?" Morgan asked, his voice hard. Where was Phil? His chest ached, threatening to split in two if the answer wasn't 'safe and sound at home nursing a cup of tea.' Unfortunately, he knew better than that. She would never leave the job unfinished, not with her brother's safety hanging in the balance.

"It's Phil," Gideon said, his voice terse. He tapped the night goggles which he was still wearing. "I finally figured out how to get these things to work just in time to see two men grab Phil as she started up the ladder."

No.

"Where did they go?"

Until Jared caught him by the arm, Morgan didn't realize that his muscles had coiled, ready to chase after Phil.

"If you leave, what will happen with the meeting? Won't Lady Whitewood get suspicious if no one shows up? She may not fall for it a second time."

Morgan shook the young man off. "We'll figure out something else." He didn't have to mull over the dilemma of serving his country or saving the woman he loved. Phil's safety was paramount. Lawks, he never would have agreed to this if he'd thought for a moment she would be in danger, out of his sight.

"Let me do it."

Morgan gritted his teeth. Every second he spent arguing was another second that Phil's kidnappers used to get further away.

"We don't have time to argue," Gideon snapped. "I can follow them by rooftop. I'll make the crow caw as I go. Morgan, you can follow that to catch up." The ladder creaked as Giddy climbed it.

"Be careful," Morgan said, an automatic reflex that his brother didn't bother answering. Knowing that Gideon was on the trail, Morgan was able to take a full breath, then another. He battled for clarity. Could they complete the mission for Britain and save Phil at the same time?

His instincts said no.

"Lady Whitewood knows your face. The moment she recognizes you, she'll realize the rumor is a trap."

"She won't see my face. She doesn't know me that well and I'll turn up my collar and keep my hat low."

Jared demonstrated. The light of the lantern, still set in the junction of the alleys, didn't illuminate far enough for Morgan to tell whether or not the ruse worked.

"If she even suspects..."

The call of a crow punctuated the air toward the north. The muscles in Morgan's back relaxed a bit, knowing that his brother was on Phil's trail. With the light-enhancing goggles, hopefully he would be able to follow Phil without trouble. He, too, was armed with a pistol, as were Phil and Jared. Morgan hadn't wanted to take any chances of something going awry tonight...as it obviously had.

"My future is at stake," Jared argued, his voice flat.

Another caw.

"I know what will happen if she suspects. She won't. She'll think I'm the English spy Phil was handing the plans off to."

Caw. Fainter, this time. Gideon was moving out of hearing distance. Morgan cocked his ears for the sound of a gun report, in case Giddy had to use his pistol to keep Phil alive. They didn't know what these brigands wanted with her. They could be opportunists or they could have been sent by Lady Whitewood.

The thought chilled Morgan.

The young man added, "I only need to fool her long enough for her to try to steal the design. Once she does, it doesn't matter if she sees my face, because I can arrest her."

Morgan didn't want to leave Jared to complete his first mission alone, but every fiber in his body urged him to go after the woman he loved. The crow calls were getting quieter and fewer between.

Lady Whitewood was only one woman. Jared should be able to handle her, even untrained as he was.

"You won't have backup," Morgan warned. "If something goes awry, it's up to you to fix it."

"Go and save my sister. I can look after myself."

Those were the only words Morgan needed to hear. Maybe he would get an earful from Phil later about leaving her brother—in fact, he hoped he did. It would mean that she was alive to berate him. Once he had her in his arms, neither one of them were ever venturing into the field again. He would shut them up in his office and lock the door. Or better yet, his bedroom. He did need to father an heir, as his mother constantly reminded him.

He handed his pistol to Jared. "Just in case you need a second shot."

The young man nodded and stuffed it into his pocket. He reached for the rolled parchment.

Morgan shook his head, pulling it out of reach. "We need to go through with the handoff. Whitewood will want to be certain these are the plans before she takes action and she is expecting Phil—or her cousin—to hand them to the English spy. By now, rumors of my association with your sister have probably circulated. I'm easily recognizable. In case Lady Whitewood has someone watching, it will look like I'm passing the designs off to you on Phil's behalf. I'll wait by the lantern. Count to twenty and come out after me."

Jared didn't argue. Good. No matter how he strained his ears, he couldn't hear his brother's call at all anymore. What if he lost Gideon's position? It would be tantamount to losing Phil.

He squared his shoulders. He had to do this right. After that, he didn't care if the world crumbled around his ears, so long as he found and saved Phil.

His heart throbbed painfully in his throat as he took measured strides to the junction of the alleys. He skirted the shadowed edge to come into the light from another angle. Once he reached the lantern, he stopped. He counted the seconds as he strained his ears for the sound of a bird call. Nothing.

By the time he counted to ten, Jared strode from the alley opposite him. His jacket collar stood stiff, shielding his neck. The brim of his hat obscured his eyes as he ducked his head, hunching as if to ward away the chill of the fog.

Jared stopped as he came apace with Morgan. "You've got it?" His voice was lower than usual, disguised.

Morgan nodded with approval. He handed the rolled-up parchment to Jared. "It's all yours," he said, trying to impress into the tone of his voice a warning for the young man to look out for himself.

Jared met his gaze, nodded, and tucked the paper under his arm. Morgan turned his back, taking the north alley away from the meet-up. The moment the shadows and fog closed in around him, he broke into a sprint.

Phil was in danger and he hadn't another second to waste.

Off the main thoroughfare, the road was packed dirt strewn with sludge, the origins of which he didn't want to contemplate. His boots squelched as he squinted through the night, trying to avoid chunks of cobblestone or rubbish that might trip him. A cat yowled as it scampered out of his way.

Ahead, he heard a faint caw. Relief weakened his knees and he nearly tripped over the pigeon carcass that the cat had been ripping to shreds. He found his footing and put on a burst of speed. Phil needed him.

He staggered to a halt as he heard another sound, this one from behind him. Was that a warbler? The thick fog obscured the alley more than four feet away.

There it was again, louder. His heart beating quickly, Morgan mirrored the call. Muffled footsteps sounded, growing louder. A figure separated from the fog, tall and lean.

"Jared?"

He panted as he slid to a halt next to Morgan, bracing his hands on his knees.

"Why aren't you at the exchange? There's hardly been time for Lady Whitewood to attempt to steal the plans and for you to arrest her."

"Bugger the exchange. My sister is in danger." Jared's voice was steely. He straightened, squaring his shoulders.

Morgan's thoughts reeled as he factored in the changes to the haphazard plan forming in his mind. The details depended upon finding Phil, first. "I thought you wanted to secure your future."

"Phil is a part of my future. We'll have to catch Lady Whitewood another way, once my sister is safe."

At least he'd finally realized that.

Morgan clapped the young man on the shoulder. "Let's not tarry." They set off at a run, following his brother's signal.

The crow calls came at regular intervals, clearly discernible. After this was all said and done, he would have to speak to Gideon about varying the signal so it sounded more natural and was less likely to be noticed by enemies. For now, he trudged toward that sound with single-minded purpose. He soon realized that it was no longer moving; he was approaching it. The call grew louder and clearer as he approached. With Jared next to him, he slowed, rubbing the stitch in his side as he searched for his brother or Phil.

The caw sounded again. He jumped. It sounded like it came from on top of him. When he craned his head back, he could barely discern the shape of the house against the foggy night sky, let alone whether or not someone waited on the roof.

He lifted his hands to his lips and made the warbler call.

No response. Had that last caw come from an actual crow? Morgan held his breath as he waited. He heard nothing else.

Chapter Twenty-Five

The brigand's grip on Phil's arm was hard enough to bruise. She shook like a leaf as he towed her through the stinking alleys, his partner on her other side with his hand bunched in her dress. Panic dominated her thoughts along with her pounding pulse and for the most frightening moments of her life, she wasn't able to think. She could only feel her kidnapper's rough skin, smell the whiskey on his breath mingled with sewage as they deterred into a decrepit neighborhood, hear the rough patter of her heartbeat and the occasional caw of a crow. The fog muffled the clomp of her captors' footsteps on the ground. The dampness chilled her skin. From time to time, they passed a window with a ghostly-pale face in it, one that soon turned away as if they didn't see her. Her tongue took up too much space in her mouth to talk, even if she could even find the breath to do so. Several times, she stumbled, her knees buckling, only to be hauled onward by the rough men on either side. They'd spoken sparingly when they'd caught her, indecipherable with the roaring in her ears. Now, neither man spoke a word. They didn't even look at each other.

The first thought that re-entered her mind was of Morgan. She batted it away, searching for something useful, but it clung to her like seaweed. The shape of his mouth, the way he fingered the white streak in his hair when he thought, the way his piercing gray eyes darkened moments before he kissed her. None of those things would help her out of this dire situation, but she couldn't rid herself of them. She wanted to see him again with a desperation that defied logic.

That desperate desire solidified, turning into a pillar around which she could build her escape plan. After all, if she was going to see him again, she would have to escape.

She was on her own. That vital thought cut her deeper than she'd thought it would. Ever since her parents had died, she'd been on her own. But now, with Morgan, she had a partner. Someone to always stand beside her. Someone to save her from danger.

Except he couldn't follow her. The fog was too thick, they were in the middle of a pivotal spying mission for Britain, and by the time he realized she was gone, it would be too late. The brigands had snatched her from the ladder when she'd gone to help Gideon don the LEGs correctly. He'd been fumbling, twisting them, getting them all wrong. Without the goggles, he wouldn't have seen her. Why had she insisted on going alone?

No, blame wouldn't help the situation. She had to think clearly. It had all happened so fast—the man's hand over her mouth cutting off her air, being ripped from the ladder and carried away. She'd thrashed, to no avail, and then the numbness had set in.

She wasn't numb anymore. And she was going to get out of this.

The men slowed their breakneck pace. Phil's legs held her better than before, but she pretended otherwise. She stumbled, letting the men catch her as she trembled. She widened her eyes so far that the sting of the stink made them water. Until that moment, she'd never seen the value of acting like a ninny. Right now, it would be to her advantage if they underestimated her.

A house loomed out of the darkness. The stucco was chipped, along with the ratty paint on the door. Were those scratch marks marring the paint? They rose as high as her shoulder. The windows facing the alley were boarded up with smoke-streaked wooden boards and rusty nails that jutted out. The brigand holding her dress released her to shoulder open the door. He preceded his cohort into the lamp-lit room inside. As she was shoved through the entryway, she stumbled over the raised lip of flooring. The brigand holding her tightened his grip. She yelped as her arm was nearly yanked from its socket. She staggered to get her feet beneath her again.

A toss of her head shook away the auburn strands obscuring her gaze and provided her the first glimpse of her captors. She would rather not have seen them. The one across the room was as tall and broad as Morgan, with a crooked cast to his nose, a short beard of unkempt stubble along his chin, and bushy hair snarled into a rat's nest. The one next to her had a patch over his eye, a pink scar poking out of the bottom. She shuddered, her mind conjuring gruesome images of the tissue beneath that black patch. In front of an unlit hearth stood the puppet master of Phil's kidnapping.

Lady Whitewood.

Phil's heartbeat kicked into a gallop as she stared into the woman's cold, cruel eyes. She knew. How had she known that this was a trap?

Ice flooded Phil's veins. The floor in here was just as grimy as the dirt outside. Her shoes scraped against it as Patch dragged her to one of two pieces of furniture in the wide room. A wooden chair that didn't even look good enough for kindling rested next to Lady Whitewood. Along the right wall, where the lamp stood, was a table that seemed to have been put together by spare boards, none the same length.

Patch shoved her into the chair. It creaked alarmingly as Phil clutched the arms for balance. Her heartbeat pounded painfully in the base of her throat. *Think.* What would they do with her now?

The reticule on her wrist weighed heavy with the muff gun Morgan had insisted she carry. She couldn't pull it out, not with both fearsome men and Lady Whitewood staring at her. She would never reach it before they snatched away her only weapon. Could she fool them and grab it in the distraction?

There were three of them and she had only one bullet. What could she do? She started to tremble, for real this time. She pressed her lips together as she examined the room. She faced the front door, where she'd come in. Both men were in the way of freedom. There had to be another door out of sight behind her but she hadn't marked where.

Lady Whitewood sneered as she sashayed into Phil's line of sight. The French spy glared at her lackeys. "I told you to bring the inventor."

Patch nodded. "You said the 'un waiting wit' the plans. That's who we brought."

Whitewood narrowed her eyes at Phil's hands. "She has no plans, you fool."

Patch looked confused. "But she had 'em in her hand afore we grabbed her."

The spy whirled to face Patch, her fists balled at her sides. "I said the *inventor*, Phil..." She trailed off, her eyes narrowing as she swung to face Phil.

Hell and damnation! She must have put together that "Cousin Phil" and Philomena St. Gobain were the same person. Phil curled her fingers toward her wrist, searching out the mouth of her reticule. It was out of reach. Could she run?

The lamp light glinted off the barrel of a pistol as Lady Whitewood withdrew the weapon from the cloak swathing her figure. "You idiots! Don't you know who she is?"

"The inventor," Patch grumbled, sullen. His expression pulled at the pink tissue peeking out from beneath his eyepatch.

"No." Irritation flashed across the traitor's face. "She's Tenwick's lover. He's a spy for England. I caught him snooping in my room."

Morgan. His face flashed across Phil's closed eyelids as she blinked. She had to think of a way to escape. Would Lady Whitewood harm him, too? Phil canted her wrist, trying to tilt her reticule near enough to pry open the strings with one hand.

Patch chuckled. "I bet she's only taking the credit and that duke of hers did all the work."

Lady Whitewood's arm vibrated with the force of her anger. Would she shoot Phil by accident?

"*That duke* was likely watching her. The Crown could be on its way here now."

Unfortunately, Phil knew the truth of that statement.

Lady Whitewood, on the other hand, looked sickly pale. Her mouth was tight and thin. She rounded the chair, striding out of sight. The click, click, click of her heels echoed off the wood floor.

"Wait until I'm gone, then kill her."

Phil's fingers slipped on the drawstring to her reticule. Her heart skipped a beat. *No.* She had nowhere to run. The two ruffians blocked her path out the front, and Lady Whitewood blocked her way out the back.

"What of the plans?" Patch muttered under his breath as he pulled a gun from his pocket and cocked it.

She still had leverage. "I have the plans," she lied. Her voice was high and thin.

Patch hesitated, waiting. His companion shifted from foot to foot.

Unfortunately, she had nothing to give them. She'd passed off the fake scroll to Morgan so she didn't have to climb with it. She didn't even have her pocketbook with her ideas in it. All she had was...

The muff gun.

"The plans are in my reticule. I'll get it for you," she said, keeping her voice small. "Then you'll let me go?"

"That's right, love. Give us the plans and we'll let you go."

Liar.

She opened the drawstring on her reticule and slipped her hand inside. Her heart pounded so loud, it was the only sound that filled her head. She only had one shot. Mustering her courage, she cocked the gun as she yanked the reticule off. She hurled the sack in the face of the nearest assailant, Bushy, and raised her other hand and aimed at Patch.

Chapter Twenty-Six

Just as Morgan's lungs started to ache from holding his breath to better hear Gideon's caw, a muffled thump rent the air along with muttered cursing. Morgan exhaled with relief. He pinched Jared's sleeve and drew them closer to the house, away from the narrow street as he squinted to see his brother.

Evidently, Gideon was able see better than he could, because Giddy muttered, "It took you long enough."

Morgan nearly jumped out of his skin. His brother was standing right beside him. Blast this fog!

"Where is she?" Morgan demanded.

Gideon lifted his arm. Morgan squinted, following the line of his sleeve as he pointed across the street. Jared coiled to move, but Morgan held him back.

"Take a breath. We need to assess the situation first."

Unfortunately, Morgan couldn't see a damn thing. With an exasperated huff, Giddy tore the goggles from his face and held them out.

"Here."

As Morgan lifted the light-enhancing goggles to his face, his brother muttered, "Wow. Those things really do make a difference."

The street, slathered in shades of gray, came into a dull kind of focus, like a blunt knife. Thanks to the goggles, he could make out the silhouette of a ramshackle building across the street. The bottom windows were boarded up. On one of the second-floor windows, a shutter hung loose. A thin, sputtering sort of light seeped out from beneath the cracks of the boards on the ground floor.

Gideon said, "She's been in there five minutes or so. No one's come back out."

What were they doing to her? Morgan examined the other buildings nearby, trying to formulate the best line of approach. With his stomach shriveled like a raisin, he couldn't think clearly. All he wanted to do was kick down the front door. Given the way Jared shifted, antsy, he had the same thought. But if either of them did that, one of the ruffians might kill her.

"Did you get a good look at her attackers?"

"It was too quick. Burly low-class fellows, though, and it sounded to me like they were hired help, from the snippets of conversation I was able to catch."

Morgan stripped off the goggles and returned them to his brother. "Stay here and keep watch. I'll circle the house and see if there's a better mode of entry than the front door. Then I'll meet you here so we can—"

A gunshot rippled through the air, cutting off his words. He clapped his hand to his chest, sure that it would be wet with blood. He felt as though his heart had burst.

Phil.

He charged across the street to the abandoned building, the other two men hot on his heels. God, what would he find inside? He banished the image of her cold, bloody body on the ground as he turned his shoulder to the door to break it down.

Please, God. Let me not be too late.

Chapter Twenty-Seven

The vibration and recoil numbed Phil's hand. The gun dropped to the ground, useless. She had no more balls or powder to reload, let alone the time to do so. The floor shook as Patch collapsed in a heap. A sharp tang stung her nose. She had to get out of here.

She bolted from the chair and dashed toward the nearest door, behind her. Lady Whitewood blocked the entrance. As wood splintered behind Phil, the French spy levered her gun and shot.

The bullet hit Phil beneath her breast bone. She doubled over, stumbling through the doorway deeper into the house as she fought to retain her balance. The pain was crippling, mind-numbing. She couldn't take a breath. White spots marred the silhouette of the corridor.

I'll need to fix that. Phil had one last absent thought before the hot flare of pain consumed her.

Lady Whitewood's footsteps grew fainter, but a stampede thundered in the front of the house. She needed a place to hide. She groped along a hall until she found another door, unlocked.

A heart-rending crash sounded behind her. The blood roared in her ears as she stumbled into the dark room and slipped to the ground beside the closed door to the hall. She pressed her palm to her middle. The lightest touch sent a renewed jolt of pain through her. She fought to think.

She'd left one man uninjured. If he barreled in, she would run past him and out the front door. Was there anything in here she could use as a weapon?

In the dark, her mind's eye conjured the image of Patch's shocked face as he collapsed. Had she killed him? Did he have a family? She wiped her damp cheeks, refusing to give in to hysteria. She wasn't done fighting yet. She had a family to return to, as well. She wasn't yet ready to die.

The swell of pain subsided enough for her hearing to return. She panted as she strained her ears. The sounds of tussling in the other room ceased. Silence rang throughout the house. What was happening? This might be her only chance to escape. Was there a back entrance through this room?

"Phil?"

Morgan? She rose onto her knees, her limbs trembling as she fumbled with the door latch. "Over here." Her voice was weak, breathless. Did he hear her?

Footsteps resounded down the hall. Morgan's or someone else's. As they came close, she mustered her strength and called, "Morgan?"

"Right here, love."

It *was* him. By will alone, she staggered to her feet and flung herself into his arms. The strong beat of his heart echoed in her ear as she laid her head on his warm chest. Tears leaked from her eyes, growing thicker. She tried to hold them back. She didn't want him to think she was a watering pot in a critical situation.

He pulled her into the corridor and shut the door. "Are you in here alone?"

"Lady Whitewood ran out the back." Her voice was a bit more wobbly than usual.

"I saw her... and I saw..." Morgan ran his hands over her face, her neck, her shoulders, then he held her at arms length, sucking in a breath when he saw the hole in the fabric of her dress right over the throbbing spot beneath her breast bone. He pressed the heel of his hand against the spot. She fell limp against him at the roar of pain that shot through her.

"Come into the light. We'll fetch a physician. You'll be fine."

Adjusting his hold on her, he half-carried her toward the main room. Her faculties returned as the shift of his palm no longer dug into her injury.

"I'm fine now." Her voice was breathless.

His arm tightened around her. He buried his face in her hair. "Yes, love of course you are. Can you wiggle your fingers and toes for me?" His voice was thick with tears. It wavered as he struggled to keep his tone even and soft.

Phil gathered her strength and pushed his hand away from her middle. At least, she tried. He held firm.

"My extremities are in perfect order."

He shifted, pressing his hand firmly against her again, and her breath fled. She weakened. Through sheer stubbornness, she forced out the words, "I can't breathe when you do that."

"I need to keep pressure on the wound."

"There's no wound." Her head spun as she gasped for air.

"Phil, love, I saw her shoot you."

"Do you feel any blood?"

His touch lightened, uncertain. She took shallow breaths. Too deep and the sharp pain stabbed her. Thankful for his hold on her, since her knees refused to cooperate, she slid her hand beneath his, groping for the bullet. It had lodged near the bottom of her sternum. Her gloves were slippery as she worked it free.

As he touched the blood-free bullet, Morgan's body stiffened around her. "How?" His voice was hoarse. He groped around the area, his fingers finding the hole in her dress and exploring the rigid material beneath. "What are you wearing?"

"An armored corset." Without the round bullet pressing against her sternum, it was easier to breathe, albeit she still couldn't draw a deep breath. She'd certainly bruised herself, and had perhaps cracked a few bones. "Tonight seemed like a good opportunity to test it."

"You didn't bloody well know if it would work?" His voice gained a desperate edge as he leaned them against the wall to the corridor.

She shrugged. "I didn't set out to be shot. And it did work. They didn't hurt me. I think I hurt them."

"That's the woman I love." His voice was warm. It granted her strength. "But please, don't ever do that to me again."

Light from the ajar door leading to the main room seeped out to frame his features. For a moment, she hadn't been sure whether or not she'd ever see him again. She reached up, tracing the line of his cheek.

"I didn't think you were coming."

He caught her hand and pressed his lips to her dirty gloves. "Always. I would never leave you. God, I thought my heart was breaking."

"I'm fine."

He helped her into the main room, supporting her weight. The longer she walked, the steadier on her feet she became. When she spotted the carnage, her knees weakened again. Blood seeped from Patch's prone body. If he wasn't dead, he would be soon. There was too much blood. Bile rose in the back of her throat and she looked away, to where Gideon was tying up the unconscious kidnapper. The man didn't look so fearsome with a gag in his mouth and his arms and legs twisted behind his back. They were the only men in the room.

"Where's my brother? Where's Jared?"

Morgan met his brother's gaze and swore under his breath. "He ran out after Lady Whitewood. We have to find him."

Gideon's mouth was thin. His face was abnormally pale, but when he spoke his voice was firm. "I'll stay here in case he wakes up. We need to send him to Strickland, right?"

Morgan nodded. "Thank you."

Turning her back on the dead man, Phil bolted for the door to the corridor. Renewed strength flooded her limbs. She ignored the throbbing in her torso. She didn't have time to fall apart just yet. She had to make sure that her brother was all right. Morgan hurried on her heels, his hand never leaving her back, as if he was afraid to be parted from her again.

Painted in black and gray shadows, the house was a maze, but not a large one. Upon trying each door, she and Morgan soon found an exit, still ajar and slapping against the side of the house with an idle breeze. They stumbled into the misty, fetid London air. Morgan caught her hand and led her onward. She hiked up her skirt only high enough that she wouldn't trip on it. She didn't care if the hem was soiled.

Faint sounds of a tussle led them onward. Her throat constricted. What if Lady Whitewood recognized Jared and realized that he'd switched to working for Britain? If she got away and told her superiors, his life might be forfeit. That was, if she didn't kill him herself. Phil put on a burst of speed, even though it made her injury throb.

She stopped short in the packed dirt alley, stumbling over her feet as a gunshot rang out. In her mind's eye, blood bloomed across the chest of a man. Only, this time, that deathly pale face was Jared. She tried to scream, but couldn't find the breath.

When she tried to lurch forward, Morgan wrapped his arm around her waist, pulling her against his body. She struggled. "Stay calm, Phil. You can't gallop into the middle of a gunfight. We have to see what's going on."

She fought tears, but nodded. "He could be hurt."

He slipped his hand into hers again. "We'll find out."

Together, they raced toward the meeting place. When they neared a junction of the alleys, Morgan slowed. He edged in front of her, blocking her view. He groped at his pocket, but didn't emerge with a gun.

She didn't have one either. She'd wasted her one shot on Patch, never thinking that this meeting would devolve into something so dangerous. *Jared...*

The thinning fog blanketed the intersection. By squinting, she discerned a tall, thin silhouette.

"Jared?"

The word slipped from her lips without permission. Morgan's hand on hers flexed as he urged her back against the nearest building.

The figure croaked, "I had to shoot her."

Relief weakened her knees. It was her brother. "Jared." She yanked free of Morgan's hold and dashed to her brother's side. The shadows painted his face in black and white. He stared at a writhing bundle on the ground some paces away. The air was sharp with a familiar, sickening tang. The bundle moaned.

"What happened?"

The gun slipped from Jared's fingers to clatter onto the packed dirt by his feet. "She was getting away. I tried to shoot her leg, but with the cloak..." He groped for Phil's hand, clutching it fiercely. She wanted to throw her arms around his neck. He was safe.

Wait...had he fatally injured Lady Whitewood?

Morgan crouched by the figure. In the dim light, the cloth bundle looked burgundy. A closer inspection showed that at least some of that was blood. A lot of blood.

The duke swore under his breath as he doffed his jacket. He wadded and pressed it against Lady Whitewood. She emitted a strangled sound between a scream and a sob. "You shot her in the arse. She'll live, but we should get her to a surgeon as soon as possible. Do you think you can find your way back to the carriage?"

"I think so."

"Then fetch it here. After that, I'll need you to run to Lord Strickland and tell him what's happened tonight. He'll expect a full report later, but in the meantime, he needs to prepare to receive Lady Whitewood and the man Giddy arrested."

As Jared bolted into the night to complete his task, Phil dropped to her knees next to Morgan. Her legs didn't want to hold her anymore. "What can I do? If you think I'll sit around—"

"Can you put pressure here to slow the bleeding? I have to return to the house," Morgan said. He guided her hands into the right position. Lady Whitewood had stopped whimpering. In fact, she might have fainted. "With all these gun shots, I have no doubt that the Bow Street Runners will have been fetched. We aren't terribly far from Bow Street. They'll likely arrive within half an hour, and I can't leave Gideon to deal with the Runners on his own."

Phil tilted her face up to his. "Do you want me to wait for you here?"

"Once Jared returns with the carriage, take Lady Whitewood to Strickland. He'll arrange for a surgeon to remove the bullet and stitch her wound shut."

She clenched her jaw. "If you think you're leaving me behind—"

He reached out to squeeze her arm. "I'd rather have you by my side. If you think Jared can handle the transport on his own, come back to the house once she's on her way to Strickland. We'll help my brother together."

Together. That was a concept Phil preferred, especially after the night she'd weathered. She was afraid to let him out of her sight. She nodded. "I'll see it gets done. You can trust me to handle this."

"I know I can. You're the strongest woman I know. It's one of the things I love best about you."

She glowed from his parting words, the warmth helping to banish the terrible ache in her torso. As he strode away with purpose, she smiled and whispered to herself, "It's one of the things I love best about you, too."

She shifted to apply renewed pressure on the wound as she awaited her brother.

Chapter Twenty-Eight

Not wanting to let her go even for an instant, Morgan nestled Phil against his side as they mounted the stairs to his townhouse. Their steps, along with Gideon who trailed them, were leaden. If it wasn't near to four of the morning, Morgan would eat his socks.

Candles were aglow in the entryway, though the butler was not at his station. The moment Morgan unlocked the door and led the way inside, Jared stopped pacing the interior. His hair stuck up at all angles.

"There you are! It's about time."

Morgan swayed on his feet, the night catching up to him. "The damned Runners wanted to take Gideon *and* his man away. It's hard to bribe a patrol with only the shillings in your pocket."

Phil patted his arm. "We convinced them we were working for the Crown."

"Yes, but only after we were detained for a few hours." Morgan sighed. He resisted the urge to rub the streak in his hair. It would involve releasing Phil, and that he absolutely refused to do.

He led the way into the parlor, so they could rest their weary legs. Without asking, Jared poured out four tumblers of brandy and passed them around. No one protested the offer of spirits. Morgan sipped on his as he settled against the arm of the settee, Phil's warm body at his side.

"What did Strickland say?" Morgan asked when he caught a second wind.

Jared, slumped in the nearest armchair, shrugged and rubbed his eyes. "He was sorry not to be able to interrogate Lady Whitewood straight off, but the physician said she would be conscious before long. Strickland told me to await instructions from her replacement."

Beside Morgan, Phil tensed, but she didn't say a word.

He asked, "Then you intend to become a double agent?"

The young man scowled. "I said I would, didn't I?"

"You did, but I won't hold you to it if you'd like to back out."

"Strickland might."

Morgan straightened, trying to infuse his stance with as much authority as he could, given the circumstances. "Let me deal with Strickland."

Jared knocked back the last of his brandy and set the glass on the table. "I want to do this. It's important work."

It was. Morgan rubbed at Phil's shoulder as her muscles bunched, trying to help her to relax.

To her brother, he said, "You proved your mettle tonight. But if you're going to do this, *I* will be training you."

Jared frowned. "You train spies?"

Morgan chuckled under his breath, but he couldn't muster much mirth, given the scare he'd had tonight. "It's what I do best. You'll be in good hands."

Beside him, Phil straightened. "If Morgan's to train you, then *I'll* outfit you."

He turned his head to look her in the face. Her mouth was set, determined. Her eyes glinted. "What do you mean?"

"My inventions can be useful."

"You've proven that already," he said, his voice dry. "I doubt Strickland will turn you away."

"Good." She raised her chin. "Jared's the only family I have, and I'm going to see him safe."

He was safe, wasn't he? Somehow, Morgan and Phil had managed to get him out from under the threat of the hangman's noose for treason. That meant... Morgan wouldn't have to do something that would make her hate him.

He thrust his drink onto the table and slid off the settee, onto one knee. He transferred his hold from around Phil's shoulders to her hand.

"He doesn't have to be. I could give you more family than you can handle. Marry me?"

His stomach shrank as Phil frowned at him. That was not the look a woman should wear when she accepted a proposal from the man she loved. She wasn't going to laugh in his face again, was she?

"Now?"

One single, incredulous word.

He cleared his throat. "Well, not this exact moment. I'll need to procure a special license first."

She smirked. "No, I mean you're asking me *now?* We're sweaty and filthy and I...I killed a man tonight." Her voice warbled, but she firmed her chin, looking brave.

He squeezed her hand. "And you're still the most beautiful and intelligent woman in the world to me. I'm seizing the moment, like you taught me. Jared is finally out of immediate danger and I can look to the future." He raised her hand to his lips. "I can't envision a future without you by my side. Will you marry me?"

She nibbled on her lower lip. "When you put it that way... Yes. Of course. I love you, Morgan."

He leaned forward, murmuring, "I love you, too," a moment before he melded his mouth to hers.

Jared made a retching sound.

Gideon laughed.

Ah, family.

When they parted, Giddy said, "Lucy is going to be green with envy over missing this. Promise me you'll make it a long engagement. And have many children. Between planning the wedding and doting on babies, that should keep Mother and Lucy occupied enough that they won't turn to harassing *me* next."

Morgan smirked and shook his head. *I wouldn't count on that.* He slid back into the seat next to Phil.

A squawk sounded, followed by the stomp of feet on the stairs. "It's the middle of the bloody night. I do *not* want to take a walk now."

Lucy, her dressing gown agape over her night-gown and her hair in a loose braid over her shoulder, paused in the doorway to the parlor. "What's going on here?"

Gideon grinned. "Morgan and Phil are getting married!"

Lucy squealed so loud, she woke the house.

Epilogue

Four months later

Morgan stretched his neck in the chair at his desk in the St. Gobain townhouse. When he had moved into the house with Phil, since the Tenwick townhouse was a tad full and he didn't have room to create a secret invention room in it, he'd brought over his study desk and chair with him. With the little devices Phil left on his desk from time to time as gifts, the study was starting to feel more and more like home.

He blotted the deciphered report with sand—the latest progress report from Giddy's field-work—and set it in the pile to send to Strickland. Lady Whitewood was well on her way to recovery and would soon even be able to sit without a pile of pillows to cushion her.   Unfortunately, she couldn't be persuaded to give them any information on the French spy network. Strickland wanted Morgan to figure out a way to get her to loosen her tongue and he thought he had an idea that might require Gideon's expertise. Ever since Tristan had returned from his honeymoon, Morgan had gladly retreated behind the desk. Not only did it keep him out of the excitement of the field, which he no longer felt as exciting, but he was never more than a floor away from Phil, also hard at work during the day.

Dimly, he heard a squawk of, "Pickle!" along with Meg's shriek.

Morgan grinned. This was his life now. It wasn't nearly as peaceful as he might have pictured it, but it was full and happy. Every day was exciting, thanks to Phil and the new family he'd inherited when he'd married her. The staff, especially the O'Neills, didn't give a fig's end that they now worked for a duke and duchess. To them, he was still 'lad' to the older staff or 'sir Giant' to the little ones. He loved it.

He glanced at the grandfather clock stuffed in the corner of the study, wondering if it was too soon to entice Phil to take a break for lunch. He hadn't seen her for well over an hour, and he missed her. Odd, considering she was only upstairs in her invention room, but it was true.

A strange whirring, flapping noise grew nearer as Morgan stirred. She must have had the same idea. He rounded the desk and leaned against it, wondering what she had for him now.

The contraption was a metal-and-canvas bird with wings that flapped. Although it miraculously stayed aloft, it had no sense of direction. Morgan lunged to save it before it crashed into the bookcase. The wings continued to flap, slowly winding down. Between them was a small wicker basket. Fishing the small bundle out of the basket, he set the invention on the shelf as he unwrapped his gift.

They were a pair of small light-enhancing goggles. He grinned, holding them up to try to peek through the lens even though there was far too much light streaming through the window.

Phil stepped into the doorway, her figure accentuated by the plain black dress she often wore to work. It looked a bit tighter than usual across her chest and hips. As she flashed him an impish smile, his heart skipped a beat. No woman could possibly be as beautiful as his wife.

Giving in to impulse, he crossed the room to pull her against him and kiss her, slow and thorough. With a sigh, he rested his forehead against hers.

"I missed you."

She chuckled. "I saw you an hour ago."

He grinned as he parted from her. "It seemed more like an eternity."

Pickle squawked, announcing his arrival in time for Morgan to step back and avoid being whacked in the head. The bird settled onto his usual position on Phil's shoulder and cleaned his claws.

Morgan glared at him. What a hog. He got her all day long.

Turning over the goggles in his hand, Morgan asked his wife, "You finished them?" She'd been working night and day, certain she was close.

Her smile grew. "I did. Do you like them?"

He wanted to sweep her into his arms, but was afraid of disturbing the parrot. The last time he had, Pickle had left an unpleasant surprise on Morgan's desk. "I love them, but my dear, they're much too small to fit me."

"They aren't for you. They're for the baby." She laid her hand on her stomach.

"Do you mean—" His breath caught. He stepped closer, startling the bird on her shoulder and earning a buffet from his wing.

Phil nodded. Her eyes brimmed with tears. "I'm pregnant."

Pickle launched into the air with an indignant squawk as Morgan wrapped his arms around his wife. His pregnant wife. They were going to have a baby.

Oh, Lud, they were going to have a baby. Morgan didn't know the first thing about infants. What if he was a horrible father? What if his son tried to do one of the hundred reckless things Morgan had as a child? Worse, what if he had a daughter and she took after Lucy?

Phil rubbed Morgan's back. "I can feel you worrying. Stop it. This is a good thing. We're going to have a family!"

He hugged her tighter. "We already have a family, my dear. But I am so incredibly happy that it will be growing. And scared."

She pulled back to rub the furrow between his eyebrows. "You're going to give yourself more gray hairs."

Deeper in the mansion, Pickle called out, "I'm pregnant! Pregnant Pickle!"

Morgan smirked. "Well, that's one way to break the news to the staff."

Phil grinned. "Imagine when we tell your family."

Mother and Lucy would probably try to move in with them.

With a wicked smile, Phil shut the door and leaned back against it. "Why don't we celebrate while we still have a modicum of privacy?"

That, he wouldn't turn down. "You were away for an eternity."

"An hour," she said with a laugh.

He stepped closer to kiss her. "To me, they are the same thing."

She gasped as he brushed his lips over her throat. Clutching his shoulders, she murmured, "Then it's a very, very good thing I only work upstairs."

The end.

Also By Leighann Dobbs

Regency Romance

***

Scandals and Spies:

Kissing The Enemy

Deceiving The Duke

The Unexpected Series:

An Unexpected Proposal

An Unexpected Passion

Dobbs Fancytales:

Dobbs Fancytales Boxed Set Collection

———

Western Historical Romance

***

Goldwater Creek Mail Order Brides:

Faith

American Mail Order Brides Series:

Chevonne: Bride of Oklahoma

———————

Contemporary Romance

***

Reluctant Romance

———

Sweetrock Cowboy Romance Series:

Some Like It Hot (Book 1)

Too Close For Comfort (Book 2)

Witches of Hawthorne Grove Series:

Something Magical (Book 1)

———————

About Leighann Dobbs

USA Today Bestselling author Leighann Dobbs has had a passion for reading since she was old enough to hold a book, but she didn't put pen to paper until much later in life. After a twenty-year career as a software engineer with a few side trips into selling antiques and making jewelry, she realized you can't make a living reading books, so she tried her hand at writing them and discovered she had a passion for that, too! She lives in New Hampshire with her husband, Bruce, their trusty Chihuahua mix, Mojo, and beautiful rescue cat, Kitty.

Find out about her latest books and how to get discounts on them by signing up at:

http://www.leighanndobbs.com/news-letter-historical-romances

Connect with Leighann on Facebook:

https://www.facebook.com/leighanndobbshistoricalromance/

About Harmony Williams

Harmony Williams once tried to be an inventor, but soon realized that she needed to master complicated things like physics and hand-eye coordination. Since wishing things into existence only works when you're writing novels, she decided to devote her career to writing instead. Although she doesn't have a pet parrot, she has a 90-lb dog who also demands kisses at inopportune moments. Visit her online at *www.harmonywilliams.com.*

Made in the USA
San Bernardino, CA
08 September 2016